ANOTHER

VIEW

Other Titles by Michaele Lockhart

Focused on Murder

A Voyage for History

Hoarding Lies, Keeping Secrets

Love at Hôtel St-Jacques

Jody's Story: A Christmas Legend

Last Night at the Claremont

Men with Black Briefcases

The Blue Guitar Literary Magazine

A Barrio Christmas

Arizona Sunrise

Nonfiction

Publishing: A Survival Guide

ANOTHER VIEW

Stories of
Loyalty, Love, & Remembrance
from France

MICHAELE LOCKHART

ANOTHER VIEW: Stories of Loyalty, Love, & Remembrance from France

ISBN-13: 978-1505521535
ISBN-10: 150552153X

Credits:
Cover design by NewGalleryPublishing.com © 2015
Cover photo: Flowering-meadow / Courtesy GraphicStock.com
            Background / Courtesy GrahpicStock.com
            Editing and book layout @NewGalleryPublishing.com

Interior text was set in Garamond.

ANOTHER VIEW: Stories of Loyalty, Love, & Remembrance from France is also available for immediate download as an eBook through Amazon.com and Smashwords.com.

To purchase a copy of this book in print, order directly from Amazon.com,
or for a signed copy, contact the author at
www.MichaeleLockhart.com

Memory & Story

The war... occurred a lifetime ago, and yet the remembering makes it now. And sometimes remembering will lead to a story, which makes it forever. That's what stories are for. Stories are for joining the past to the future. Stories are for those late hours in the night when you can't remember how you got from where you were to where you are. Stories are for eternity, when memory is erased, when there is nothing to remember except the story.

—Tim O'Brien, *The Things They Carried*

❖

THE STORIES

1 The Day of the General

Douvré, near Lyon June 1940

IT WAS THE FRAGRANCE OF FLOWERS—probably of lilacs and roses mingled on rain-washed spring air—that beckoned to him and why General Kurt-Griebel Heinrich Von Strauchen ordered his driver to stop exactly where he did. The discomforts of his headquarters in Lyon, the once luxurious, late-nineteenth century DuClos mansion, had become more irritating and frazzling than the field hardships of the past year.

The unerring efficiency of the world-renowned Krupp cannons had collapsed the cobbled boulevard into a main section of public sewer, backing up raw sewage into the house and bringing its predictable stench.

Furthermore, it had rained for an entire week. A non-stop, pounding deluge of unchanging tempo and steady sheets of water cascaded down the gables and enshrouded him in the stinking miasma of Lyon's city center. He was in France at last and this was what greeted him. It should have been the charming countryside of his university holidays and wedding trip, not this dreary reality.

This morning, the first day work was feasible, he had dispatched thirty-five men, his soldiers as guards plus a detail of captive labor to clear out the sewer. If the problem was not re-solved that day, his men had memorized their orders long ago, the sequence of executions that would follow. Another detail was digging a trench for their bodies at a distance, and thus the smell of decay would not further offend him. Labor was cheap; an-other group would be collected and assembled for the following day. Von Strauchen would not tolerate inefficiency of any sort and his men knew it.

The troop of guards left in the dark of early morning, the moment the rain stopped, their boots clattering through the bricked and cobbled streets. Pleased with the day's promise, Von Strauchen had breakfasted later on the terrace, avoiding the foulness that permeated every breathable cubic centimeter of the mansion. At the general's command, his driver Schulz had brought the sleek, black BMW-327 around to the front portico. The leather top of the convertible was relaxed back into graceful pleats, readied for him to enjoy the sunshine that promised to appear. Accompanied by his personal guard and driver, the general headed out and away from the city.

This was his Führer's new country, at long last. Inhaling great gulps of fresh, non-sewage laden air, he roamed the countryside, exploring one lane after another. To his astonishment, Von Strauchen discovered the surrounding areas not only less rain-soaked than the city, but pockets of charming, bucolic beauty remained intact, unmarred by fire and bombs.

As they rounded a curve on one back road he called up to his driver. *"Halt!"* Generals commanded; they didn't ask.

Schulz complied instantly and brought the long, black vehicle to a smooth stop.

The general stood, turning around to survey the pleasing country that spread out around him. Fields and pastures stretched across gently undulating hills in a burst of soft new growth; to one side, a copse of poplars clustered near a small stone house.

"Right there! Down that drive!" He pointed toward the farm. "That smells much better than headquarters, *jawohl?* Secure it, now!"

An unexpected luxury of victory, which Von Strauchen was only now discovering, was the permission to be homesick. By June, his family's estate near Baden-Baden would have transformed into deep, lush greens everywhere, with pastel blossoms bulging forth on the tulip trees. The gardens at their manor house would already be a rainbow of colors and a heady competition of perfumes. Whatever was at the end of this drive, which appeared even more primitive than the country lane they were traveling, was where he now wanted to go. It was his right after all. He would experience the profusion of colors and scents he was certain awaited him there.

His personal guard Dieter grabbed his automatic rifle, vaulted over the car's door, and darted down the muddy drive. Schulz followed, his Luger drawn, zigzagging purposefully in the other man's wake.

Little Camille's mother, Odile Mauriat, had watched the long black convertible pass the drive leading down to their house. There was no petrol to power their one small automobile and no tires to replace the old ones. All four were worn fragile and threadbare, and the spare was useless. Fortunately she and Roger both could ride bicycles, little Camille perched on her husband's handlebars or tucked into the shopping basket. Thanks to the small generosities of her husband's congregation, they had been able to patch the tires of the bicycles.

Odile had anticipated this intrusion would come: it was inevitable. Knowing that it would happen did not make the sense of impending violation less acute. Remote as their cottage was they would have been noticed in time. Hitler's bright red flag with its black geometric figures already hung on the town hall of their village of Douvré. She had listened to stories, accounts from the Reverend Mauriat's congregation, and tales shared on market day, but nothing could have prepared her for the eventuality.

Today she had been trimming the roses, at least those she could reach. The bushes had straggled up the western wall of the cottage, long ago escaped from their trellises. Lilacs were encroaching too, threatening to cover the front door. That task must wait until she could borrow a ladder. Her arms and apron billowed with roses—many past their prime, others she would place in bowls throughout the house, but most she would use for making rosewater.

The gleaming convertible, bearing military insignia and the small ensign flags of a Nazi general fluttering near the headlights, must have turned around because now it had parked on the upper road, wisely not venturing down the rutted country lane to the Mauriat cottage. No German driver would risk damage to this expensive piece of machinery or the desecration of its metallic perfection with the dirt of a French farm.

Breathless, her heart racing, Odile's instinct was to run, but to where? "Roger?" Her voice trembled with panic. *Where was he? Where had he gone? Was he in his study?* Camille, she was certain, was at play in the garden. She slipped off the apron, gently enfolding the roses, and stepped back to the porch.

In the seconds before a German soldier burst through the trees and into their yard, she prayed. That was what Roger would have asked of her. Of that she was certain. She took a deep wavering breath, let it out as slowly as she could, and began to whisper, "The Lord is my shepherd…." Nothing else came to mind. Then the soldier was rushing up to her, shouting, his rifle aimed at her heart. His language was so execrable she couldn't understand a word. If possible, his breath was worse, exploding in fecal gusts from around rotting teeth.

Steadying herself, Odile tried to reply to what she assumed might be his question. "Yes, my husband is here too. That is all." Would not admitting to her daughter's presence be punishable? Camille could play for hours at the bottom of their garden in her solitary world of make-believe with her doll and new pet kitten, hidden in a bower of berry bushes and surrounded by beds of aromatic herbs. Any childlike sounds might be masked by the clucking of their three aged hens and the burbling and cooing overhead from the modest dovecote.

Her answer proved unnecessary. Another soldier, less aggressive than the first but armed with a pistol—his handheld Luger deadly nonetheless—was bringing Roger through the front door. He forced Roger and her off the porch into the grass, guarding them at gunpoint.

The soldier was tying Roger's hands behind him, but hadn't yet touched her. *What were they doing to him?* For some reason she could not have explained, she was still protectively holding onto the apron filled with roses. The other soldier, whom their guard addressed as Dieter, barged into and through the house, emerging again within minutes. Theirs was a small cottage, but his brusque inspection made it seem of doll-sized inconsequence.

"*Mein General!*" The rifle-bearing soldier turned and called up the drive. "It is now safe."

The German officer came striding down the drive. Dappled sunlight flickered through the trees and winked off the insignia of stars and gold embroidery, his immaculately combed blond hair, and the blue-black polish of his side arm. His high-necked uniform, too, was impeccably tailored, unlike the clothes of the two soldiers who had rushed the house. Knee-high boots of supple leather rippled and gleamed, complementing the detailed perfection of an officer in Hitler's elite.

Oh my, he's so tall! Odile thought. Seeming unconcerned, he came forward, walking with care and purpose. He was almost like a god—the unwelcome reaction startled her. Holding the bundle of roses close, she stepped forward, only one step. The Luger pressed against her ribs.

"*Bonjour, Monsieur, comment allez-vous?*" she asked pleasantly, gasping as the pistol left her side. "It is a beautiful day, is it not? Would you care for some refreshment?" The same words would have come from her naturally, for guest or for enemy. Odile had learned well the art of welcome, to offer caring and sharing as befit a pastor's wife.

She glanced back at Roger. He was trying to control his trembling, and in his murmured prayers he was begging for the sweat of fear that was pouring off him to stop.

General Von Strauchen, pleased that everything about him was gleaming in the early June sunshine, stopped a dozen feet from the dooryard. He smiled, wondering which actually held the woman captive: was it Schulz's Luger or the vision of him? He'd been told often enough that he possessed a "commanding presence," as well he ought. Hands locked behind his back he tilted his face toward the sky to survey the morning's clearing rain clouds, now scudding away to the west and moving out as if at his command.

Dieter, with the automatic rifle, stepped forward to confront Odile, brandishing the long weapon in her face. He barked at her in more roughly rendered French. "Refreshment is not yours to offer! This is already the general's home, as is all of Lyon. *Heil Hitler!*" The soldier threw back his head and brought his heels together smartly; the effect was muffled by grass and mud. He returned to attention, the rifle positioned high across his chest.

"Dieter," the general spoke at last. "That is unnecessary. Surely this fine lady is aware of the Victory of the Armies of the Third Reich over all France." He turned to Odile and addressed her in nearly flawless French. "I apologize for Dieter's rudeness, Madame."

He inclined his head slightly, studying her. *Blond—good. Blue eyes—very good and quite pretty. Slender, perfect posture, and graceful—a rare jewel in a rough setting. High rounded breasts.* Distracted for a moment, he considered the deep plum-pink of each areola that was suggested through her white blouse. *Rounded rosy cheeks, good teeth—all these even better.* Her wavy blond hair was pulled back with tortoiseshell combs to reveal the ideal Aryan bone structure. Her hands were fine and nicely formed. *Lovely indeed.* Despite her delicate appearance she radiated inner strength, and, most importantly, she didn't appear in the least afraid of him.

"General Kurt-Griebel Heinrich Von Strauchen, Madame." He presented himself formally. "Yes, indeed, a glass of beer would be most welcome on this glorious spring day."

"Odile Mauriat." Camille's mother introduced herself in return, extending her hand.

He noted her voice didn't shake. *Good.*

"My husband, the Reverend Roger Mauriat."

He found the economic gesture that included her husband to be charming too. Only then did Von Strauchen actually take note of the man standing slightly behind the enchanting woman: a slight, pale country parson wearing glasses, his shirt collar open.

"Ah!" He snapped his head authoritatively in the man's direction. "Schulz, unbind him."

Roger slumped to the ground at his release, then pulled himself up and leaned unsteadily against the edge of the porch. The Luger that was aimed at him never wavered.

"General," Odile said. "As you might understand there have been... *eh,* some shortages. I regret we have no beer. May I offer you a cup of tea perhaps?"

Von Strauchen was half-listening. There had been that infernal rain for seven days until the sun appeared today at last and the skies cleared, like an omen. The morning had begun as an outing; now the day held promise for more pleasure. If his officially acknowledged genetic purity were to be combined with this woman's beauty, health, and perfection.... He continued to speculate. Any child thus produced would be a glowing, valuable contribution to the superior race destined to follow in the wake of the Führer's ethnic cleansing and rebuilding of France and of all Europe.

His wouldn't be the crude lust of the conquering soldier forcing himself on any available female. As a general, his was a nobler, gentler, and higher calling. His grandfather, the renowned Karlsberg jurist, would probably have declared, "It is not without historical precedent." The old judge would undoubtedly have rambled on, expounding at length on the ancient laws of *ius primae noctis*—the "right of first night" granted to the superior and the conqueror. General Von Strauchen was as certain of duty as he was carnal desire.

The general's plans were but slightly hindered by the presence of the woman's husband. *"A Reverend," she'd called him.* They would need to check him carefully. With Mauriat and his men conveniently away from the house, Von Strauchen thought, all the better. An officer and a general, especially a member of Germany's once aristocratic old families, must be held to higher standards than those who served him and not seen rutting like common soldiers who often behaved like goats in a barnyard.

A piercing yowl temporarily intruded into his strategic and logistical planning as a small gray form, hurtling like a furry projectile issued from hell, streaked between him and the woman. *What was her name—Odile?* The minuscule bit of gray fluff trailed a white streamer and was frantically trying to hide under the house. Dieter leapt after it, firing his automatic rifle at the front stoop.

Odile screamed. Roger dropped to the ground and rolled in the grass, dodging the bursts of strafed plaster, shards of wood, and lilac blossoms that scattered in all directions.

"Put the rifle down." The general's words sliced through the chaos of the moment, cold as steel, scathing, evenly spaced, and heavy with portent. He addressed, but didn't look at, his personal guard. "It is only a kitten. You will learn self-control, Dieter." It was not a question, but a command, laden with consequences.

In the moment's turmoil he almost didn't notice the child.

A blond little girl had come running up from the garden, looking frightened and bewildered by the gunfire, her eyes brimming with tears. She was holding out her right forefinger that was trickling blood. Von Strauchen had been focused only on the woman, for the expression on her face changed in an instant, her eyes wide, seeing beyond him.

The woman barely spoke, softly breathing out words of warning. "No, Camille, no."

Von Strauchen turned and finally saw the little girl.

"Katrina?" The father in General Kurt-Griebel Heinrich Von Strauchen whispered the name. *Was it a passing thought... or did I actually say her name too?* "Oh, *meine kleine Katrina*," he said to the child before him. For the moment he was seeing her, the daughter he had left behind.

Within some of the most brutal of warriors, there seemed to remain secret hiding places guarding the affection that belonged uniquely to fathers for their daughters, the young charmers who could forever enslave the sternest heart. Von Strauchen's son Günther, twelve years old and one of the finest boys ever born, was his pride and joy. He would be a credit to the Third Reich, but his baby girl Katrina would forever be his little princess.

His focus strayed temporarily from plans for the pretty blond woman. She had gasped softly, her whispered words involuntary; it was the first indication of her fear or weakness. Von Strauchen could not abide weakness. *But this child....* He turned back to Camille. *Mein Gott*, how much she resembled his own Katrina.

Half-kneeling, he squatted down nearer to the child's height, taking care not to smear his neatly pressed uniform with the day's omnipresent mud. He reached out to the little girl. "*Mein kleines Mädchen,*" the once steely voice crooned, soft as a lullaby, then, realizing his error, he returned to French. "Here, my child, I won't hurt you."

Camille, her eyes filled with uncertainty, clutched what remained of a torn doll dress, the scratched finger held upright before her face, the blood-streaked talisman her immediate concern. She glanced from her mother, to her father, and back to this tall man who had appeared on their farm from out of nowhere. Once more she turned away.

Was she seeking her mother's approval? he wondered.

Marginally aware of their interchange Von Strauchen remained transfixed by the loveliness of the small oval face and the piquancy of the child's wide-eyed innocence. Odile's tension appeared to have eased and she'd nodded. He approved. Maybe the mother was not weak and frightened after all. Perhaps she would be allowed to bear his child, the matter postponed but for the moment.

Slowly, one small step at a time, Camille advanced toward him, behaving like a typical child of her age, half-shy among strangers. She seemed convinced of the importance of her message and her mission. The shredded white doll dress dangled and trailed forgotten in the mud, but the right index finger with its solitary, diagonal scratch was extended toward this man.

"Babette scratched me. See?"

Von Strauchen scooped the child up, swinging her off the ground and propping her against his hip. He braced her with easy familiarity in the crook of his arm. She even felt like his own Katrina. His little *schätze* would be a year older now, for he hadn't seen her since she was just like this, her small, sturdy legs resting naturally around his waist.

In the midday sunshine the girl's hair glistened like spun gold, pale wisps highlighted as they escaped from braids that skimmed her shoulders. Even her skin was warm, soft gold, and her cheeks sun-kissed to rosy perfection by the spring that stubbornly evaded his headquarters. It was lovely skin, just like her mother's. But this little girl… he'd noticed her one defect immediately. Her eyes weren't blue like her mother's or like his Katrina's, the deep, pure blue of the hand-painted flowers on his grandmother's Royal Meissen china. He glanced up at Odile and her eyes met his. Thoughts of postponed pleasures returned, his duty and obligation quickly recalled.

"Pretty." Camille drew the word out, one of those new words a child would discover and subsequently apply to everything. She stroked his gold-embroidered shoulder boards. With her uninjured finger she traced the outlines of more decorative metallic embroidery on the points of his collar. Innocently she picked up the cross, the award of the Knight of the Iron Cross, one of Germany's highest military honors. She traced the gold border that surrounded the enameled center, then examined the cluster of diamonds above the cross and the crisp ribbon of red, white, and black that secured it close under his collar. "Very pretty," she repeated and stroked his cheek.

Von Strauchen grasped her wounded finger, still extended so it would not be forgotten in the order of importance, and examined it. Small wonder the child's finger was scratched. Even greater wonder the irate kitten had injured only her finger, if the shredded remnants of the doll dress were any indication of what she'd been doing. He sighed, relieved: at least her injury was not the result of Dieter's wild gunfire.

"That is not too bad. You're a big girl, aren't you?" He waited while Camille bent her head with great solemnity to this question. "And your name, my little one?"

"Camille." She appeared quite unaware of her present situation. "And Babette a bad boy!"

"But Camille is a good girl, *non?* And Babette—she is a little girl too. *Non?*"

"She insisted, Monsieur." The blond woman stepped forward

uncertainly. She let out a breath and glanced back; the soldier with the Luger had not followed. "Babette is a little boy kitten, as Camille said. It was the name she chose." She smiled and shrugged.

The girl's mother was even lovelier, Von Strauchen concluded as he studied her more closely. Her dismissive shrug had released the perfume of fresh roses, soft and sensual. Thoughts of his plans returned, accompanied by a decidedly warm physical response. This child that he would create within her would indeed be a credit to the Master Race. Somehow, in this war-torn country, he would impose order here, protecting the child he would sire for the country's future. He would dictate these conditions to his aide upon return to Lyon, already dreading the stench of his rain-soaked headquarters.

"A beer would be much better," he announced, a rough plan forming as he contemplated strategic options. "But we will accept your offer of tea. *Merci beaucoup*."

Odile smiled graciously in reply and started toward the porch. "May I?"

Von Strauchen nodded and followed her, a smiling Camille balanced in the crook of his arm. He ducked to enter the dim foyer of the small house but turned back to his driver, whose Luger was pressed against Roger Mauriat. The brown eyes on the otherwise perfect blond French child had come from that man. Any child he bestowed, planting the pure seed of his precious German genetic legacy within this French woman, would require a father of record for legitimacy, for the child could never claim the noble Von Strauchen name. Certain matters remained to investigate; he would need to be absolutely certain. He didn't want to risk, as Himmler expressed it, "contaminating himself."

"Examine that man, Schulz," Von Strauchen commanded.

The door to the house closed behind them: the pastor's wife and the general who was holding a little girl in his arms.

———

"Surely you can't remember all this!" Louis had said when Camille finally shared the story with him. "You were just three and a half!" They were finishing lunch, about a year before they were married, in those early days when each was learning about the other's family, and she was still in medical school.

"Nearly four," she corrected him patiently. "No, but I do remember the general *exactly*. The color of his eyes, his shiny blond hair, a scar on one cheek, a sweet smile, the military decorations that looked like baubles to me. He was the tallest man I'd ever seen... but most adults seem tall to a child." She shrugged. "He had a certain presence. Even to my child's eyes he was also the most handsome man I'd ever seen." Camille hesitated, as though ashamed of her admission. It was men exactly like him, she'd learned, growing up and studying history, who had been Hitler's chosen, his elite, both symbol and promise of the Führer's Master Race and his Golden Supermen.

"And I don't remember what he ordered his soldiers to do then either," Camille said. "I learned later. My father suffered a heart attack just two years ago. My mother and I sat together for hours in his hospital room, whispering and sharing memories as if he had died. It was urgent for her, I think. She felt compelled to share things about him right then, while he was with us."

Louis studied her carefully. "But, 'examine'?"

"My father has dark brown eyes, very dark—like mine—and a more than typical Gallic nose." She laughed nervously, studying Louis's nose for a moment. "And his complexion was slightly darker than most from our region, although he was blond when he was younger too. I think there might be some Italian heritage in his family, being close to the south of France. Of course, they didn't believe he was a Protestant minister. The two soldiers stripped him."

Louis shuddered in premonition.

"They wanted to see if he was circumcised," she finished simply, more comfortable with this quasi-medical aspect of their conversation than the rest of her account.

"But... you once said that what you remembered most clearly was when you were beaten?"

"Ah, no, those were not my exact words." Camille paused for a sip of wine, then reached for the carafe of water in the center of the table and refilled her glass. She drank thirstily, and then swallowed several times against the lump in her throat, feeling that even in the telling, she would betray her kind, gentle father. "Of course, I don't remember my mother serving tea either."

———

In the Mauriat kitchen Von Strauchen raised his eyes toward the ceiling, amused at the guttural curses that burst from the cramped space scarcely qualified to be called an attic. His guard Dieter must have found what he was searching for up there, those concealed niches where the *Résistance* would hide their loyal followers.

With Camille balanced on one knee, he was waiting for the water to come to a boil for the tea he'd been promised. He admired Odile's grace as she moved to a cupboard, measured out a pittance of tea leaves, and placed the crockery teapot on the table before him. She'd earlier laid the roses aside, but as she reached across he could still smell where the petals had touched her skin. Occasionally his pleasant domestic idyll was broken as Dieter's crashing about from above reached them.

"A cradle!" Dieter boomed, his voice carrying through the house. This frustrating discovery was followed by a string of convoluted obscenities. "Two broken chairs! And jars!"

The sound of shattering glass penetrated downstairs, and Odile flinched.

"Oh, no! My jars for the preserves!" She gasped, just as the water in the kettle began to boil, as though shrieking distress in a way that she could not.

"Mein Gott!" The guard Dieter's satisfaction bellowed throughout the cottage at his next find. *"Was ist das?"*

Von Strauchen tried to ignore the noisy solider and his muffled litany of crude, highly improbable, exclamations. He wished he'd get done upstairs and leave him alone with this woman. The search must be completed however: Lyon was the center of the *Résistance*. His desires must be set aside for the moment, because he could not chance walking into a trap.

Another crash was followed by another sequence of profanity. Von Strauchen chuckled at the particular German words and tried to suppress a grin, but Camille glanced up and smiled back at him. He continued to follow Odile's every movement, finding even her simplest gestures charming and erotic, as he waited patiently for what would soon be his. He wondered idly whether she understood German, but as yet she'd given no indication that she did.

Cursing, blood from a head wound trickling down past his collar, the guard Dieter clomped downstairs and into the small kitchen carrying two boxes. He beamed with satisfaction, appearing convinced that he possessed proof of this French family's traitorous activities.

At the discovery of seditious materials, Von Strauchen deduced, his guard had probably raised up suddenly, ramming his head against the low ceiling. That must have caused the most recent outburst.

"These are in code!" Dieter proudly displayed one box to his general who was holding Camille close in his left arm while she played with the polished buttons on his jacket. Von Strauchen had prudently crossed one leg over the other, plunging his free hand into the box, extracting pages at random, and letting the discarded sheets flutter to the floor.

"You don't read French, do you, Dieter?" The guard could barely speak it.

Odile reached to fill the pot, steam rising as water surrounded the tea leaves, while Von Strauchen read out loud—a line from one of the papers here and another paragraph there. He looked back to her each time, enjoying her reaction. Had she flushed just coming near to him? Could that have been from the steaming water, or was it only embarrassment? She certainly would recognize her husband's early exercises and attempts at sermons. Because of the repetitious nature of certain phrases, one might believe they were in code, he acknowledged. The man was outside under guard, and this woman should be grateful. Whatever else transpired today, her husband would be spared at least this one taunting exposure.

"And the other box? There are even more seditious materials?" Von Strauchen's sarcasm was lost on his devoted guard, who stood by idly picking at a pimple on his forehead. "Dieter!" The single brusque word carried a warning.

Dieter quickly lowered his left hand from his face and then tore into the second box. Why anyone would have kept its contents was a mystery. The general recognized old hymnals, published in 1908. The yellowed paper crackled apart as his guard delved through them, looking for whatever secrets they concealed.

"Dieter, you will return both boxes to headquarters for further inspection. Place them in my car now." The young man's loyalty was simple and touching, and he was a superb marksman, but Von Strauchen was certain his staff would enjoy a hearty laugh this evening at the soldier's expense.

Trusting in a child's innocence to betray any further hiding places, after tea he proceeded to carry Camille throughout the house, cradled high in his arms, turning their search into a novel game. "Here, my little one, touch here." He instructed her to touch the ceiling in one spot and then in another. "And now, knock on this wall, right there." Giggling, Camille would do as she was told.

The house remained exactly as it appeared: a tiny country farmhouse with barely enough room for the present occupants.

"And is this your room, little one?"

Camille nodded.

Von Strauchen placed her gently on the bed. Camille giggled again. "This is part of the game we're playing." He studied the pretty child for a moment, so much like the woman who would be waiting for him in the next room. "Shh," he whispered.

"Shh," Camille repeated after him.

He pulled the door closed behind him. The child would probably take a nap. Most children would be exhausted by the excitement of what was undoubtedly an unusual day for any country family.

The long June day came to an end at last.

The boyish, pug-nosed Schulz spent most of the afternoon doing little and staring off into the distance. He squatted near the back of the house on the pile of Roger Mauriat's clothes. Dieter lounged on one elbow, the rifle by his side, and picked at the swollen pustules on his cheeks and forehead. Occasionally he lobbed a pebble at the chicken coop, laughing at the birds' cackles of alarm. Both men had grown disinterested in examining Roger because the possibilities for the particular task were limited. They had also been instructed to take their time and thoroughly check the grounds.

Leaving Roger bound and naked, they had earlier wandered down to the river bank for a swim that they'd followed by a nap, taking turns guarding the prisoner, and then completed their inspection of the gardens behind the house. Quite late in the day, during their final exploration, they discovered a low door into the Mauriats' insignificant root cellar.

Bundles of garlic and strings of onions hung from the supporting rafters; potatoes and turnips lined shallow shelves in neat rows; and a half dozen jars of fruit preserves and mustard were set apart beside several small unfinished baskets.

"*Mein Herr! Mein General!* Look what we found!" The two soldiers burst from the bottom of the yard holding the baskets, strands of ribbon partially woven through the handles waving wildly behind them.

Odile had stepped from the house last, absently smoothing down her rumpled skirt. She glanced about anxiously and sighed with relief: Camille appeared unharmed. She and the gray kitten Babette had reconciled. Her daughter cuddled the small, furry bundle in one arm, foregoing any doll's clothing, and waited beside her parents in front of their cottage.

Roger, allowed to dress himself, stared down at the ground, silent and not raising his eyes. They were gathered like any family bidding farewell to their guests of the day, yet they were unlike any other hosts, for their guests were uninvited.

Wilted and subdued, Odile remained still as a statue. She had done what she must, obeying in total silence—except the once—even when the general demanded more and more of her, again and again.

"*Was ist das?*" Dieter rushed forward to challenge her. "Just what is this?" He shoved the unfinished baskets close to her face, delivering another gust of halitosis.

Overcome with fatigue, Odile sighed, unable to answer for the moment. The day weighed down on her as though she were wearing a too heavy woolen coat. Somehow she'd managed to remain aloof and detached throughout the long hours alone with the general. He had been gentle in his mockery of the act of love and had stopped only at her body's final betrayal. He'd smiled then, pleased with himself and pleased with her.

She brushed at her lips with the back of her hand, but couldn't remove the taste of him. Some small essence of her former being might still exist deep within her, somewhere, but at the moment it seemed miles away. A voice that sounded like hers was trying to speak, yet she felt that nothing she might say could possibly matter, not anymore.

Von Strauchen had just noticed that the small tortoiseshell combs which earlier restrained the waves of Odile's pale golden hair were lost or had been misplaced during the afternoon. The mother of his new child should receive fine new ones; he made a mental note of this. Curls fluttered around her face, lifted in the early evening breeze that rose from the Sarène, the small river beyond the house.

He could still taste her body's sweetness and inhaled again the perfume of roses that had been a part of her too. More than ever she resembled Botticelli's Venus; it was how he would remember her. He had never been more certain of the good he'd accomplished that day: once for his Führer—and the other times for himself.

With her head held high, her posture regal in unnatural contrast to the semi-barbaric surroundings of armed men and mud, Odile stared past the general, focusing on a distant tree beyond his left shoulder as she tried to find words to answer.

"I have explained that my husband is a minister." She finished answering Dieter's question, speaking very slowly. "When someone in his congregation is sick, or there is a new… baby—" Her voice caught as she uttered the last word, hesitating a fraction of a second with the fresh, raw memory of the general's body invading hers and his certainty that she would bear his child. "Or a death in someone's family," she continued more rapidly. "Then I bring a small token—a basket that I've made with a jar of preserves, some herbs or flowers, a fresh loaf of bread—little things. We are not wealthy. One does what one can. It is a thoughtful gesture of caring from me and from us."

But Schulz was streaking up the drive toward the general's car, the baskets' multicolored streamers fluttering behind him. What they would do with the baskets, needing more of the supple young stems plus Odile's talented hands to finish them, was anyone's guess.

Dieter was next, trained soldier that he was, crouched and running low, machine gun aimed to the right, to the left. At last they were alone.

Von Strauchen faced Odile and Roger, but it was to Camille that he addressed his farewell. "You are a very good girl, Camille. You will become a really good girl, like one of us."

The general shook her hand, examining once more the kitten's scratch, now pink and swollen but no longer bleeding. Then he straightened, the stern general once more, his military bearing absolute perfection. Pulling his heels together with some difficulty, since mud would cake around the soles of even a general's boots, he extended his right arm, hand stretched forward formally, addressing all three of them, but looking at Camille. *"Heil Hitler!"*

Camille smiled back at her new friend. In perfect imitation of Von Strauchen, she stretched out her arm, raised at an identical angle, and repeated, *"Heil Hitler!"*

General Von Strauchen turned sharply and was past the bend in the drive and nearing his car before Roger's hand came down across Camille's upraised arm. He slapped her once, twice, three times, as though summoning all the violence he could muster, this man of peace who had never struck anyone or anything before in his life. Startled, Camille burst into tears as the terrorized kitten yowled and leapt from the comfort of her embrace, as bewildered and offended as she was.

"Oh," Louis had said when Camille had finished her story. "I'm sorry." He reached across the table to place his hand over hers, the right hand that once saluted the German general. Feeling the stiffening and pull of her hand, he removed his own. Just talking about this part of her past seemed to have strained their fragile new relationship.

"Did he—the general—did he come back?" He wasn't sure he wanted to hear the rest of the story.

"No. That is, I don't think so." She sighed. "But now I'm certain he meant to."

Louis considered this for a moment. "I wonder sometimes. Is it better to have experienced something or try to believe the stories you hear, always wondering what's been left out?"

Camille shrugged. Small as this event appeared in the larger context of war, it was significant enough. Her mother had spoken of that day only once, the visit of the German general and how they had treated her father, but omitted any mention of how it had affected her.

Years later, she would ask her mother again, but her answer was one Camille had come to recognize all too well in her medical practice.

"Really, *ma chère,* that was long ago. I don't remember much about it."

Rape? Camille had thought at the time. *Who wouldn't remember rape?* But she had respected her mother's unwillingness to discuss that day or relive it.

Several years after her mother's death, she was talking with her father one evening. She had discovered that her men patients most often endured the recurring nightmares, the dreams they wouldn't speak of, about a past they couldn't forget. The haunting nature of war memories was a common thread.

"Papa?" she'd asked. "What do you remember from that time?" As a minister Roger had been burdened with the pains of others, assuming them selflessly, but what of his own suffering?

"Oh, there's really not much I remember from those years. It was so long ago."

The same answer. Just like my mother's. She heard those exact words too often, typically from men who concealed some deep inner pain they were unable or unwilling to share. Then there would come that faraway stare as they looked back into a past that refused to disappear. She was usually capable of helping those patients talk, those who were traumatized to the extent they were hospitalized. She would not and could not do this to her own father.

"Papa, surely...?" Camille encouraged him and reached across the dinner table to caress his hand. "This is me, Camille—your daughter. Not the doctor... please?" She'd looked into his deep brown eyes, mirrors of her own, beseeching.

"Of course, near Lyon, close to the Demarcation line, there were some young men I tried to help." His words were modest, understated. "Every day there were younger and younger men, only boys, pressed into forced service for the Führer for the *Service du Travail Obligatoire.* The STO was one of the concessions created by Pétain's Vichy government." He tried looking away but Camille's straightforward gaze must have pulled him back. "I didn't share my activities with your mother. I bore the weight of my actions in secrecy and silence. They must have been successful in their escapes—*Dieu merci!*—for none confessed to my involvement. Most faded into the woods and hid in deserted hunting cabins, returning as part of the active *Résistance.*"

"Yes?" Camille studied her father. Clearly he was hedging. "And so...?"

"*Eh....* There were hardships, of course. The major ones—for all of an enemy-occupied France. Like the lack of food and fuel. But our farm was small and remote. There was no good space for soldiers to camp or to hide tanks… even if the Germans had chosen it as important. We had no vineyards or fields to ravage. We existed, largely ignored. But in 1945 I began to worry again, wondering if whatever orders of protection the general had given would turn against us, when discovered by the Allies."

Ah, at last, Camille thought. *What did finally happen? Does he know that Maman has already told me part of this?*

"Bien. The war crumbled to an end but nothing changed immediately, not for this poor preacher and his family." Roger's laugh was gentle and self-deprecating. "At long last we had food! The drunken headiness of victory ebbed, but it gave way to something else. Those who'd endured the pains of loyalty longed to take revenge on their countrymen who collaborated. Women suffered the most. Their heads were shaved when it was discovered they had satisfied the needs of German soldiers, some in return for their own safety."

Camille gasped. *Did it happen to my mother? Was there a pregnancy? Certainly, I would have known, somehow.*

"In my pastoral duties I saw them, heard about them, and prayed with them and for them. But I worried again. What about the three weeks that the Germans brought us food, afterward? That one group with the general and his staff were transferred to the Russian front we learned later…. He was killed at Kiev, I think."

Her father had hesitated before adding this afterthought. She wondered why he'd mentioned it at all. How had he possibly kept track of one man in the vastness of war?

"Did our distant neighbors perhaps notice what happened then, maybe report us? The thirst for revenge can fester. It smolders until it grows as fierce as it once was for liberation."

"Yes, those years after the war were not some of our country's proudest moments," Camille said.

"Could it be understood that what happened to your mother—quiet and selfless—was no less a rape? We waited in terror, *ma petite,*" Roger said.

"Papa," Camille finally said, confronting him. *"Maman* did tell me some of it—about that day. What happened? Afterward?"

Her father sighed in sad resignation. He hesitated, staring beyond the partially cleared dinner table. He picked up a coffee spoon, put it down, and then laid his hand over hers.

"For me, 1940 will forever be the year that June contained but twenty-nine days." Roger looked away from her and then down at the table and their intertwined hands. "I tried to push that one day, the day of the German general, so far back into my mind that I need never think of it. Not ever again."

Camille nodded, smiling her encouragement, but didn't let go of her father's hand. She hoped she was doing the right thing. Would her curiosity excuse the pain she was causing him to relive?

"Should I have fought and resisted, naked and guarded by two armed soldiers?" He shrugged and was silent.

They both knew the answer to that impractical question.

"My wife and my only child were inside my house with another of them, even though he was an *officer.*" He spat out the word. "I remember waiting, listening, uncertain whether I hoped to hear Odile's scream or not. It was a scream that never came. Then there was that hideous moment of the general's farewell, when for the first and only time in my life I raised my hand in anger and struck another person—you, my very own precious daughter."

"Papa." Camille smiled gently. "You know, I really don't remember that at all."

"Your mother and I never spoke of the incident. I'll admit now that I hated her for what she had done. My hatred for her was greater than for the German general!"

Shocked at the vehemence in her father's words, Camille was certain he was finished.

Roger was silent for several long moments. "We didn't touch or speak at all for over four months, amidst the noisy chaos of war, in our house that had grown totally silent. They're four months I can never give back to her," he said sadly. "She awoke one morning, cramping and in terrible pain. Blood had begun staining through her night shift, into the bed. I was ashamed of my hatred that hours of constant prayer could not assuage. Now I was embarrassed at my relief. The general would no longer be a permanent part of our lives after all."

"But—?"

"I begged for God's forgiveness. I whispered to her how much I loved her. I held her in my arms for hours until all the bleeding and the pains and the cramping finally stopped."

Camille squeezed her father's hand. Tears that he'd never before cried in her presence brimmed, but he blinked them away. She leaned across the table and brushed a kiss on his forehead.

"She understood. I understood. We both knew she had saved all of us." Her father turned away from her and spoke so softly she almost didn't hear him. "But I could never learn to accept it. I could never forgive her. I'm so sorry."

"But... never, Papa?" Camille faced him, certain she had heard incorrectly. Two people broken by that one day they had all survived but suffering from it the rest of their lives. Tears stung her eyes.

"I told you," her father said. "I'm sorry."

❖

2 The Homecoming

Paris, 1945

MAJOR MACKENZIE EMERSON CROSWELL of the United States Army Reserves studied his reflection in the only piece of partially intact mirror that remained in the old house at No. 1, Place du Chêne, Paris. He glowered back at the crooked image that faced him. With its uneven diagonal crack, the mirror made his head appear offset, resting slightly over his left shoulder.

He addressed the gaunt man with gray eyes and graying hair who stared back at him. "Look like a goddamn dressed-up scarecrow." Croswell's hair had been a solid if nondescript brown when he was called to active duty; only during the past months had it started to turn gray. He attempted a smile into the mirror, concluding that helped some.

As he adjusted his belt, his hand brushed against the leather holster and the coolness of dark, heavy metal. Each time that he passed a proficiency test with the weapon, he'd always surprised himself. The presence of the service revolver bothered him from time to time, but it was required, a part of the uniform. Especially today, the pistol added a vaguely threatening note, inappropriate for peaceful occasions such as this. All of France was still considered a war zone, even after Germany's unconditional surrender four months ago in May. Therefore he followed orders, carrying the loaded weapon at all times.

Mac Croswell had chosen to wear full uniform, what the military casually referred to as "pinks and greens." His aide Private Alderman had helped oversee the project: polishing the brass oak leaf clusters, aligning the major's meager rows of service ribbons, and making certain the curly, metallic embroidery on his cap was cleaned and shining. During the twenty months since Croswell had been called to active duty, he had rarely worn the full uniform since reporting as ordered to Fort Dix, New Jersey.

Stationed in Paris, in the last months at the end of the war, he had received no invitations to dine with other officers; apparently none were forthcoming. He had not been summoned to participate in a court martial board, and he had not been forced to formally surrender to anyone either. It was odd how those random and extreme occasions stuck in his memory, bits of information that rattled in his mind like loose coins in the bottom of his pocket. Officers' training seemed so many years ago he'd forgotten why else he might have needed the full, heavy, woolen outfit, but the Army manual made it quite clear what was required. *Regulations,* he reminded himself and grinned back at his crooked twin in the pier glass.

The trusted Army manual also had no specified protocol for occasions such as today either, but he was considering it a special event, requiring a display of respect. The owners of the still grand old house where he and his staff had been quartered while serving in France were coming back, returning to their home. During that time, the place had become his home too; it seemed only proper that he should be there to welcome the family back and to thank them, even though they had not invited anyone to occupy it in the first place.

Yesterday, he'd informed his commanding officer of his plans.

"Major, there will be two guards stationed there to prevent looting until the authorized civilians present themselves," Colonel Gardner had said. "Staying there isn't necessary or regulation."

To Croswell it did seem necessary. Fortunately the colonel hadn't ordered him to not proceed; that would have made a difference. If required to obey a direct order from the colonel, he would have felt that his part of the war was incomplete. He wanted to apologize to the owners about the damage and destruction the elegant mansion had suffered, although almost all had occurred long before the Allies had retaken Paris in August of 1944. Croswell and his staff had occupied No. 1, Place du Chêne, ever since.

He glanced back at his reflection one last time, attempted another smile, and decided that it was a significant improvement. Studying his sunken cheeks, he thought the morning's shave would pass too—just one nick. Cautiously, he removed the piece of tissue clinging to his jaw. That was as good as it would get.

A tall and lean man, Croswell had always worn his clothes well. Unfortunately, since he had long arms, long legs, and a slender waist, everything he'd ever worn required custom alterations, even for the United States Army. Slacks that had fit him twenty months ago were gathered around his waist, and the jacket draped from his shoulders in loose, unmilitary folds. He hadn't actually suffered the deprivations of war; he just looked as if he had. Of course the food didn't compare to his wife's cooking either, but he'd grown accustomed to it. His work here had been emotionally draining, not physically difficult. He'd eaten poorly and slept poorly, and about fifteen pounds he could ill afford to lose seemed to have vanished.

After most of his staff left the day before, his aide, Private Alderman, had stayed on with him. Boxes and crates filled with documents and records had been transferred to some other headquarters, moved up the line of command to become Colonel Gardner's responsibility, no longer his. Little had remained but their cots, duffle bags, mess kits, and a single footlocker. With just the two of them, the vast eighteenth-century building had seemed even larger and more grand than before.

At Croswell's insistence, Alderman had unpacked the uniform yesterday. He'd pushed aside the major's neatly tied stacks of letters—every soldier's treasure regardless his rank—and extracted the heavy wool service jacket and pants from the depths of the major's footlocker. He unwrapped the uniform, and waves of eye-stinging naphthalene from mothballs filled the room.

"Sir?" The private addressed his superior cautiously. "I'm afraid this smells terrible, sir."

"Alderman, that's what I'm wearing tomorrow when I meet the owners. Do the best you can."

"Yes, sir." His answer was respectful but underscored with doubt. The young man had settled to his task.

———

The day dawned with promise, a bright, cold October morning. Clouds were clearing, their shadows marking the older areas of the city, shifting across the sky and highlighting nearby clay chimneypots and the glorious landmarks of Paris that gleamed in the distance.

Major Croswell leaned against the opened doorway and stared down the long cobbled drive. Shifting a few steps to the right, he could see past the iron gate of the crumbling front wall where several determined vines struggled to exist in the neglected gardens. From there he glimpsed the slight rise where a narrow street twisted and climbed as it approached the entrance to Place du Chêne. At first he'd found it amusing that this one short drive, which emerged from another minimally wider and bricked street, had been given the address of No. 1. It was the only building on the circle drive except for its old carriage house, which the Germans had used for jeeps, motorcycles, two heavily armored cars, and ammunition storage.

Croswell would be going home in two or three months, he'd been informed. Why they wanted him to stay on was a riddle of military reasoning. Perhaps it was a matter of timing and availability of ships. As far as he could understand his orders, his job was complete.

"Intelligence?" he said out loud and laughed, because that had been his assignment. Part of Hitler's high command had used the building for the same purposes, as interpretation of abandoned documents had easily proved. But this wasn't just a building, he reminded himself; the ravaged structure at Place du Chêne was a family's home.

The occupying Germans had been caught by surprise in the Allied Armies' rapid retaking of Paris. The mansion's interim occupants had been captured during a disorganized attempt at escape, as had been many important and sensitive documents, not collected in sufficient time to be destroyed.

The majority of Croswell's staff, twenty soldiers and several junior officers, had moved out three days ago. Yesterday, another appropriate group had presented orders—in triplicate, of course—and he'd relinquished his command. Members of the Army's Signal Corps had dismantled their communication equipment and carried away coding and decoding machines. Trucks had rumbled from the yard, taking rolls of cable and transformers, telegraph connections, and a generator to wherever these essential components were needed.

Major Croswell shifted, folded his arms, and eased back against the heavy stonework. "Alderman?" He called to the young man who was lounging against their jeep.

The open vehicle overflowed with their duffle bags, crates, cots, the one remaining footlocker, and perched precariously atop the olive drab heap was his aide's small portable typewriter. The private's relaxed slouch, completely at ease, contrasted with the major's more ascetic and nervous stance, his hands clasped behind his back.

"Sir?" Alderman had taken advantage of the opportunity to light a cigarette, but he came to attention, the glowing cigarette cupped in his hand by his side.

"At ease, Alderman. And you may smoke." The major sighed. "Any sign of them yet?"

"Thank you, sir," Alderman replied. "I'll check again." The soldier walked down the drive to the gate and stepped out into the narrow street. He waited there several moments, first glancing up at the nearby buildings and houses as they'd been trained earlier, remaining alert for the stray, occasional sniper and then peering down the hillside to his left. There was little point in checking downhill to the right, because the slight rise dipped back down and away, on one of the many rolling hills that Paris concealed so well, except for those who walked them. It was also, in principle if not in actual practice, a one-way street.

"No, sir. Nothing yet."

"What time was their train due to arrive this morning? Nine thirty?"

"Yes, sir, it was. Not everything is running on time yet."

"I'm surprised they're running at all," Croswell said. He called after the soldier as he strolled back toward the jeep. "Do you know yet if you're going home after this, Alderman?" Orders were generated elsewhere. With his command dismantled, he would probably never learn where any of his men went, dispersed onto the dying winds of war.

"No, sir, I got at least six months to go." He dropped the cigarette and ground it into the packed, cobbled drive. He glanced up; the major was watching him. Alderman bent and picked it up automatically; he should have known better. He dropped the offending cigarette butt into an empty flower pot. "And you, sir?"

"They've said I'll have another three months before I go home."

Home. The word had been on every soldier's mind since the day he enlisted, was drafted, or called up from the Reserves. It must have been the on mind of the owners of this place too. He and most of his staff had received letters; they had some idea of what home would be like for them, even though it was usually idealized and oversimplified. What about this French family, the Duchênes?

He was fairly certain of what awaited him back in New Jersey. He and Lorraine had even spoken twice during the past six months. Their words would scratch and pop through the static of trans-Atlantic connections. These brief telephone conversations consisted of frequent repeated questions—"Sweetheart?"

or "Hello? Hello?" and an occasional "Are you still there?"—mixed with truncated sentences. Still, he had been reassured.

Life should be comparatively normal after his return. However, he was an intelligent, educated man and a professor of history: following a war—any war—everything about life would inevitably change. Unlike the owners of this house, he assumed he would find adjustment relatively easy. How would it be for this family? He would still have his professorship. He would probably not retain his position as Assistant Department head, but that was all right. Students, he knew, would have changed, because the world around them was altered forever. Others would never come back, but they would live on in his memory and in the memories of many of his colleagues.

Lorraine would be there: steadfast, loving, and still the prettiest faculty wife. His daughter Suzanne had promised she would wait to marry until he returned. That was typical of her, always loyal and devoted. The war had helped manage her engagement too, because her sweetheart had been called up, later in the war. Spared from the worst, Suzanne's fiancé would be coming back from the Eastern Theater later this year.

His son Tom had wanted to enlist. Keeping him home and safe was his youth, reinforced by Lorraine's steadfast refusal to sign the special parental waiver required. By then the United States' armed forces had needed a different kind of experience, something a fresh high school graduate couldn't offer to the meat grinders of war.

Croswell glanced up at the peripatetic skies. The sun was struggling against the light clouds and had chosen to hide once more. He checked his watch and again leaned back into the cool stonework of the entryway, lost to thoughts of elsewhere and a new life that would resume.

Once again there would be the faculty teas and cocktail parties with Lorraine beside him, warmly welcoming the newly hired younger professors and charming the older staff as she always did. There would be vacancies and constant reminders of sacrifice, empty places where certain faces should have been. He'd known some of these men and would learn of others only later. His homecoming would not be all joy, because there would be fresh opportunities to mourn.

The low-lying clouds that clung to the small hilltops of Paris parted at last and the sun sliced through, shining down on him and reawakening the pungent scent of mothballs. He shifted again, stepping closer to the broad steps that led down from the double oak doors.

"Anything yet?" Croswell called to his aide for the second time.

Private Alderman again strolled down the sloping drive toward the gate. "No, sir." Back at the jeep, he leaned against it, at ease once more.

Croswell surveyed the devastation surrounding him. He'd ordered his men to neaten up the place, but what could they do? Untended struggling shrubs in dire need of trimming or replacing, martyred stumps of trees, flowerbeds that gaped forlorn and barren.... His backyard would probably need attention too, but at least he still had a garden. Croswell wondered whether there would be any shortage of seeds this year. Had Lorraine been able to manage the weeds while he was gone? Most importantly, his home—perhaps needing a bit of work that wartime shortages and rationing had postponed—would be there for him, intact, unlike here, at the home of this French family with the curious surname of Duchêne.

"I think I see them coming, sir." Alderman had returned to the gate, pointing down the hill and squinting into the distance.

Croswell joined him and stepped out into the street. At the bottom of the street, where Rue de Ste-Claire entered the sloping road that climbed the small rise to Place du Chêne, a group was huddled around a railroad cart. Croswell blinked, straining to focus, but in the deep shade of an early fall morning details were hidden against the smoke-darkened old brick of nearby buildings.

"Should I go down and help them, sir?"

Croswell wasn't certain this was the family. "No, let's wait." He remained by the street, watching as grayed forms separated from shadows. A young, teenaged boy from the railroad struggled to push the baggage cart uphill, but the grade was proving too steep. Another boy wearing a jaunty cloth cap, sturdy, dark-haired, and pink-cheeked with the healthy flush of youth, was about the same age as the railroad helper. He ran around to the rear and pushed with him.

An older man, whose hair had once been dark like the boy's, held the arm of an attractive, fair-haired woman. She seemed much younger than him, but then Croswell recalled how he had looked in the mirror this morning. They might say the same about him and his wife when he returned to the university. Walking beside the couple was a young girl carrying a child he guessed to be about three, maybe four, years old. Biology waits for no one and certainly not for war. He smiled at the thought of new life, rising Phoenix-like from the ashes. Strange though, he thought, he had been informed that this was a family of four.

"That's good, Alderman. I'll wait by the door now."

"Yes, sir," the private acknowledged.

The girl who was holding the child stepped into the courtyard first. She was a lovely girl, about the same age as the dark-haired boy. Unlike him, her skin was pale olive, and her long, dark, wavy hair was pulled back at the nape of her neck. It fell between her shoulders in a cloud of curls. At first Croswell thought her hair was black until a furtive ray of sun touched it, awakening rich highlights of copper and deep auburn. The child, a little boy, wriggled free of her arms, sliding to the ground, and landed running. Light-haired and fair, he had cheeks that were brushed rosy pink by the brisk morning air. Strangely, the girl had stopped at the gate and stood unmoving, as though without the child in her arms there was no point continuing on.

"Maman!" the little boy called. He whirled about and rushed back to the gate. The others followed quickly behind him.

Now the pretty, fair-haired woman was smiling. The little boy's hand was grasped in hers, and he tugged at her, leaping about excitedly. *"Marc."* She bent to kiss his forehead. *"Calmes-toi! We're home, mon chéri."*

The man beside her glanced up too, years and worry dropping away from his face. He was much younger than Croswell had first guessed and probably younger than him. He was a nice looking gentleman; like all the family he was dressed in the sturdy, warm clothes of a traveler.

The railroad baggage cart rattled in next. The two older boys helped unload the suitcases, setting them down one by one, building a monument to what was left of the family's worldly possessions in the middle of the courtyard. The older man, who must be Henri Duchêne, handed some coins to the lad from the railroad. The boy turned his cart, and soon the clattering of wheels against stone and broken sidewalk echoed back up, filling the empty yard.

So this was the family. They were here, home at last. Croswell wasn't sure whether what he was about to say would be proper or well taken. These matters were often touchy.

He walked toward them, down the last steps, and crossed out into the courtyard. "Monsieur Duchêne?" He extended his hand. Stepping closer, he was again acutely aware of the uncomfortable presence of his service side arm. "On behalf of the United States Army and the Allied Forces, welcome back to your home. We thank you for the use of this marvelous house."

The man standing before him in the courtyard started to grasp Croswell's hand and then stopped, hesitating, as if the simple gesture of courtesy might be more complex than it seemed at first.

"*Oui?*" He responded at last and clasped the other man's hand in his. Finally, too, he smiled in response to the major's greeting. "So…. Does this mean—? May we live here again?"

The woman, who surely was his wife, faced Croswell expectantly, blue eyes brimming with tears. The tall boy stood by his father's side, waiting and respectfully attentive. The excited younger child bounced up and down like a jumping jack, but the dark-haired girl who had carried him had still not moved from beside the gate.

"Of course." Major Croswell wondered whether he might have said something foolish or incorrect. "This is your home."

The three members of the family whose attention were focused on him let out a collective sigh. Little Marc continued to skip and bounce, trying to break away.

"Major Mackenzie Emerson Croswell of the United States Army. There have been twenty-six of us using your home for headquarters for the past fourteen months. I wanted to be here to welcome you and meet you. That is all." He paused, confused by the expressions on their faces. Had they understood him? He had spoken in English and in French. "I'm afraid there is extensive damage, but almost all had occurred before we arrived in August of 1944."

"But it's still here!" the woman exclaimed in disbelief. She whirled around, one arm extended, pointing to the carriage house and then up at the façade of the two-story mansion. "Look, Henri, it's all here!"

Croswell watched her blink several times, clearing away tears, and then noticed Henri Duchêne's expression.

The man had not forgotten how to smile after all, but now he looked embarrassed. "Please, excuse our manners, Major. Yes, I am Henri Duchêne. My wife, Cécile, and my son, Louis."

The lovely woman extended her hand and warmly clasped Croswell's.

Their son stepped forward, a well-mannered young man, and shook his hand. "Pleased to meet you, Monsieur," he said, a smile creasing deep dimples in his cheeks.

"And the little one who won't keep still is our younger son, Marc." Cécile bent down to scoop the wriggly little boy into her arms; he faced Croswell for a brief second and then shyly buried his face against his mother's neck. *"Henri?"* Cécile whispered to her husband and tilted her head, indicating the girl who waited by the iron gate, still as a statue.

"Françoise, ma chère?" Henri called to her gently but she did not respond. "Major Croswell, the war has been more difficult for some children than others." He sighed in resignation and shrugged. "May we go in now? Perhaps she will follow us."

"Oui," Croswell responded, continuing without hesitation in French. "But there is much destruction throughout." Hands clasped behind him, he began a tour of the war-ravaged mansion.

"You... you speak French?" Duchêne sounded incredulous. Like many of his countrymen he had expected the occupying army, liberators though they might be, to speak only their own language. The lessons of history and experience had taught him this.

"That is a matter of constant debate in our home," Croswell commented vaguely. "My wife would probably disagree with you."

"So your wife—" Duchêne smiled broadly, not hiding his amazement. "She is French?" His eyes widened; his eyebrows were raised in question.

Croswell could read undisguised delight in the other man's approval. He was very glad that he had stayed, regardless of lack of protocol and the lack of formal orders.

"Yes, from the Bordeaux region. There was once another war...."

"The war to end all wars," the two men quoted and finished the phrase in unison.

There was no bitterness in how they said it or what they'd said, only acknowledgement and recognition of its irony, the reality that there would be other wars to come. Worldwide violence and strife would not end now either. The Second World War, not yet even termed that by historians, had been officially over in Europe since May and in the East since August.

"What was your work here?" Duchêne's gesture encompassed the house as they passed a stunning view of Paris and the Seine from one of the few unboarded windows on the second floor.

"A history professor like me, you mean? What could I do in a war?" He smiled. "I've wondered myself. I was in the Army Reserves and they assigned me to the administrative staff for Intelligence. Debatable, wouldn't you say?"

Duchêne laughed. "Like with all armies, I suppose."

The exiting occupant and the home's returning owner continued a slow tour of the mostly boarded-up residence. Duchêne said little, because the devastation spoke for itself: obscenities in German scrawled on the walls, wooden floors scarred and gouged by heavy boots, shattered chandeliers, bullet holes in the ceiling, crumbling pilasters, splintered mirrors, broken tiles, and dangling chunks of plaster.

"I apologize there's no furniture. There was none here when the German command... er... vacated." Croswell hesitated over the choice of that particular word to describe the former occupants' hasty attempt at flight. They had all been detained in prisons. "So...?" He shrugged. "I have no idea what happened to any of it. I can only imagine, Monsieur Duchêne. Firewood, barter—who knows?"

"Ah, but, please—*s'il vous plaît, mon ami*—it is Henri." He tilted his head and looked up at the tall, lean major, eyebrows raised again with the informal question.

Croswell grinned, relaxing for the first time in how long he couldn't remember and cherishing Duchêne's simple gesture of friendship. "Either Mac or Mackenzie. Scottish names, you know. Difficult in French."

Duchêne replied comfortably. "Mac. Not that difficult. I had a business associate whom we called Mac because it was easier. His name in French was too long!" He chuckled and Croswell noticed he was quite a bit younger than he'd first appeared, yet war had certainly aged them both.

"As for the furniture, many of the most important pieces are safe," he continued. "You see, we have practice with this thing called war, and we have trusted friends."

During the Hundred Years War and later the Revolution,

Duchêne explained, gesturing through the large, sadly emptied rooms, when the estate was still in the country, loyal and trusted friends among their tenants had hidden treasures against the mad pillaging that war would always bring.

"There would be one piece tucked under the thatched roof of a cottage, another behind casks of a home's personal wine production, still others in smelly unused root cellars, paintings hidden within walls."

"My wife told me about this once, but I didn't really believe her." Croswell laughed. "Then—I was a much younger man—I probably had other things on my mind, with a beautiful young woman beside me. But it really works?"

"Almost two-thirds of our home's contents were returned to the family, even the silver, gold, valuable paintings, furniture. The last war was no different. The beneficent loyalty of friends, once established, seems to be passed through generations like a genetic trait."

Croswell shook his head, amazed. "But Paris wasn't occupied then, was it?"

"No, but still, we took the precaution." Duchêne smiled. "I'm surprised too how often it's worked. We will wait and see what comes back this time. It is too soon to know. Otherwise, my own treasure is safe." He gestured, indicating the joyful racket that rebounded through the empty rooms.

Young Marc screamed and shrilled as he played hide-and-seek with his older brother. Although Louis must have been quite young when he'd lived here, Croswell assumed that he surely recalled every possible place to locate the little boy. Giggles and shouts drifted down the long staircase, the sounds of young Marc's hiding, then being found by his older brother: the delighted sound of discovering a home he'd never seen or known.

"Oh, non! Henri!" Cécile's sob echoed from the adjacent room. Henri rushed to her side. His wife was gazing toward the courtyard from a rear window; he looked to where she pointed. "Our tree!" she cried. "They cut down our tree."

"That, too, was gone before we arrived, Madame," Croswell explained. "I'm sorry. It must have been very beautiful." A broad stump, over five feet across, remained. On pleasant days during the summer some of his staff had chosen to eat lunch there.

"It was the only one left," Duchêne said. "Once, a very long time ago, this was a country estate surrounded by a vast oak grove. Then, there was just that one huge oak left, between here and the carriage house. It was possibly 200 years old or more. That's where our family surname comes from. La Place du Chêne—the place of the oak—shortened, of course." He turned back to his wife and enfolded her in his arms. "Cécile, dearest. We will plant more. The house is here and we are safe." He bent and kissed her tenderly, brushing her tears from one cheek and then from the other. She nodded, sniffled once, and pressed her face against his shoulder.

Watching them, Croswell felt vaguely like a voyeur; it also made him terribly homesick.

"We'll be leaving then," he extended his hand to Duchêne. "Oh, one more thing. It was done before the US Army occupied here as well. This is truly a desecration. That ceiling—painted by Watteau or Boucher, I think. It's in your grand salon."

Duchêne followed as Croswell spoke, looking up as the major raised a long, thin arm and pointed toward the ceiling.

Painted in the glorious tradition of the eighteenth century, the swirling cherubs and birds encircled a *trompe-l'oeil* space in the ceiling where once a chandelier had hung from the artist's softly rendered, pale blue sky. The occupying Germans, bored and in want of target practice, must have aimed carefully: all the cherubs sported blackened bullet holes for eyes and most, in addition, suffered from another wound, expert shots through their belly buttons. Many of the birds had also been killed in their flight.

"Watteau?" Duchêne was curious. "*Eh*... so you are familiar with French art as well?"

"My undergraduate minor in college—art history," Croswell explained. "One of my great loves, but not one that makes a living."

"No." Duchêne laughed, apparently enjoying this new discovery. "It was an apprentice of Watteau, not the artist himself. But rather good, *non*? It can be repaired. It has been before." His tone was bitter and resigned. "The art students at the *Académie* are excellent and will be glad for the work. But we always leave one eye, just one small part, not repaired. As a reminder."

Croswell wasn't sure whether he could withstand the violation of family and home with such dignity and equanimity and then deliberately choose to "keep a reminder."

Squealing and laughing, young Marc rushed down the broad steps of the central staircase, short legs pumping as fast as they could carry him. Louis followed, in the benevolent tradition of older brothers, allowing the younger one to gain a minor lead. Marc stopped at the base of the stairs, hugging his father's legs, protection against unknown terrors—perhaps tickling or capture by the brute of a big brother who was chasing him.

"*Arrêtez—mes enfants!*" Duchêne admonished the two boys. "*Silence, s'il vous plaît.*"

Breathless, they halted their game long enough to wait by his side. "Papa? Which room will be for Françoise?" Louis nodded politely toward Major Croswell. "Excuse me, Monsieur."

"Your daughter? I haven't met her yet," the major said.

The girl, whose dark hair was pulled back at the base of her neck so it flared out like a wide, curling fan, was standing immediately inside the front door, staring out toward the circle drive, past what remained of the iron fence, past everything. It was as if she was looking everywhere but seeing nothing. Once relieved of little Marc when the others came inside she had moved only this far, now clinging to the door as though entering further might leave another world behind forever.

"*Non, mon ami*," Henri Duchêne replied. Croswell watched the man's face darken, transformed by some deep, hidden pain. His words were soft, low, and tender. "Françoise, *ma petite*, please come here for a moment."

The girl moved slowly and uncertainly, first across the short distance between the archway of the foyer, then in timid steps toward the base of the stairs, where Marc still tugged at his father's trousers, clinging to his knees for sanctuary.

"Major Croswell," he said, once the girl joined them. "I should like to present Françoise LeBourget. Françoise, this is Major Croswell, of the United States Army."

Shy and hesitant, the girl extended her hand and then smiled, a small tremulous smile.

Major Croswell bent to grasp her hand, noticing the richness of her hazel eyes, the curly, dark brown hair, the pale olive skin. He decided that if she was related to this family, it was not by blood.

Duchêne must have read his question. Marc and Louis galloped up the staircase once again, and Françoise drifted slowly back to the foyer and the open doorway. Their eyes met for a moment. "She is so much like her father—sometimes I think I'm seeing him." Duchêne stared down at the floor. "We will try to locate her parents. It might not be possible."

"Is there any way we can help?" Croswell offered, uncertain how much help it would be and how long any search might take. There were so many missing, so many dead, so few records.

"Perhaps, but I fear they have already died. Françoise will want to know someday. Maybe she'll need to know." He cleared his throat and continued. "Charles LeBourget was my close business partner for ten years and a brilliant young man. I tried to help them all, but my position was precarious too. If only they had left early, like we did."

The vast house, devoid of furniture, offered no welcoming place to sit and talk. The major, still acting as host although the rightful owner was present, motioned toward the stairway. Duchêne followed and the two men eased down side by side on the steps.

"I was condemned for being unpatriotic, disloyal, and cowardly. Those were some of the nicer accusations!" he said. "I had started transferring our companies' financial assets out of France to Switzerland by 1936, when Europe's attention was focused on Berlin and the Olympics."

Croswell said nothing, recalling America's financial crash not that much in the past, a short sixteen years ago. Governments would naturally want to prevent a frightened run on their banking institutions and a stampede-like exodus at the borders. Europe was small. Where could farseeing businessmen like Henri Duchêne run to?

"I had a Swiss passport and identification papers—my mother was from *la Suisse Romande*. The French part of Switzerland, you know," he added. "Then I worked to obtain forged documents for my wife and Louis. They were really quite good." He grinned. Perhaps this was the first time he had ever divulged the secret to anyone, and it seemed as if a part of him had been liberated too.

Croswell was curious. "But when did you leave?"

"We left—for a 'ski vacation'—in March of 1938 and never returned. Until now."

"You should have been praised for your foresight," the major commented. "But?"

"Not at first, *certainement*. Later others begged for my help. Sometimes I could assist with an escape, but other times I could do nothing at all. At last Charles and Geneviève wanted to leave, but it was too late." Duchêne sighed, as though reliving the pain of the past. "Geneviève LeBourget's predicament was complicated. Although she was born in France, a citizen, a baptized and confirmed Catholic, *her* mother was half-Jewish. After Pétain, citizens would get extra points with the Germans if they revealed their neighbors' secrets."

"We've heard some of the stories," Croswell said.

"Françoise's mother was required to wear an armband with the yellow Star of David. Their daughter was only five then." He tilted his chin toward the open door, where Françoise stood now, a rigid silhouette against the flat light of late morning. "We were able to save her."

"I will report their names, Monsieur. We can always hope."

"It would be appreciated." Duchêne hesitated. "If her family is found, *bon*. Otherwise, she is our daughter now. Equal in all ways to our two sons."

Oh, dear God, Croswell thought, images from treasured, recent photographs of his own son and daughter filling his memory. In the strained silence that followed he reached into his shirt pocket and pulled out a package of Lucky Strikes. He offered a cigarette first to his host, and then took one himself. They leaned close, cupping a hand to share the flame of a lighter, and then eased back against the stairs.

Croswell inhaled deeply. "May I ask how you managed to rescue her? If you don't mind?" Familiar with logistics and border guards, it seemed like it would have been nearly impossible.

"Once we were in Switzerland, I could hear and read the full truth," Duchêne spoke slowly.

"The French press had tried to mislead everyone, didn't they?"

Duchêne nodded. "Our government too. What all of France received was sugar-coated, so our country wouldn't panic. They designed stories that made everything that was happening sound 'reasonable.'" He sighed. "Then I discovered my country had valid reasons to panic."

"The United States didn't grasp the full extent of what was happening here for quite a long time either," Croswell said.

"It was very complicated and dangerous for the LeBourget family. Charles had waited too long. And he refused to leave without Geneviève. And then, even paying the bribes, she was not allowed to leave. It broke my heart, not helping them. They would be at the mercy of whoever could gain by betraying them."

Duchêne stared out the door for a moment. "By then Louis was already a student, in Switzerland. As a Swiss citizen—my dual citizenship—I requested that friends ship a trunk full of his books to me." He sighed deeply, exhaling the tension from long ago. "It was fortunate she was a small, quiet child."

"No!" Croswell gasped. "You couldn't have!"

"It was a risk they all knew and accepted, Françoise and her parents. There's a short railroad line and crossing near Châtelard—it's in the mountains. Louis was waiting by the tracks in his school uniform at the first station, where the train stopped for water. I was a few hundred yards further on, parked in the woods." Duchêne shrugged. "She's been living with us in Geneva ever since."

The shrieking of young voices echoed through the top floors and then, like a stream of sound, it poured down the stairs, the two boys chasing each other once more. First the small, determined, running steps of Marc, then Louis galloping in his wake, past the major and Duchêne.

Louis turned as they rushed by. *"Pardonnez-nous—Papa, Monsieur!"* They ran on through the house.

"Please excuse the noise," Duchêne said. "It's exciting for them. Especially after the long train ride."

The major smiled, nodding in complete understanding.

"Did I say they would be equal?" Duchêne mused aloud and shook his head. "Françoise is much quieter. Louis?" His voice echoed through the rooms and the boys came back quickly.

"Mes enfants," Duchêne instructed them. "Louis, you should remember which room was the nursery. That is for Marc. You know which rooms have always been for *Maman* and me. Take Françoise upstairs and the two of you should choose which room each of you would like. Françoise, *ma petite*, this is your home now." Duchêne and the major waited, watching the two young people depart. "It probably isn't really important now, but it might help her adjust. As you so aptly reminded me, there are no beds."

No beds. That's right, there aren't any beds. Not when they arrived and certainly not now. Everything his staff had brought with them had been removed. Croswell turned on his heel and strode back to the foyer. "Alderman!" he barked into the courtyard.

The soldier lounging against the jeep snapped to attention. "Yes, sir!"

"How many cots are in that damn thing? It's too full anyway.

Stuff will fall out of it all the way down the hill, don't you think?"

The soldier regarded his commander curiously for only a moment, until he realized what was being asked of him, and then smiled. "Oh, yes, sir. Yes, indeed, sir. Absolutely correct. No excuse for such a poor packing job, sir."

Within moments, duffle bags and boxes, and finally, three army-issue cots, their wooden legs neatly tucked within the self-contained sack of their canvas, had been unloaded onto the cobblestone drive.

The jeep's contents were quickly reassembled, minus the cots. "Doesn't it fit better now?" Croswell teased his aide. The portable Royal typewriter was replaced atop the surroundings of lumpy olive drab.

The two men exchanged a most unmilitary goodbye. Mac Croswell and Henri Duchêne had known each other less than an hour, but Duchêne offered first, extending his arms to grip the majors' shoulders: the traditional greeting and farewell, the brushing of cheeks, the embrace of friendship.

Major Croswell returned the gesture. *"Au revoir, mon ami."* He climbed into the cleverly lightened jeep and took his place beside his aide who would drive them to headquarters. The engine roared to life and they headed for the courtyard gate. Croswell turned in his seat and called back. "Henri!"

Alderman brought the sturdy little vehicle screeching to a stop, then jerkily reversed until they were parked before the door once more. Croswell had pulled a small notebook from his coat pocket and was writing in it furiously.

"Henri? It won't be too many more years before Louis will be in university, correct?"

"Maybe four years." Duchêne walked down the steps, headed toward the jeep.

"Your family—all of you—you're invited to come stay with my wife and me, any time. Here's our address." Croswell handed him a page torn from the notebook. "Perhaps Louis might like to spend a year of college at Princeton? Remember us!"

"You already know our address." Duchêne waved to where *No. 1, Place du Chêne* could be read through a haze of cracks in the ceramic tiles mounted on the side of the house.

The jeep growled into gear and completed the circle drive, bumping along the small rise that was Place du Chêne, and continued down to Rue de Ste-Claire. *It's just three more months,* Croswell was thinking as he tried to swallow against the lump in his throat. *Damn, I'm a lucky man. I'll be coming home too.*

❖

3 Afterward

St-Etienne-des-Près, Normandy 1949

STRETCHED OUT IN THE GRASS, with one arm propped behind his head, Louis Duchêne was enjoying a break from hard work and gazing up into the clouds that feathered across the pale canvas of Normandy's sky. All around him the warm sweetness of summer seemed to rest upon the field like a gentle caress. Here and there graceful spikes lanced high against the blue, hardy poplars leading up to what remained of his grandparents' family home.

His Grandpère Maurice and Grandmère Hélène were safely returned from England and now living close to his family in Paris. Louis was familiar with the aftermath of war, although the topic was never discussed; such matters were common knowledge, part of their country's shared history. Until the summer of '49, when he helped in the rebuilding of his grandparents' home, he hadn't yet witnessed the fullness of terrible destruction brought to the Normandy countryside and the small village of St-Etienne-des-Près.

With difficulty he tried to summon up an image of the sprawling manor and its lands. He would have been about five or maybe six, the last time he and his parents visited, before the war. Most everything was carved into memory that way, as "before" or "after."

The old house had had a high-pitched slate roof and a stone-flagged kitchen with a huge open fireplace. He recalled playing in one corner of the cool hearth when he was a toddler, then receiving quite a scolding when he'd emerged hours later, smudged black with soot. On three sides of the old home, tall windows opened into a garden filled with rose bushes. As a child he'd imagined that the lush pastures stretched on forever, their broad expanses of gently rolling hills scored with tall white fences. Next there were orchards that surrounded the horse pastures as far as his young eyes could see.

Hand in hand with his grandfather he'd often strolled across the grassy fields. They would pause at the tall hedgerows to listen while he pictured entire families of cheeping, chattering birds living in the dense growth, much as people lived in houses. "Where are their beds, Grandpère?" he'd asked him once, peering inside the dense growth. His grandfather patted his hand. "But they all sleep in there too, *mon petit.*"

The gentleness and beauty of his grandmother's horses at her breeding farms had awed him too, and, even ten years later, thinking about their cruel fate always brought him pain. No amount of reconstruction could bring them back to her. The rambling estate—its houses, barns, and outbuildings—existed no more, reduced to scattered piles of stone and rubble. Somehow the old country manor had withstood the previous centuries of armed conflict and emerged relatively unharmed.

That was before the most recent war, when this one portion

of the countryside was the battleground where the Allied Forces fought Hitler's German Armies. It hardly mattered now which one was responsible for its ultimate ruin, but five years ago the Bertrand Estate nearly ceased to be, living on in name and memory only.

At home in Paris, the Duchênes' family life had resumed slowly, solemnly. By the end of 1945, the dining room furniture was somehow returned to them. Piece by piece, item by item, the big, empty house began to resemble a home. Occasionally a piece of news arrived too, and his father would spend the day nursing some personal sadness, silent and deep, but then he'd resume work. At times another message would reach the family, and Louis would notice how a great weight of concern was lifted from his parents. His father spoke rarely of the war he'd fought and even less of the small victories he had achieved.

A cloud passed in front of the sun, briefly throwing the pastures into welcome shade. His sister Françoise was like that from time to time. She'd be laughing and playing with his brother Marc, but her smile would fade, only for a moment, and she would seem to stare away at nothing at all. Then she would brighten, smiling once more, pretty hazel eyes twinkling, and it was as if the sun had reappeared, just like it was doing today.

Louis's summer job, his last carefree year before university, had brought him north to Normandy. Joining a group of other young men he would work at the site, helping to collect whatever remnants of the original structures and crumbled barns they could. Next they would excavate more chunks of native Caen stone. The creamy gold limestone, the coveted material of cathedrals and grand manor houses throughout France and England, was buried like a treasure beneath layers of soil, theirs for the taking and rebuilding.

It was the most physically demanding work Louis had ever known, but he welcomed the relative anonymity provided by his obligation, that summer of 1949. The assumption, one he did not try to correct, was that he was one of them, a boy from nearby St-Etienne-des-Près or one of the other neighboring villages.

Monsieur Pagnol, the stonemason in charge of his grand-parents' rebuilding project, either was unaware of Louis's connection with the Bertrand family or it had slipped his mind, a mind that also seemed to have a slippery grasp of other matters. Pagnol's main concern, like many who were struggling to rebuild a life postwar, was basic economics. If he could hire schoolboys to complete a portion of the unskilled labor, so much the better for his profit.

In the evenings, Louis relaxed, enjoying the camaraderie and bawdy humor of the local boys. They bemoaned the same blisters and the same aches; they shared and smoked the same rough, unfiltered Gauloises when permitted a respite from work. Had the other lads suspected he was related to the local squire, the man who owned the replanted orchards that sprawled around them and who employed a large percentage of the villagers, the freedom offered by the days of summer would not have been possible.

Pagnol had just called an immediate halt to all work. The sun beat down on them in the stillness nearing noon while Louis and the other boys waited, one or two still watching and leaning on their shovels. Everyone gladly accepted the merciful interlude allowed from digging up charred blocks of old stone and hacking into the ancient rock beneath. A sturdy lift-truck was hauling the results of their labor to the construction site where the old manor house had started to take form, one stone at a time.

Louis turned to his side, listening. Even the stonemason's truck had stopped, its groaning engine stilled to join the quiet of midday and the hush of anticipation.

The most recent discovery of a bomb in the fields late this morning would cause yet another delay. Louis imagined the stonemason grumbling and grousing once more; he was always complaining about something and today would be no exception. However, the work crew had fortunately received explicit orders, commands that superseded anything from Pagnol. Louis sighed and lay down again, pressing his back deep into the earth against crisp tufts of spring grass, the cool damp a welcoming balm against sweating skin and aching muscles.

A week ago, one of the boys had unearthed what eventually would prove to be an unexploded grenade. While Pagnol was taking one of his frequent "little naps," they had tossed the small, round, dirt-encrusted object they'd found back and forth like a ball, running forward to play catch. Behaving like unthinking children, not responsible young adults, they had not even suspected what it was. Gavin Norbert, who'd unearthed the novelty, ultimately reclaimed ownership and carried his prize home at the end of the day.

The boy's father reportedly had pointed with trembling hand at the object his son casually displayed on their mantelpiece. "*Mon Dieu!* Gavin?" By then the dirt-covered ball had lost some of its hard, outer crust, become less round and slightly cone-shaped. "*What* do you have there?"

Monsieur Norbert, who had survived the war years in Normandy, hustled his family from their home and urgently reported his son's discovery to the local authorities. Following that episode, if Pagnol's lads discovered an intact bomb or a grenade, they must wait until it was safely removed by experts, not by a crew of adolescent stoneworkers.

Many years later, grown to more responsible adulthood, Louis would read the daunting figures, estimates that out of every ten grenades or other small ordnance fired during the war, by either the Allies or the Germans, an average of only eight exploded. Bombs seemed more reliable: out of twenty dropped or launched, a "statistical average" of eighteen had exploded correctly.

"That left behind at least two, but only one 'statistically,'" he would remind his friends with grim irony, "a dud, while the remaining one was live, very much alive." As they were digging in his grandparents' pastures, each time he and the other boys unearthed an unexploded grenade, they might have faced a fifty-fifty chance of serious injury or death. The destructive possibilities of even one undetonated bomb boggled his mind.

One of the grossly underestimated advantages of rural life, Louis was discovering that summer, was the efficacy of the grapevine and neighborhood gossip. He turned on his side and pushed up on one elbow to watch the crowd that traipsed out from town, always following the munitions handlers when they drove through the countryside to the Bertrand properties. He'd listened to the officials and could have repeated their warnings, much like his catechism.

"*Mesdames et messieurs,* you must understand this is very dangerous work, *eh?* We are trained in the safe removal of armaments. It is most important that you stay here, in your homes." The munitions handlers, dressed in severe uniform coveralls and wearing helmets with hinged-metal faceguards, would stop to deliver the perfunctory words, thereby only raising the level of fascination.

Their safety lectures were largely useless. The local folk would hear the heavy trucks lumber through town, and curiosity would spread from house to house like an epidemic of measles. As routinely as the villagers were cautioned and instructed not to leave town, most would predictably abandon whatever they were doing and find some means of transport to come observe what might be happening at the Bertrand Estate.

They're crazy! Louis thought as he rolled onto his back. Face to the sky, he gazed up into the dome of summer blue, closed his eyes in resignation, and dozed off again. Pagnol would wake him once the munitions workers left and declared the field safe.

This morning he had unearthed the item in question, his shovel clanging off the unmistakable resistance of iron and steel. He'd earlier isolated and pried one block of the house's original carved stone from the earth. It was a lintel from the front doorway, rich loam clinging deep in its crevices, the carved date of 1736 worn so smooth he wouldn't have been able to read it but for the dark stains. Then he stopped and pulled away, holding his breath in alarm. The ominously dark, oval, and pointed object he just exposed beside the stonework was clearly a bomb.

After the previous week's episode with the grenade, local law enforcement handed the lads crude illustrations as a precaution to help them identify what they might find. This, too, proved only moderately useful. Despite their good intentions, the officials failed to indicate any relative scale: a hand grenade was drawn the same size as a bomb, a bomb the same as a bullet. The boys also received vague instructions "to maintain a safe distance."

What was a "safe distance" anyway? No one had ever clarified that for them either. They had all wondered and asked, but each arrived at his own private decision of what seemed safe. No one offered any further suggestions, and by sheer luck no one had been injured. The low stone wall separating the pasture from the replanted and restored orchards provided as much protection as anything else. Therefore most of them were joining Louis, sprawled about on the carpet of fresh new grass, shovels and picks dropped by their sides. Each moment of rest was a treat because Pagnol was a rigorous taskmaster.

"Anyone got a cigarette?" someone nearby called out.

Louis yawned, reached into his pocket for a half-empty packet of Gauloises, and tossed it in the general direction of whomever had spoken. He watched as the cigarette pack sailed through the air, a small pale blue missile disappearing against the sky, and listened to the murmured *"Merci!"* indicating that the cigarettes had found a home. He closed his eyes once more.

The music of a gentle female voice awakened him.

"Bonjour? Hello?" A girl knelt beside him, her cool, small hand resting tentatively on his forehead. "You feel hot."

Louis blinked, awakening with a start. He tried staring up toward the girl's face, but she remained silhouetted by the sun whose angle indicated an hour well past noon. He glanced around, feeling muddled and sluggish from sleep; the others must have returned to work. Sighing, he sat up. Sleeping on the job wouldn't look good, not to his fellow workers or to the grumpy old stonemason. He raised a hand to shield his eyes against the glare of midday.

"I was wondering," the girl began, her voice rising hopefully but then faltering. "Would you like to have lunch?" She remained kneeling beside him.

"*Merci,* but I must get back to work," Louis responded in a rush. He sat up quickly and groped around on the ground, quickly locating his shovel and pick.

His visitor pushed up and stood, now bubbling with excitement, happy and assured, the bearer of news. "Oh, but no! They've only now left with the bomb!"

Turning away from the sun, Louis could finally see the girl's face. He shouldn't call her a girl, he supposed, because she was probably but a year or so younger than him. She had light hair and eyes the color of the sky above them. Her fair slender arms were turned pink from standing a long time in the day's sun, and she grasped a picnic basket, extended before her and offered up like a gift.

"It took them longer than usual," she continued eagerly. "Ah! I've never seen one that big before." She placed the basket on the grass and gestured, trying to encompass the dimensions of the huge object and create a vision for him. "The soldiers dug and dug. For a long time and *so* carefully." Her eyes widened in amazement as she described the excitement of the day's events that Louis had slept through. "So many men too! It was like they were wearing armor. And then, they needed to send for a different truck to take it away!" The girl concluded her account, breathless from the retelling.

He scrambled to his feet, brushing grass and twigs from his work clothes and knocking stray leaves from his hair. He flicked away several curious ants that must have considered him part of the landscape since he had been there so long, occupying their terrain.

"But where are you going?" the girl persisted.

"Back to work," Louis said. "With the others, my buddies—*mes copains.*"

"Oh, no. I think there will be no more work today!"

The girl laughed and only then did Louis notice how very pretty she was. Like his mother and grandmother she carried the same fair Norman genes, a delicate, soft coloring that his younger brother Marc had inherited too.

"The others—they are eating lunch now. Monsieur Pagnol says he might not work the rest of the day himself. I think he was very frightened." She gestured toward the picnic basket, glancing up at him through lowered lashes. "Today, we decided to bring a lunch for all of you. My name is Nicole."

Louis extended one hand to her while he casually indicated himself with the other. "Louis. *Enchanté, Mademoiselle.*" As usual he didn't offer the family surname, hoping to protect what anonymity he could while here with the local young men, many of whom he'd come to consider his pals. For this summer, but probably never again in the future, he would be "just one of the guys." It wouldn't help if he were recognized as the grandson of the local squire. Even in absentia, his grandfather Monsieur le Seigneur Maurice Bertrand of the Bertrand Estate—or what was left of it—would forever be regarded thus.

Nicole blushed at his formal greeting but smiled again. "*Bon.* Do you want to eat lunch with the others?" She motioned toward a group in the distance. Teenaged girls in the pastel, full-skirted dresses of summer, like blossoms that billowed from the grass, were sitting about under the trees in the orchard, chattering with Louis's work crew.

"Here's good enough." Louis eased back into the grass, yawning and leaning against the rock wall. "Unless you prefer to join the others, of course."

Nicole's shy smile provided an answer, her cheeks turning the pale pink of the new apples ripening above them. She reached into the basket and handed a bottle of cool cider to Louis. "Can you open that?" A note of uncertainty caused her voice to rise.

Louis nodded confidently. If the summer's work had done nothing else, it was developing new muscles and rough calluses in places he couldn't have imagined before. He often ached at night. "It builds character," his father had reminded him before he left Paris for Normandy. Character must hurt one hell of a lot, he would think many times during the summer.

He pushed at the cork, pried, and wiggled the bulbous top. At last, at the moment when he thought he would need to admit defeat, the cork slipped out with a slight *pffft*.

"*Voilà!*" he exclaimed, not concealing his pride and relieved surprise. He reached to pour the bubbling cider into the cups Nicole held out for him.

"Did you notice the label?" Her cheeks dimpled when she spoke. "It's from here, from the Bertrand Orchards." She waved toward the young trees around them, as though the gesture and the deed were assuring his approval and complicity. Depending on the species of tree some were already producing small pink and yellow fruit while others still fluttered in blossom.

Right then, especially before this pretty girl who clearly was flirting with him, it would have been natural and ever so tempting to divulge his connection to the estate, but Louis reconsidered. Whatever he said would not stay with her, of that he was certain. "Yes! Well, so it is!" He grinned and touched his cup to hers. "It seems proper to toast finding yet another bomb at the Bertrand Estate with Bertrand cider!"

She tore off one end of the baguette she'd brought and handed it to Louis as she focused on preparing their meal. He was finding this plain fare, especially on a warm day like today, quite appealing and a refreshing change. He munched on the crust of bread and watched the girl bend over her task, spreading the two halves of the slender loaf with a creamy local cheese and layering it with slices of ham.

She glanced up through her eyelashes as she handed him the simple lunch. "There. It's not much."

"Thank you." Louis sipped at the bubbling cider and bit into the open-faced sandwich. He chewed thoughtfully for several minutes and sighed. "This is very good."

"Do you live here in St-Etienne?" Nicole asked at last, after they'd eaten together in silence. "I don't remember you from school."

"I know some families in the area," Louis improvised. "I came here for the summer work."

She looked up, her sky blue eyes meeting his. "Oh, I see."

Had she guessed somehow? Louis wondered if she really did understand. His accent was an easy blend of Paris schooling, influence from his maternal grandparents who had lived in Normandy most of their lives, plus the seven years his family had spent in Geneva. He was certain his speech wouldn't reveal anything about him. Their eyes met and remained that way until she turned, shyness pulling her gaze away from his.

"Some of us were going to bring a picnic supper out here one evening, if you think Monsieur Pagnol won't mind. A little party, perhaps? Because it stays light until so late."

Pagnol, Louis knew, liked to retire early thus to enjoy the companionship of a bottle of Calvados, another local product, the brandy which probably also wore the Bertrand label. "I don't think he'd mind if it's after work." He hoped their boss wouldn't object. "Should I tell the others?"

"Oh, no." Nicole blushed furiously, the pink deepening on her cheeks and spreading up the sides of her face, a slash of vermillion against the mottled shade. "My friends are doing that now. We decided our plan before we came out today. Next Thursday—exactly midsummer."

"Unless we have another bomb, of course." Louis smiled and began to reach for her hand, but she had pulled back. "That'd be nice. The guys will like it, I know. This is hard work." He leaned back against the wall, ripped open another package of Gauloises, and lit one, pulling deeply against the rough smoke. He replaced the cigarettes in his shirt pocket, but then remembered he hadn't offered one to his lunch partner. He could hear his father's stern etiquette lecture starting, "Always offer your guest a cigarette *first,* Louis."

"Mademoiselle?" He held out the package to her, one cigarette tipped forward in invitation.

Nicole shook her head. *"Non, merci."* This time she leaned in closer to him, almost as if she were reconsidering his offer.

Louis casually stretched his arm in her direction, a movement of deliberate nonchalance, and, almost by accident, he touched her at last. He felt her hand resist at first, then suddenly melt into his—soft, tender, and ever so small. They sat that way for several minutes, hand in hand. He moved his fingers until they touched the inner place on her wrist where her pulse beat, and he felt it race forward, as though he'd somehow got hold of her heart. He firmed his grip and pulled her toward him, increasingly aware of how small and delicate she was.

At the moment it seemed the most natural thing in the world to do. He turned to her and cupped her face in hands roughened by hard work, taking care to hold the cigarette away from her, and brought her nearer. With his thumb he caressed her round pink cheeks, first one and then the other, his touch trailing across her lips. Her eyes never left his, wide and fair and blue and innocent. Uncertainly, she leaned into him but paused, her parted lips waiting a fraction of an inch from his.

Louis also hesitated before completing their link, resting his lips against hers for a second before he kissed her: first gently, then harder, probing, seeking, questioning.

Nicole gasped and pulled away. Breathing heavily, she leaned her face into his shoulder for a moment. "I'll come back next week," she whispered, her hand clasped over her mouth.

Was she trying to guard his kiss? Louis smiled at the thought. He'd certainly liked it well enough.

Covering her confusion, Nicole reached to collect the remnants of their lunch, hastily gathering napkins, cups, and the empty bottle into her basket. She scrambled to her feet and left. Louis watched her run away, waiting for her to turn back, but she never did.

———

Rain, a steady downpour, interrupted work for the next two days, an unpredictable force of nature even Pagnol's impatient grumbling couldn't control. Standing water soon filled the crater left by the excavation of what everyone would refer to as Louis's bomb, a very much alive piece of ordnance the authorities had quickly identified as German.

Once the rain stopped, the boys returned to digging in the muddy earth, easily discovering more leftover ammunition. Pagnol managed to circumvent his official orders by inventing a new one, just a bit of a variation. "Instead you will mark the spots where you have found grenades or other military weapons. Then dig elsewhere."

Unless the entire estate was pockmarked with these things, which would eventually prove to be the case, the stonemason decreed they would interrupt work but once a week. Mid-August would come all too soon, when Pagnol would lose his cheap workforce. The boys would return to other villages, some to school, and at least two—which ones he could never remember—to university.

The sun stayed with them, their daily companion, blazing through the spiked poplars and trailing through the newly-leafed orchards. The soft pastels of late spring matured, painting the fields and hedgerows a deep, rich green.

One of the boys shouted up from the fields. "At least the ground is drier, *eh?*"

"You think this is easier than lifting mud, *mon ami?*" A good-natured reply teased the other lad across the heavy air of summer.

On June 20, Pagnol allowed the munitions experts to return and retrieve what they must. "Quite a day today. So many finds."

The officer stared at the stonemason, his appraisal curious and slightly suspicious. He gazed out over the fields where dozens of small white streamers attached to twigs fluttered beside the discoveries of the past week.

Pagnol shrugged in dismissal, his gesture noncommittal. "There must have been heavy fighting. Just right here. *Non?*"

The military captain in charge of munitions recovery shook his head at this explanation. There wasn't much he could do about it. Out in the countryside, without constant surveillance, Pagnol ruled. The captain shrugged in response and directed his crew to begin work.

Thursday, Midsummer's Day, dawned hot and still, the air hanging heavy over the fresh, raw excavations. Breezes that usually drifted in, flowing over the low hills from the Channel and easing down into the countryside, remained stalled off the northern coast. By early afternoon, the stoneworkers were struggling against the resistance of heat and humidity. Most would lift a shovel or a pick only when someone noticed that Pagnol was watching.

Sound seemed to travel easily on a warm still evening. Rémy, one of the work crew, triumphantly called up to the others, "Pagnol just drove away!" His voice rang out across the fields and through the trees. He'd been down by the road cleaning tools, while most of his fellow workers were acres away, either in the far pastures or up in the orchards, probing with care around the roots of replanted trees. Shovels clattered to the ground, and the lads hurried down to the stream to wash as best they could before the girls arrived.

"They're coming!" another boy shouted. "I can hear them!"

Like the treble notes of a melody, their voices carried on the first chance breeze of early evening. The sound of teenaged girls, high and sweet, sailed out from St-Etienne toward the Bertrand Estate. Music from a tinny car radio eventually joined them, a popular song that everyone seemed to know for they all quickly clamored to its chorus, the high happy notes of the carefree and young.

Someone else in Louis's group, a boy named Pierre, spotted the vanguard of the cavalcade as it moved closer. "Here they are! I can see them now!"

Teenaged girls in an ancient car were leading the group, followed by a horse-drawn wagon carrying the beer and most of the evening's picnic. Crowded on the wagon were more party goers, brothers and sisters and cousins of the workers. Since the beginning of time, where there were young men inevitably there would also be young women, and here they were on a Midsummer's Eve, drawn together as though dictated by nature.

Louis watched them move in, a few stragglers following the car slowly. Several boys jumped off the wagon before it stopped and pulled onto the verge of the pasture. One by one, the girls disentangled themselves from the car; others climbed down from the wagon, trailing the picnic baskets.

Two boys carefully helped Yves Pomereau down from the wagon. He was a tall, gangly youth on crutches; his left trouser leg was pinned up halfway, and a guitar was slung by a strap around his neck. He had not stepped on a grenade in the Bertrand fields: six years ago a wall had collapsed on him during an artillery barrage and crushed his leg. Others carried the beer and cider down to the stream where Louis was helping stack the bottles in the chill water, wedging them with care among the rocks.

He searched for the girl he'd met before, but didn't find her. *Must be too young,* he thought. She probably couldn't come out for an evening party after all. The others quickly paired off with the friends they'd come to know over the past few weeks. The lad with crutches and guitar settled down against the rock wall where he plucked at the strings, expertly tuning the instrument.

"*Heh!*" one of the boys called, shouting in Louis's direction. "Any wood up there?"

"For what?"

"A fire, *mon vieux.* We'll need to build a fire."

Louis shrugged at the sweat trickling down his back, wondering why they could possibly want a fire in this hot weather, when the sun would shine until nearly nine o'clock, but he helped gather stumps of dead trees, fallen branches, and twigs needed for tinder.

"Attention!" He called to others plunging through the orchards and tearing into the trees. "Pagnol will report any damage up there," he reminded them. Once again tempted, he'd almost admitted that this was, in some sense, his property too.

A crude suggestion as to what Pagnol could do about it was proposed, but the pack dispersed, searching for firewood elsewhere.

Within half an hour they'd collected enough for a bonfire, and the boy with the guitar was soon strumming familiar songs that everyone knew. The girls, a few wearing stylish pedal pushers and halter tops, were seated by their boyfriends, some already enfolded in familiar arms.

Louis was sipping on a beer, chilled from its bath in the stream, and picking up half a sandwich. "Not bad," he commented, unaware that he was interrupting the young man to his left who was paying serious homage to the lips of the girl seated across his lap.

"Eh?" Antoine said, breaking away from a particularly lengthy kiss and turning back to Louis. His arm rested possessively around the girl.

"Do you do this a lot?" Louis asked. Their family was casual at the seashore, at Cap Ferret, but never had he been with a crowd like this one. Any picnics he could recall were relatively sedate affairs by comparison.

Antoine laughed. "Not as often as we should, *mon ami.*" He turned back to embrace the girl, allowing his hand to slip casually down through her halter top.

At that moment the cooling breezes of evening finally arrived, stirring the fire and sending up bright cinders that swirled high into a spiral of light and sparked the sky above. Someone seated to Louis's right spoke in a whisper. "Now, I'm cold."

Had she been there all the while? The girl from last week smiled back at him.

"Nicole? *C'est vous?*" he asked. "It's really you? You came out here?" Unlike the others, who easily lapsed into the familiarity of *tu,* he had not yet done so except among the guys at work. Especially not with the girl.

She nodded and smiled.

Louis, aware once more of how lovely she was, glanced back at the group. One couple was leaving the circle at the now welcome fire, laughing and stumbling as they walked, the boy's arm surrounding the girl's waist, her hips pressed close to his.

"Where have you been?" he asked.

Nicole indicated the sandwich in his hand,

"Oh, here." He offered the other half to her. "Are you hungry?" he said, feeling dull with his lack of originality. There was no telling what she might make of his unbrilliant repartee.

"Oh, no. I was helping with the sandwiches."

She was shivering. He removed his shirt as he'd watched the other boys do and draped it around her shoulders.

The breeze, steady and cool, a gift borne on the changing of tides from miles away, had shifted and would be theirs for the evening. They leaned close together in the twilight, music and soft voices drifting over them, the young men and the girls who needed to be together.

They were all so very alive and so very glad of it. Now and then, Louis noticed other couples slip away from the group, the boy's arm encircling the girl's waist and pulling her firmly against him. Other couples would return sometime later, clinging to each other as though they'd become one. They huddled nearer to the warmth of the bonfire, eyes aglow in the reflected flames.

Louis set his unfinished sandwich aside. He reached for Nicole; she was still shivering. He pulled her into his arms and held her close. Her pretty sky-blue eyes met his as they had on the day last week. He leaned down to kiss her, just as he had before. She allowed him to slide his hands up through her blouse until they rested around her waist, just for a moment. He pressed her tightly against him and moved his palms upward, caressing her small firm breasts, the nipples arousing to his touch. She trembled and sighed, breathing faster, but relaxed into his embrace. They kissed again… and once more.

"Ah…." Nicole sighed and whispered against him, after a while. "I wish this could last forever."

"Hmm?" Louis responded lazily. *"Mais, oui."*

Life was good. There was no war. All about them only the warm sweetness of summer lay upon the pastures of Normandy. He was certain this was one part of the months of hard work he would always remember.

❖

4 Nicole & Annette Chaumont

St-Etienne-des-Près, Normandy 1950

IT WOULD HAVE BEEN DIFFICULT for a teenager in those times, as 1949 became 1950, when the myth persisted that good girls—virtuous girls—could never have a baby out of wedlock. Nicole's mother would have scolded and the neighbors would surely have stared in disapproval, but the bulky clothes of winter helped conceal the baby that was growing inside her. She hid her pregnancy as long as she could, until February.

Icy fog had settled upon the countryside. The grim shades of early dawn, square panes of black and gray, were outlining the window of her bedroom; frosty condensation was refreezing along the edges, tiny icicles forming in contrast to the fiery, griping pain in her belly. Could it have been dinner last night—her mother's delectable *pâté maison*—that disagreed with her? It was always one of her favorites.

Still half-asleep she curled into the pain, guarding the swollen tenderness of her abdomen, trying to protect herself. Why was it so bitterly cold, so suddenly? It could not get any more frigid, she was thinking, until she fully awakened to chilled bed clothes, soaked in blood. The slightly metallic scent was unmistakable and, in the semi-darkness, she could make out the clots of dark red clinging to her fingers.

Nicole's terror shrilled through their house. *"Maman!"*

Annette Chaumont rushed to her daughter's room and stared disbelieving at the scene before her. Realization dawned, followed quickly by despair. Blood was soaking through Nicole's bed clothes; one small, congealed puddle lay on the wooden floor.

Even before the latest war, St-Etienne had never had any medical facilities. Old Doctor Arnaud died in 1937 and no one had come to replace him. As the village struggled to heal its wounds afterward, even fewer resources remained. *Of course, there's Marie Grandbois,* she thought. The name filtered through Annette's haze of shock and disbelief. The local nurse who had served during the Great War was much older now, but Marie was the only possible medical help for miles. Although her main experience had been treating battlefield casualties, she surely would know what to do.

Shivering with dread as much as from the cold, Annette ran back through the dark and silent village streets. She paused, breathless, at the first group of houses then raced over the final stretch of war-pitted cobblestones. She hammered at the shutters of the old nurse's modest cottage. *"Au secours!* Marie, help me!" Jarred from sleep, the older woman grasped the urgency in Annette's voice, if not her jumbled words and what she was trying to convey, and joined her in another frantic dash along the deserted streets of St-Etienne.

Help for Nicole arrived too little and too late. The healthy pink skin of a fifteen-year-old, in the bloom of youth and glow of pregnancy, was already fading to pale gray, a match to the dimness of the room. Splotches of fresh blood were one of the few signs that life was actually still there. Annette and Marie rushed to the bedside, and Nicole groaned again, a forceful expulsion of the agony gripping and tearing at her from within.

Marie jerked back the sodden sheets. *"Mon Dieu!"* she exclaimed, her horrified words sliding up the scale nearly a full octave. She stared down at what lay between the girl's legs: a tiny, blood-covered infant, its miniature chest heaving in a supreme effort to inhale its first breath.

Annette stood by the nurse, silent and in shock, but automatically making the Sign of the Cross, while Marie instantly grasped the urgency of the new crisis before them. Annette would always remember what followed as a single ruthless and ultimately useless series of events.

Marie Grandbois severed the infant's umbilical cord with the sewing shears she always carried in her skirt pocket. She jerked free the black ribbon used to secure her gray hair into a prim chignon and tied a knot around the baby's earlier anchor to life, what now lay deflated and limp in the spreading blood. She hastily wrapped the baby in her shawl and thrust the bundle into Annette's arms. Last, with both fists she began what appeared to be a violent assault on the girl's flaccid, empty abdomen.

Annette later imagined she had screamed, "Stop! Stop! You're hurting her!" Coming from the frozen void of her consciousness, there may have been no sound at all, the words locked somewhere between mind and voice. She could never be certain whether she had called out or not.

Marie continued, frantically pummeling and kneading at the girl as the blood kept flowing. "Pay attention!" she ordered. "You must help me! Annette, your daughter's dying! She's hemorrhaging! It's the only way to stop the bleeding—if we can. Raise the end of the bed!"

Following the old nurse's instructions, she jammed Nicole's school books under the bed frame, angling it slightly, still grasping the baby in her left arm. Surreally detached, she watched blood ease up the incline: a bright red that was turning darker as it pooled in a mass near Nicole's limp, white hands.

Not comprehending that Marie was trying to preserve circulation to her daughter's brain, Annette had mistakenly assumed the blood would flow back inside. "Does that really work?" she whispered. She stood by watching, immobile, numbed and disoriented.

Marie ignored her. Despite the chill of the room, sweat was beading on her forehead as she massaged deep, begging the girl's body to respond and for her traumatized uterus to obey. "*S'il vous plaît, mon Dieu!*" She grunted a prayer to the veins and arteries before her and to any available power in her attempts to stop the life-stream that poured forth, determined to empty the childlike vessel of all it contained.

Nicole opened her eyes once and stared upward. Her eyelids fluttered as if seeking something among the dark spots that would have dominated her vision, the consequence of heavy blood loss. She seemed to have difficulty focusing and frowned against the pain. "A girl?" she whispered, her pale lips barely moving.

Annette lifted one corner of Marie's shawl, looked, and nodded, temporarily unable to say anything more.

"Louise…." Nicole breathed out the single word, voice and life ebbing from her as one. The agony that had gripped and torn at her was gone at last and she lay dead.

The brusque efficiency the old nurse had focused on the dying girl was immediately transferred to the new development—a baby, obviously premature. Later, Annette would reflect back, identifying this as the moment too when the town's ostracizing and recriminations subtly began, what would be perfected and refined in the days to come. In that instant Marie changed from using the familiar *tu,* speaking to Annette stiffly and coldly as *vous.*

"It's a miracle the tiny infant is breathing on her own," Marie stated, her tone crisp and businesslike. She peered closely at the small chest that rose and fell, rapidly but curiously without strain or effort, a newborn baby girl, mercifully unaware of how close to death she, too, had been.

With total disregard for the newly deceased, Marie grabbed the blankets flung aside during her earlier attempts to halt Nicole's bleeding. She raised one finger in admonition. "It is most important that you keep the little one warm, Madame." She spoke formally to Nicole's mother, whom she'd addressed familiarly, as would a friend and neighbor, calling her by her given name mere seconds before.

"Empty that drawer." Marie nodded toward the small chest by the bed. "Follow me. You must warm your kitchen." She fired off orders as would a drill sergeant, accustomed to unquestioned obedience.

Annette could picture her, among the hospital tents of France and Flanders during earlier wars, directing, managing, expecting action, and saving one life out of four or five, not wasting energy on what had happened, only on what could be helped.

Within minutes the premature baby was swaddled in clean dry towels and lodged neatly in her first crib, the emptied drawer that her young mother had once filled with a teenager's treasures of blouses, sweaters, and trinkets, this new home placed on a kitchen chair near the open stove.

Marie Grandbois rubbed at her arthritic back and collapsed onto the other chair. Long, lank gray hair drooped around her shoulders, accentuating her exhaustion. She accepted the cup of tea that Annette held out for her, but waved away her other small offers of hospitality.

"You are a wanton woman, Madame Chaumont." She sniffed in disapproval. "You are without shame. Only a wanton woman would allow such a thing to happen, isn't that so?" She finished the tea and set aside the cup and saucer, sighing as she pushed wearily to her feet.

"The babe must eat, Madame," she directed. "At first, you must mix sugar or honey with water. Boil the water, but let it cool until it's slightly warm. Use a clean handkerchief, dip it in the sugar-water, and perhaps the babe is old enough to suck. How old is she?" She shrugged and raised both hands, indicating her inability to even guess.

Shaking her head, Annette shared her ignorance.

"Maybe six months?" Marie continued. "Ernest Branchet... he has goats. I will send him to you with goats' milk. Most babies can drink goats' milk." She paused, groaning with fatigue. "I will ask too if someone in the village has baby bottles. You must keep her warm." She repeated the reminder for the grieving mother and stunned new grandmother. "Do you have enough fuel? For *this* many will share, I think." She arched her eyebrows meaningfully to specify that any generosity would be intended for the baby, not in acknowledgement of the death of Annette's teenaged daughter. She stood to take her leave, reaching absently for her shawl.

Annette pointed to the blood-stained clothing, tossed aside in a corner of the kitchen. All harried activity had subsided, and her tears had begun after the initial shock.

"I'm so sorry, Marie, but it's ruined. I'll try to wash it for you. Please, wait! You can't go out like that—it's much too cold." Sobbing, she returned to Nicole's room. "Her sweater?" she whispered, handing the old nurse a gray cardigan.

Marie accepted the small sweater without comment and wrapped it awkwardly around her broad shoulders. Through her tears, Annette reached out to embrace the other woman. "Thank you for coming, Marie. Oh, thank you so much," she sobbed

The town's nurse raised both hands and violently shoved her away. Startled by the forcefulness of the blow, Annette stumbled back but caught herself before falling.

"I find your conduct offensive. I do not approve. Goodbye, Madame." Marie Grandbois nodded stiffly, pulled open the door and, stepped out into the freezing gray February dawn.

Annette watched Marie walk away, holding herself primly erect, distancing herself from a premature baby and from death and from the stain of sin. She'd offered no words of consolation. Annette waited by the door, hoping, but Marie Grandbois never turned back. The fingers of icy gray fog that lay upon the land seemed to have reached inside, wrapping themselves around her heart.

❖

5 Monsignor Guichard

St-Etienne-des-Près, 1950

MONSIGNOR ROMAIN-PAUL GUICHARD was certainly not the oldest member of the priesthood in France, but he felt like it, thoroughly exhausted and entitled to weariness. Nearing the age of seventy he often imagined that the Church might have overlooked his existence. In a village of fewer than four hundred souls, it seemed unlikely that his superiors would have allowed a monsignor to remain. A young seminarian, assigned to the countryside and responsible for two or three villages of the same size, would have been a more appropriate choice for the Roman Catholic Church in postwar France. Yet here he was still, in the rectory of L'Eglise-de-St-Etienne-des-Près.

Bracing his arms on the worn oak desk, he faced yet one more tiring, draining dilemma as he struggled with God and his conscience and Annette Chaumont.

Annette had been there in his study for the past half hour. She sat before him, hugging against her chest a very tiny baby who was red and quite wrinkled. Luckily the infant was quiet; he thought it was almost too quiet.

"Surely, Madame, you must understand that she has sinned," he was explaining, for at least the fourth time. "Had sinned," he corrected himself. "A mortal sin in the eyes of the Church. She has borne a child without benefit of Holy Matrimony, and…." He sighed because by now his explanations, although correct by the teachings of Holy Mother Church, had begun to sound weak and inadequate to his own ears.

"My daughter was but a child," Annette begged, tears coursing down her cheeks.

Guichard sighed and leaned forward, head in his hands. What was he to do? By the grace of God and the most Blessed Virgin Mary—automatically he made the Sign of the Cross in gratitude—he had survived two wars. During the Great War, the war which was to end all wars, he had served as an army chaplain but had also fought in the trenches with his unit. Armed like the rest, his purple *stola,* small prayer book, and chaplain kit were additional armament, issued as though by another Commander.

Throughout the years that followed and the next war, Guichard tried to bear his old war injuries quietly, without complaint, offering up each ache and pang as penance. Pain was a reminder of the losses of war and of the men he surely must have killed. Each bout—some much worse than others—might bring him closer to death any day, at any time, or so the doctors had told him. He had been wounded at the Battle of Verdun in 1916, and those injuries had ended his short military career. One fragment of shrapnel remained lodged in his lower back.

The doctor had shaken his head apologetically. "Too close to the spinal cord to operate, *mon père.*" His further pronouncement was more discouraging. Perhaps one day the small piece of metal would decide Guichard's fate, abruptly and without surgery, he'd been told.

Another piece of metal he carried even closer. It was a sliver of tin from the chaplain's kit in which he had carried the Holy Sacrament at all times; it had lodged under his ribs, near his heart. The small kit, with its round container protecting the Host, had saved his life once, deflecting the trajectory of a bullet. That one sliver lingered within him—always a threat, always a reminder. When the fragment chose to migrate inward toward his heart, Guichard accepted that his life would be in God's hands.

In his long years as a priest he had endured horror and mayhem. He had blessed the dying, both friend and foe, buried his friends and neighbors, and comforted the grieving. More and more the thought came to him that his fatigue was well-earned. When it was cold and damp and grim like today, the pains plagued him even more.

Guichard sighed again, out of habit placing one hand over his heart questioningly, before turning back to contemplate the problem at hand. *What would a younger priest do?* he wondered. *Someone who has not seen or suffered as much?* However, there was no other priest, only him. Feeling increasingly harassed, he resumed his struggle with God and his conscience and the woman with the baby. She represented a moral and theological dilemma.

"But, Madame, surely you must understand your daughter had sinned." The words sounded hollow since by now he had repeated himself five or six times. He was losing count.

"She didn't have the chance to confess." Annette shook her head. "I wish I knew the name of the father, but I don't. She bled to death! For God's sake, *please* Father Guichard. Please, *mon père*," she sobbed.

Guichard felt overwhelmed.

Just a few years ago, he had walked through the bomb-pitted, blackened fields, all that remained of the countryside's lush orchards and horse paddocks, anointing and granting absolution, and giving Last Rites to all who lay dying, the killers of innocents and innocents alike. Now he was withholding this simplest of consolations, a Christian burial, from one of his own.

Annette was a good woman. She'd been widowed as Hitler's armies forced their way across the countryside and claimed Normandy. Nicholas Chaumont was the first of their village to die in its defense. His, too, would be the first name on the village's war memorial once the town had the funds to rebuild; it was also missing its top ornament and cross years after the Bosch had used it for target practice. Guichard's wars were done, quite over; he was too tired to fight anymore.

The sight of Annette in her agony, as she grasped the premature baby in her arms and pleaded for her daughter, was moving something deep within him. He wondered briefly whether it was the shrapnel or the piece from the round tin box. War was a strange conditioner. It would either harden one to everything or leave one so fragile that the slightest touch could cause one to crumble. He was certain which he had become and at last felt powerless in the face of so much. There were the many parishioners and others he'd buried in the past fifteen years. All those young soldiers—French, English, Canadian, American, Australian, and German—to this day their blood saturated the soil around him. He had blessed all he could in their dying, regardless of their faith. And now this....

.   He had known Annette, her daughter Nicole, her husband, and their entire family as far back as he could remember, for all their lives and a good many years of his. She continued to rock the strangely silent bundle in her arms against the physical warmth of empty breasts. The baby had made but one sound—soft, rather like the mewling of a kitten—then was quiet again. Relieved, he released the breath he'd been holding. At least this one child was alive. He looked up finally, his tired gaze meeting hers. Annette's pretty blue eyes—they were so like the girl Nicole's—were rimmed red from crying.

Annette's voice was no more than a whisper. "Please, I beg of you." Silent tears were running steadily down her once soft and lovely face, grown haggard with grief.

Guichard started to protest again but sighed in resignation. "*Oui, Madame*. As you wish." He raised both hands in defeat. "Tomorrow morning, early. Very early, if you please."

He was thoroughly exhausted by life, by war, by his own pain, by tragedy, and now by this woman. Her arguments were valid, after all: "She was but a child," "It was an accident"—he would concede that much—"She'd had no chance to make confession" or receive the Last Rites. Thus he would enter her death in the church registry of St-Etienne-des-Près: Nicole Chaumont, age fifteen, died of an accident.

"However," he added, "you must find someone to dig the grave."

He sank back against the wooden chair, the protesting creaks and groans of its aged joints matching his own.

———

The following morning Guichard watched from the old rectory as Annette, with baby Louise clutched tightly in her arms, arrived just at dawn, a hint of steel gray lighting the horizon. Next came two laborers, young men whom he thought he recognized. Wasn't that Thierry, the tall fair lad? The shorter, darker boy was

Rémy, strong, muscular, and dependable. He was certain of his name. How had they been hired away from restoration work on the grand old Bertrand estate? There, acres of orchards were being restored and the old manor house was gradually rising once more, rebuilding from the ruins of war.

Their shovels turned and lifted in a practiced rhythm, soft dark mounds of soil growing around the edge of the new grave opening. Perhaps, Guichard considered practically, this was an easier job than hauling chunks of stone for the head mason at the big estate, old Monsieur Pagnol.

Finished digging, Thierry and Rémy stood by, leaning on their shovels and waiting. At a nod from Annette, they abandoned their tools, propping them against a nearby headstone, and carried the plain wooden box from the horse cart in the street and back around to the graveyard.

Guichard shivered as he stepped out into the morning chill. His surplice and *stola* fluttered and flapped about him like streaming wings in the icy breeze that whistled in from the Channel with each change of tide. He solemnly intoned the Church's brief final words, and the boys lowered the bloodless body of the young girl Nicole into consecrated ground.

He was curious, stray bits from the confessional flitting through his mind. If either of the lads recognized her as one of the group who spent part of last summer with them, relaxing and laughing after a hard day's work on the Bertrand property, they didn't say. Respectfully, Rémy and Thierry had made the Sign of the Cross, but neither uttered a word. At a nod from him, they started replacing the moist earth, soft clumps thudding against the wooden lid of the coffin. Cold silence returned to the churchyard while Guichard stood by, clutching his prayer book.

A frail sun at last pierced the leafless canopy of the surrounding plane trees, mottling the ground with light, the pale
gray patches set against the darker tones of winter. The girl's
mother Annette seemed numb with grief as she turned, nodded
to him once, and walked slowly away, passing between the headstones. Occasionally she would pause, kicking off the mud and
pebbles that clung to her shoes, aiming the clods at one grave or
another.

The tall headstones amplified her words and the sound
carried well, although the path of fallen leaves had muffled her
footsteps. "Charles Baudel, 'Faithful Husband.' Ha!" she said,
and at another, "Mathilde Courvoisier, 'Pious and Virtuous'! We
all know how virtuous you were—and so do the men in the
nearby villages!"

Guichard was shocked. *She knew about them!* He wondered
what other "secrets of the confessional" were not so secret after
all. If fornication and adultery really kept people from a Christian grave many others with such a past would not lie beneath the
grounds of his church. *Her poor daughter....* His eyes burned and
watered. The icy wind always affected him this way; surely that's
what it was. He brushed at the tears with the back of his hand.

Annette had stopped briefly between two tall headstones. She
was crying, her shoulders heaving and racked with sobs, tears
falling on the infant in her arms like a warm, salty baptism.

He watched until she'd finally left the churchyard, a woman
hopeless, bereft, and stunned. The horrendous task of burying
her only child was behind her, but ahead loomed the task of
raising another. *What would this lone woman do about Nicole's baby?*

Guichard returned to the rectory, grateful for the blazing fire
at his hearth.

In traditional villages, the priest decided, the small minds of even smaller towns could be unpredictable. In the space of two months the entire village seemed to have adopted the little infant. She became Annette's baby, almost as if an actual birth mother had never existed, although everyone referred to her now as Grandmère Annette. To Father Guichard's greater surprise, the small town rallied around the fatherless, motherless, and undeniably beautiful infant, quickly grown past the stage of dry, red wrinkles.

Given how Annette and her daughter Nicole had been treated—first by the old nurse Marie Grandbois and then by those with whom she had gossiped—he would have expected the town's self-righteous condemnation to continue. Would the censure and disapproval have been any different if the town folk had even suspected the identity of the child's father? The pregnant girl never uttered a word, never let drop the slightest hint, a secret she took to her grave. Or had she? She did name the child, he recalled. Without success Guichard tried to think of anyone in the village the baby might resemble. Was there a boy or man named Louis? Perhaps the girl had a friend from school, another Louise, the name Nicole had chosen.

Still traumatized and partially in ruins from the onslaught of two armies in a past so recent, the village seemed to view the death of Annette Chaumont's only child as the ultimate of her multiple compounded tragedies and a completed penance for the sins of her daughter, because she faced a more immediate challenge.

Local gossip and chatter on the streets easily filtered through the rectory walls.

"After all, Nicholas was such a brave man! Oh, so brave." Guichard heard this frequently, as day followed day.

"The first to give his life defending St-Etienne-des-Près."

"With the *Résistance* too!"

"Her daughter may have sinned—*mais oui!*" The speaker would shrug meaningfully. "But Annette? There is a good and virtuous woman."

"Widowed too! Her husband killed.... May God rest his soul."

"The babe... it's not her fault her mother was a...." The words were never quite spoken. Sentences would trail away with a shrug and the occasional lift of an eyebrow, but Baby Louise was welcomed, a symbolic breath of new life arising after the horror of war.

———

Her baptism was scheduled the first Sunday after Easter, because the Church was very strict in those days. Monsignor Guichard allowed no baptisms during Lent—unless the infant was ill or dying. That, *bien sûr*, was altogether a different matter, and then the Rites of Holy Mother Church were an obligation.

The next Sunday arrived and with it came the matter of godparents, and Guichard faced another battle. There were so many of them they wouldn't fit inside the narrow, fourteenth century stone chapel. He struggled weakly, then abandoned the issue to the inevitable.

It had started with the protests of Erneste Branchet. "Without the milk from my goats, my little Louise would not have survived," he said. "The best, the richest, in all of Normandy!" he proclaimed a bit truculently, as if someone might have been about to dispute it.

The old farmer Pencheret donated his christening gown. For some reason never quite explained it had been stored under the thatched roof of his cottage and smelled strongly of molding hay and gunpowder, even after many careful launderings. The thought of the stocky old man in anything but farmer's work clothes—especially in something white with yards of handmade lace—seemed inconceivable, nearly ludicrous. He naturally insisted on being in the baptismal party.

Catherine Bricard was adamant. "My supply of bottles and nipples allowed Louise to suck that precious goat's milk." She faced Erneste Branchet, hands on her hips, challenging him to compare the value of her contribution. She must be a godmother too.

Monsieur and Madame Rampillon, their age and arthritis preventing them from any other work than maintaining a small home garden, fed and cared for Louise during the day while Annette returned to work, riding her bicycle to a neighboring town where she joined other women employed in the region's revived textile industry. Madame Rampillon insisted that she be allowed to hold the infant on her special day.

Even Marie Grandbois seemed to have finally accepted the irregularity of the baby's birth. She would proudly recount her part in saving the child's life to anyone patient enough to listen to the retelling. Eventually she allowed the carnage of that icy morning in February to dim in her memory, joining other blood-soaked images from another war where soldiers died in tent field hospitals, their arteries spurting wildly after crude amputations.

A grumbling Claude Villet vehemently restated his claim to be a godfather. "Bah!" He glared at the others crammed into the rectory office. "Without my gift of fuel oil, that tiny infant might just as well have frozen to death!" And so it went. None of them would come alone; all would be accompanied by their extended families.

Everyone, it seemed to Guichard, claimed some right to this child. Everyone except her father. However, the gift which Baby Louise bestowed was one of joy and the belief that St-Etienne-des-Près did have a future, and she was a symbol of its beginning.

Father Guichard surveyed the crowded church; on a typical Sunday it would overflow with forty worshippers. There were at least four times that many claiming spiritual responsibility for this orphaned child.

The tall windows were propped open so that those who didn't fit within could peer inside. No one wanted to miss any part of the ceremony. The interior was so tightly packed that Guichard feared for the welfare of his flock. Should one of his elderly parishioners faint the person would be held erect by the sheer density of the crowd.

Abandoning any attempt at mob control, he proceeded with the Sacrament of Holy Baptism. Reading from the prayer book, he asked, "Who presents this child?" The thunderous reply from the crowd was unsettling, not the expected meek murmurings of typical godparents, the *maraine* and *paraine* who would hold the infant while the parents stood by, worshipful and silent.

At one point Father Guichard lost his place in the prayer book and actually dropped his missal once. Parishioners leaned in at the narrow slit windows, shouting their responses. He looked out on the sea of faces and chuckled. They would stand in line for hours, signing the parish register, before they could join the festivities set up in the village square. On this one day, more pages would be filled in that book than had been over the past ten years.

Eleven years later the fragment of shrapnel low in the old priest's spine had finally accomplished its damage, what the doctors had predicted years ago. Father Guichard could no longer walk. Half-blind with cataracts, his fingers gnarled with arthritis, and fighting a losing battle with emphysema, the old priest had insisted on being brought back to L'Eglise-de-St-Etienne-des-Près for the Confirmation of his Louise, for he felt that she belonged to him too.

Two younger priests supported him as he placed his hands on the young girl's head, her glossy black curls crowned with fragrant apple blossoms. She faced him with the same pretty smile she'd always had since she was a child, dimples in her rosy cheeks. While she was kneeling before him he looked back into the dark blue eyes that were fringed with heavy black eyelashes. Just for a moment, he thought he recalled who she resembled. *Ah, yes! That was the boy who was probably her father....* The boy's name was there, flitting and skittering through his memory, but the thought drifted from him, and he concentrated again on the Holy Sacrament of Confirmation. He struggled through the motions for several more blessings of those who had once been his parishioners, then he was carried out of the church to his wheelchair. Apparently at peace, he died in his sleep the following week.

For nineteen years, Louise had belonged to the village of St-Etienne-des-Près until she married and moved away in June of 1969. It was hard not to share in her happiness, but everyone would miss her. She was marrying the only son of a modestly prosperous fishing family originally from Caen.

"To our Louise!" Toasts, many and long, were raised to the bride and her husband by her family, which consisted of the entire village of St-Etienne-des-Près.

The bride's grandmother, Annette, stood and raised her glass of *cidre bouché*. "To Father Guichard." Her words inspired another round of toasts. The old priest was remembered, over and over; many lamented that he should have blessed the wedding, not some stranger who hadn't always known their Louise.

A festive procession had traveled to the nearby town for her wedding, but it might have been a funeral cortège on its return, straggling back across the countryside at dusk. Some of the younger men had driven long flatbed trucks, borrowed from the Bertrand orchards, allowing the older men to sprawl out behind them in a maudlin, drunken stupor.

"What are you crying on about?" Pichot, who was nearing the age of seventy-six at the time, pushed up on one elbow and turned to his friend, the octogenarian Raymond. "She wouldn't have married you." Philosophically, each gulped another hearty swig of Calvados. Many of them would suffer a mighty hangover the following day.

Although she had promised to return and visit often, their precious Louise had left them, and the village would seem lonely and empty without her.

❖

6 Camille Mauriat

Grenoble, 1962

I

WHEN CAMILLE WAS A RESIDENT in medical school, it was only natural she would remember the first time she lost a patient. Death was not unexpected in intensive care units; however, but this day's events would prove to be of a quite different nature.

The morning had not begun well, as she dealt with an influx of trauma cases fresh from surgery, but that she had also met Louis Duchêne, unconscious and critically injured, on the same day she would recall only later.

Duchêne was one of the new arrivals to her service that morning. After reviewing his chart, she planned to continue to her last patient, an elderly gentleman in the next bed of the ward. With the ritual of morning rounds nearly finished, Camille pulled the curtain between the beds, stethoscope readied, and glanced through the chart, briefly noting the new patient's date of birth and admission data:

> Duchêne, Jean-Louis. Age 31. Cit. fr. Mountain climbing accident. Airlifted previous day at 1328h to Grenoble from rescue station in Chamonix. Loss of consciousness related to massive head trauma/concussion. Blunt trauma rib fracture, left side, numbers seven and eight. Left pneumothorax, probably related to corresponding rib fractures. Total dislocation of left shoulder. Compound fracture of right tibia; closed fracture of right femur. Status: post open reduction of compound fractures; closed reduction of femur fracture and dislocated left shoulder.

The clipped, terse, medical jargon categorized and summarized the man's life, all she needed to know.

Behind the curtain that separated the ward, the neighboring patient, the slightly disoriented eighty-five year old Monsieur Latour, was chatting with his visitor, a gentleman of approximately equal vintage and questionable hearing. How his friend had managed to circumvent the nursing sisters and the hospital's iron-fisted visiting rules Camille couldn't imagine.

Amused, Doctor C. Mauriat allowed their deep voices, scraped ragged from a lifetime of cigarettes, to blend into the background noise. The sound joined the hiss of humidified oxygen and the beeps, ticks, and whirrs of monitoring equipment that filled the room like a living hospital presence.

The two men boomed non sequiturs at each other in what could scarcely be called a conversation. "*Eh bon, ça va, mon vieux?*" Latour's question of "How's it going, old friend?" was met with the unrelated response from his visitor Monsieur Fournier, "It snowed in your village yesterday," to which Latour said, "They won't let me smoke here," and Fournier countered with, "My wife thinks the berry crop will be good this summer."

Her new patient Duchêne might have been a very handsome man. Without consciously doing so she was relegating him to the past. He had wavy black hair and broad cheeks which even now were slightly pink. His routine temperature checks confirmed that he was not and had not been febrile, and therefore this must be his natural coloring. Long, thick black eyelashes extended from flaccid eyelids, curling against unresponsive cheeks. She lifted one eyelid, then the other, checking for pupillary reflexes with a small flashlight and noting an ominous "no response." The eyes were blue, a deep blue, but the pupils that ignored any stimulus were inky blue-black, nearly as dark his hair.

Each time she touched him she carefully explained her examination and what she was doing. Unconscious or not, there was always a remote chance that the mind would pick up words heard, as patients all too often would report immediately after surgery. Brain activity, even when documented by a continuous EEG, an electroencephalogram, could only hint at journeys through the maze of the human brain and was never a complete map of its territory. Strangely, despite his significant head injury, this man had no such monitor.

A muscular right arm and shoulder protruded from bandaging that swathed his chest, splinting and stabilizing fractured ribs as well as the dislocated left shoulder. Beside his bed was a large jar connected to the tube coming from his chest. The casted right leg was suspended in traction, quite a lot of weight at nearly seven kilos. She dodged the frame and avoided the dangling weights while assessing the circulation of his toes, comparing the left to the right.

The adjacent gravely voices reached easily through the barrier of the muslin privacy divider. *"Un cognac...?"* one of the men rumbled.

"My coat...."

Fragmented, unrelated comments flowed on while the two old men continued to talk at each other. Behind her, Monsieur Latour coughed occasionally, a rattling and raspy cough that was improving as it gradually moved fluid from his lungs and the space around his heart. Even while examining the victim of the mountain climbing accident, she was listening to the monitors, her ears attuned to both patients' heartbeats. Curiously, Latour's rapid, irregular, and laboring heart rate was changing, ever so slightly, and was joining the single reassuring rhythm of Duchêne's healthy and regular 74–82 beats per minute. In this regard at least, the victim of the mountain climbing accident was stable.

"What a sad waste," she murmured, unaware she had spoken out loud.

A deep voice scratched, questioning her from the other side of the curtain. *"Eh bien, quoi?* What's that?"

"Nothing at all, Monsieur Latour," she replied pleasantly, speaking into her side of the muslin. She had been thinking about Pierre again: he would never have taken such risks like this mountain climber, a man who might have had a full life ahead of him otherwise. She sighed: time was mercifully granting her some peace. Day by day Pierre was less and less in her thoughts and for this she was grateful. Soon, she hoped, she would stop finding and making these comparisons. Someday he must surely fade from her memory altogether, but for the present he remained there, lurking, waiting, her basis to judge every other man. He had been a part of her life for nearly fifteen years, since they were children. But he'd left her six months ago and married someone else; his wife was pregnant with their first child. She tried forcing his memory away.

By mid-morning sunlight had begun to pour into the far end of the hospital ward, glowing creamy and white through the muslin curtains. From outside, light reflected off the crown-like peaks gleaming with fresh snow, the tiara of white jewels that surrounded Grenoble. The shutters should be adjusted against the glare, at least for the conscious Monsieur Latour, although the two old men were silent now and might have fallen asleep, lulled by the soothing warmth of winter sunshine.

She wrote on Duchêne's chart that, if there was no change in level of consciousness and still with absent bowel sounds, the patient should have a nasogastric tube to decrease the abdominal distention that had already begun; it should have been placed in surgery. Finished, she planned a cursory check on Latour, then a brief visit to another cardiac patient who was recovering from recent surgery. Then she would need an assistant, one of the nursing sisters, to help insert the tube down into the stomach of the comatose patient. She glanced back at Jean-Louis Duchêne, his face slack with a heavy stubble of black beard. It amazed her how a conscious mind, even in sleep, could bestow the gift of grace and life to the human face. Where and how did this connection occur? The phenomenon fascinated her, what she would always consider one of life's beautiful mysteries.

She turned away from the unconscious man and pulled back the curtains. That was when she discovered that not only was Monsieur Latour gone from his bed, but both old gentlemen had disappeared. Camille pulled the red cord designated for emergencies, sending bells clamoring and reverberating throughout the long corridors of the old hospital. She had unequivocally lost the elderly patient.

Acutely embarrassed, she described the morning's events to her supervisor, the twenty minutes of neurological and circulatory evaluation of Monsieur Duchêne and the conversation of the old men as much as she recalled. Very little would prove useful, unrelated and sporadic as it was. None of the staff in Intensive Care had observed the men leave. A thorough search of the hospital's main building, including storage closets and little used hallways, turned up nothing. No one on the ground floor had seen two elderly men walk out the main entrance, certainly no one wearing pajamas.

The next logical step was to alert the local police. The two elderly truants were easily found two blocks from the hospital, sipping coffee, smoking, and enjoying an early morning cognac. Relaxed and jovial, they were seated inside the front terrace of a cozy brasserie. Sophisticated detective work hadn't been needed. What had given them away was the large, upright, glass bottle of intravenous fluid, slowly turning red as Monsieur Latour's blood backed up, an incongruous, ornamental centerpiece placed between the two on the round table. Why the young man who served the gentlemen hadn't noticed this curiosity was never addressed.

The young Dr. Mauriat would learn that Monsieur Latour's visitor was not as disoriented as she'd first assumed. A notoriously brave and clever demolitions expert during and after the last war and then a licensed electrician, Fournier had easily bypassed any alarm systems on his old friend's cardiac monitors and spliced the wires to the monitor of the neighboring patient. The technology itself might have been unfamiliar to him—what the machine was supposed to do and how—but the basic principles must have seemed nearly the same as disarming or arming a bomb. There was the matter of sharing his overcoat, and then they were gone, happy as two school boys avoiding the confines of a dull classroom.

———

By twelve thirty Camille had completed the reporting required to describe the escapades of her lost patient, who was now secured somewhat more effectively in bed.

The nursing sisters were most displeased, as if Latour's actions had been Camille's doing. "We find this highly unacceptable, Dr. Mauriat." The sister in charge always spoke in the imperial "we," while the wide, white wings of her starched *cornette* seemed to quiver with disapproval. There was much they disapproved of about her on principle: she was a Protestant and a Protestant *woman* doctor in the hospital that their Roman Catholic nursing order had ruled with an iron-like fist for over one hundred years. Accepting her was one more adjustment among many they were forced to accept with the changing times.

The comatose patient Duchêne would still need the nasogastric tube. Another, but less severe, nursing sister waited quietly at his bedside, the necessary equipment neatly assembled on a tray.

"Thank you," Camille said to her helper, a nurse of the old school who would speak only when asked a direct question. The nurse nodded, sending the wings of her starched headdress flapping wildly.

As she had before, Camille talked to the unconscious man, speaking softly, explaining what she would be doing as she positioned his head and neck. "Monsieur Duchêne?" Her voice was gentle and soothing. "I am your doctor. Dr. Mauriat. I will be inserting a tube that goes through your nose and down into your stomach." She gripped his chin, positioned his neck, and reached back for the cool, flexible tube.

"*Mon ange?* My angel…?"

Someone was speaking, but it was not Monsieur Latour's gravely baritone. It sounded constricted, as though there was serious damage to the vocal cords, whoever it was coming from. The nursing sister whirled about in confusion, sending her veil flying as she looked around, searching.

"My angel, please?" It was Duchêne. The words were coming from him, but with difficulty.

Camille, intubation equipment still held near the man's face, looked down into the deep blue eyes she had checked twice during the day, eliciting no response whatsoever, eyes that were not only moving together, but were focused directly on her.

Recovered from the moment's shock, she decided that he must have suffered significant brain trauma. He was talking out of one side of his mouth, much like patients who had suffered a stroke. Again, she felt the recurring pang of waste, that a thirty-one year old man would live the rest of his life with this level of neurological damage and disability. Not letting go of his cheek and jaw, she gestured with the tube, splattering water and lubricant over his face, into his eyes, and onto his pillow.

Finally setting aside the equipment, she indicated the name on her white coat while she wiped water from his face. "I'm Dr. Mauriat." The head injury must have blurred his vision as well. She experienced another twinge of remorse at the young man's fate.

He ignored her correction. "Angel, your hand's pressing on my throat," he managed, the words coming out with difficulty.

She had not been aware of the intensity of her grip on his face and neck. Uncertainly, she released the tension.

Duchene sighed, took a shallow breath, and winced at the discovery of fresh, new pain. He exhaled slowly and cautiously. "That's better."

His voice was instantly normal, speech and sound coming from lips that moved equally, both sides, the left and right. His right arm twitched against its restraints.

Camille studied him for a moment. "If the nurse releases those ties, you must move very carefully. There is a needle in your arm now." She nodded to the nursing sister. "Also, do not even try to move your left arm." The chest bandages would probably prevent any movement, but she warned him anyway.

He moved his good arm tentatively, reaching up and massaging his throat. "Angel," he said, "for someone so small, you've got quite a grip."

She wondered briefly why he was calling her "Angel," but dismissed it as unimportant. Perhaps the nurse's white headdress had confused him; it was always best to allow some leeway following head trauma.

Intubation was temporarily postponed with the need to repeat a neurological evaluation of her patient: reflexes here and there, the small flashlight once again beamed into his eyes, assessing the grasp of the fingers of his right hand, and guessing at the strength of the left. The deep blue eyes smiled back easily into hers.

"Angel?" He continued talking as she worked. "Does everyone you bring back to life tell you how beautiful you are?" He glanced down at his leg encased in a heavy cast. *"Merde!* That hurts. Those mountain roads to Chamonix were too damn icy. I missed a turn, didn't I?"

So memory would be his challenge, Camille decided. "You were mountain climbing, Monsieur. You fell over 600 meters down a rock face, through a *corniche."* She waited, allowing her patient to process the information.

He shook his head, but seemed to regret having done so instantly, and reached for his temples. "Oh, *mon Dieu!"* He continued more slowly, uncertainly. "No, I don't remember that."

He had mentioned driving; that was a good place to start. "Do you remember driving to Chamonix?" Later she would ask whether he had been in car accidents before.

"Yes, I think so...." He hesitated. "I was meeting someone. My guides?"

"Perhaps," Camille said. "You were fortunate. There was a crowd below watching Jean-Claude Killy at training. Some of them had binoculars and watched you fall through the snow ledge."

"This hurts like hell."

"It should hurt, Monsieur," she replied primly. "You might have killed yourself on that mountain. The nurse will get you medicine for the pain shortly."

With one hand he pulled the nearby overbed table closer and flipped up its small mirror. "I need a shave."

Camille turned away, ignoring him while she wrote in the chart. She would need to notify the chief resident next.

"And I'm hungry too."

"You may need to wait a day or two for that," she stated, the words automatic. Once more that day she pulled a cord, alerting staff at the desk of the Intensive Care ward.

An elderly nun named Sister Marie-Jeanne was stationed there, answering summons and relaying messages. She responded, her tone phlegmatic. *"Oui?* Has *Mademoiselle le docteur* lost someone again?" It was her rough attempt at humor and reproach.

"Oh, no, *ma soeur.* I have found someone instead." She smiled at her patient. "He tells me he's hurting and he's hungry. Could you please contact Dr. Viénot?"

II

Every inch of him hurt. Taking a deep breath, which even more doctors insisted upon as they returned in droves, brandishing their stethoscopes, was a particular torture.

For an eternity Louis had waited for the jab in his hip, the promised injection for pain relief. A nurse, not as pretty as the blond doctor with tender brown eyes but not as grim as the nursing sister, had repeated the lengthy assessments that he was assured were necessary before administering any medication that might sedate him or skew the results of other examinations.

He was in a hospital—that much was evident. For the life of him he couldn't figure out how or why he had gotten there, then wondered vaguely, as the medication began to take effect, which car he might have wrecked. He was very protective about his cars. And where? No one could tell him. Perhaps no one here knew.

Slowly, ever so slowly it seemed, he was finding pain relief as the morphine trickled across his consciousness. The throbbing in his leg, shoulder, and ribs gradually subsided.

Through his pleasantly altered state Louis Duchêne stared up at the wall clock mounted opposite his bed and at the second hand swinging around and around in a hypnotic circle. He may have lost a car—although he'd been told that he'd fallen while mountain climbing, he was sure he must have crashed the car—but he had the feeling of finding something too. In and out of the shallow dreams of narcosis drifted a golden angel, enfolded in the white wings of a starched lab coat; she would float toward him briefly carrying a long rubber tube and then float away. They were very strange dreams.

III

Duchêne was transferred to the hospital's main ward and from Camille's service in intensive care after two days. She remained curious about his case, wondering whether his episode of normalcy might have been only the lucid interval after a head injury that could occur before internal bleeding created permanent brain damage. Another obvious concern was his memory, but she was relieved not to have his attention focused on her. His body may have been traumatized, but his need to flirt constantly remained unscathed, even after tumbling down a mountain and narrowly escaping death. Considering the extent of his injuries, his recovery had seemed nearly miraculous.

Camille was still not recovered from her own wounds, a different sort than her patient's. She wondered when she would heal, if ever. It was now eight months since Pierre had left her.

Two months after Duchêne was transferred from her care, she visited her parents in Douvré and arrived back in Grenoble late the following morning, relaxed and refreshed. A car she hadn't seen before was parked near her apartment, its length occupying two coveted parking spaces. All parking was becoming a serious challenge, with furiously paced construction continuing night and day as the city prepared for the upcoming X Winter Olympic Games. The streets were increasingly crowded and chaotic, and she was forced to park over three blocks away.

Waiting on the sidewalk and leaning casually against the wall of her building were two men she didn't recognize, although one of them seemed somehow familiar. One was a young man with tousled light brown hair, very tall and gangly in the way a young colt is, still waiting to grow into limbs that had grown too long for the rest of him. He was holding an armful of roses and daffodils and tulips. The other man was slightly shorter and had darker, wavy hair; his leg was in a cast, and he wobbled uncertainly on wooden crutches.

"Mademoiselle?" He lurched forward but caught himself before falling, then tried to extend his hand in greeting. One crutch slipped away and clattered to the sidewalk. He remained balanced on one leg, supporting himself against the wall.

Automatically Camille reached down to retrieve the crutch and handed it back to him.

"*Merci!*" He smiled broadly, his eyes meeting hers. "Dr. Mauriat?"

She nodded. "*Oui.* How may I help you? The hospital is less than a ten minute walk." Hesitating, she glanced down at his leg encased in a heavy cast. "Do you need someone to call for help? A taxi, perhaps?"

He turned to the young man burdened with flowers. "Marc, she's the angel I told you about."

There was something vaguely familiar about the dark blue of his eyes, the heavy black eyelashes, and his smile, yet she still couldn't place him.

"Louis Duchêne." He grinned, lifting one finger from the crutch but not letting go in his greeting. "I was your patient. Remember? This is my brother, Marc."

"*Enchantée,*" she said politely, nodding and smiling up at the young man who extended his hand, weaving it through the bundles of flowers.

Louis Duchêne, the mountain climbing accident, unconscious, then the strange psychological affect… ah, yes, I remember now. "How did you find me?" Her innate politeness was shifting to mild irritation. The nursing sisters frowned on this type of conduct, patients with staff and vice-versa.

"Sister Marie-Jeanne, at the hospital. She told me where I could find you."

Deeply reserved by nature, Camille reacted first with an instinctive feeling of violation, then she realized that he had only to ask at the hospital and they would tell him her full name. From there, she realized there was probably only one Camille Mauriat living in Grenoble who was also a physician. She shrugged in defeat.

If that day marked the beginning of their courtship, it hadn't gone well, but it had introduced her to the wildly exuberant nature of the Duchêne family. Marc thrust the flowers into her arms and bowed, much like a gallant, Renaissance courtier.

"Now, get lost," Louis genially instructed his brother after handing him a wad of 500 franc notes. "Angel, may I take you to lunch?"

Why does he keep calling me Angel? Camille wondered. Their current situation already seemed too bizarre to ask. There were times when she cursed the niceness instilled into her as a child, what had been required of a preacher's daughter. Here was this young man, alone in Grenoble while he recovered from an accident and endured treatment for his injuries and probably therapy for brain trauma as well. It would be rude to say no. She gestured toward a bistro a half block from where they stood. "La Brasserie du Mont, perhaps?"

"Absolutely not! Let's drive up to Chambéry!" Wobbling again, he gestured toward the clear and sunny sky. "The weather's perfect."

The winter day could have leapt from a tourist brochure. The mountains presented themselves like a stage backdrop, the ragged crown of snowcapped peaks outlined against a sky of cobalt blue. The route to the historic Roman town of Chambéry, only 58 kilometers away, was a pleasant one, passing through a national park where picturesque mountain villages clustered near small lakes.

"But… but you can't drive," Camille protested, peering over her armload of flowers. She glanced down at the broken leg that she knew well—medically, at least—as pieces of the day's scenario and drama began to fall into place. Was she the only person in this cast of three characters who had the slightest grasp of reality?

"Oh, I know that." Louis's tone was cheerful, matter-of-fact, and confident. "But you can. You *can* drive, can't you?"

She nodded. "My car is down there." She motioned toward the speck of faded blue that was her old Renault 4CV.

"Let's take mine." He waved expansively and lurched toward the long, silver Mercedes Ponton, the car occupying the two parking spaces. "More room for this *maudit* leg."

The vehicle was huge, and he was right: the casted leg would need extra space. If they were going anywhere, it would of necessity be in his monster of a car.

They stopped before reaching their intended destination of Chambéry and had eaten lunch at an inn that overlooked a mountain lake of deep, deep blue—the color of his eyes actually.

Camille wouldn't recall what they eaten for lunch, except that it had been quite good. Conversation was pleasant, although Louis continually startled her with his brashness.

She judged that he was probably drinking too much, especially if he was still taking any medications. At one point he complained of an itch under his cast and grabbed a long implement from the bouquet of fondue forks in the center of their table to poke about under the plaster. Appalled, she'd delivered a stern lecture.

He smiled at her again, his eyes twinkling with mischief. "Angel, I swear I'll never to it again."

Before they left, he'd reached into his pocket and brought out two white tablets, pain pills she assumed, recognizing the imprint of LaRoche codeine, and swallowed them with his third beer. He'd fallen asleep in the seat beside her as she negotiated icy mountain roads in the unfamiliar car. After depositing him into his brother's care—she wondered where Marc had waited while they were gone but didn't ask—she vowed that she would never go out with him again. He was most definitely unstable mentally.

Besides, her one good deed should be sufficient for many days to come.

❖

7 Camille and Louis

Paris, 1964

I

IT WOULD BE A YEAR AND A HALF before Camille Mauriat agreed to marry Louis Duchêne, although he'd proposed the day when they'd gone to lunch. She would discover that he was brash, impetuous, and probably quite spoiled, but he was a kind, generous, tender, and gentle man. Some of his eccentricities she attributed to the one year he had spent at university in the United States. He was boisterously childlike in the way he charmed others, and she had somehow finally learned to love him.

As they neared Paris the knot in her stomach had tightened further. She wasn't inclined to chatter under normal circumstances, but shortly after leaving Grenoble she'd retreated into total silence. Her lips felt numb, and her throat was dry: she probably couldn't have spoken if her life depended on it. The kilometer posts flickered past as the prospect grew increasingly intimidating. She had never been taken home to "meet a man's family."

Pierre.... She wondered whether she would ever cease to think about him. She no longer loved him—of that she was certain. Disappointment and jealousy no longer troubled her. His family had been members of her father's congregation, thus she and Pierre had known each other since childhood. There had never been a need to be introduced or presented to anyone. Pierre had shared her dreams and her passion for medicine. Together they endured the many rigorous national qualifying exams before leaving home for school. Time passed; becoming lovers was simply something that happened.

She had no idea what to expect today. Trying to share in Louis's euphoria, she could only worry, huddled next to him in another of his many luxury cars. Importing and distributing cars was his business, but his love affair with the automobile she had also traced to the year spent in America.

Exuberant and expansive, Louis was nonspecific when she'd asked in particular about his mother and father: "They're great, Camie, you'll love them" and "Of course, they'll be crazy about you."

That was no help whatsoever. The Duchêne family was wealthy, that much she had deduced. Would they look down on her humble background? They were Catholic and she was not. Although her father was a minister, to say she was Protestant was a stretch, for she actually held few religious convictions, except that she believed in God. However, she was *not* Catholic, and that alone would preclude a church wedding. Religious differences were a serious consideration, especially since his parents had been married in the Catholic Church. Fortunately, according to

French law, the civil marriage ceremony was the only legal requirement; anything conducted in a church was above and beyond, carried out for the sensibilities of those involved.

She tried to swallow, her mouth progressively drier. "Louis?" she whispered. "Are you sure? I'm so nervous."

"They're regular family." He placed a hand on her knee. "Just like your folks."

II

Introducing Louis to her parents had been altogether different. Whoever she loved, she believed that they would also love unconditionally, and they had. As she'd discovered, it was nearly impossible not to be charmed by him.

Initially startled by his brashness and childlike ebullience, they had accepted his behavior as part of *him,* part of the man their daughter loved and would marry. The Reverend Roger Mauriat would have found some kindly manner to mention his reservations, and Camille would have noticed any unspoken clues. Her mother, like all women apparently, had fallen immediately under Louis's spell.

Strolling the familiar village streets, Camille basked in her father's pride as he introduced Louis to their friends. "Meet my daughter's fiancé, Louis Duchêne. Camille's a doctor now." Slightly over two years ago she had faced the fear and agony of almost losing her father. Now their time spent together seemed sweeter still as she watched him, robust and aglow with renewed health.

Upon their arrival, her mother Odile had escorted Louis upstairs. "This is Camille's room. I hope everything's arranged so you'll be comfortable."

"But—? What about Camie?" Louis stared down at the single narrow bed but must have decided against any further protests.

"Don't worry. She'll sleep downstairs, in the sitting room. On the couch, of course." Odile placed her hand on Louis's arm in reassurance. *"Ne t'inquiète pas du tout."*

———

Their ancient horsehair sofa might have predated the old house and maybe several preceding wars. Camille, as she had become accustomed when her father would ask a visitor to stay, made peace with the lumpy, sagging piece of furniture. She was just falling asleep when the creaking of stairs awakened her. All the floorboards of the house were noisy. Grown accustomed to the undercurrent and sounds of a city, she discovered that quiet was disturbed by much less, once again in the country. The creaks and groans of the old house came closer, then Louis was touching her shoulder.

"Angel?" he asked. "Can you move over?" After the first day in the hospital he'd rarely called her anything but Angel; only on rare occasions would he use her nickname, Camie.

His question must surely have been hopefully rhetorical: movement on the old divan was nearly impossible alone.

"Louis! For God's sake, what are you thinking? We.... We can't possibly—not here!"

"No," he agreed equably, but attempted to squeeze onto the couch anyway. "You're right about that." He had wisely brought the pillow and blankets from her bed upstairs.

"Louis!" She continued to protest in an exasperated whisper. "No!"

It seemed that he always knew how to cope, no matter the situation. He was already arranging their bedding on the floor beside the sofa, pillows and blankets strategically placed for optimum comfort.

"I've pitched tents on mountainsides that were about this soft." He wrapped himself around her, supporting her in his arms.

Desperation was creeping into her voice. "What will my parents think?"

"They won't come downstairs in the middle of the night," he stated with absolute conviction.

How could he be so certain? Camille didn't ask.

"But if they do, they'll think that I love their daughter and I can't sleep without her. And they'll be right." He kissed her gently. "I'll be back in up your bedroom by morning. Promise."

And Louis had kept his word.

III

"Angel? Are you all right, Camie?" His left hand was draped casually over the steering wheel, so he pulled her closer with his right arm. "You haven't said anything for the last half hour."

"Oh, Louis, I'm scared. Talk to me, please. Tell me what to expect. Who'll be there? Who will I have to meet?" Why could she talk to total strangers—any patient—and never feel a moment's shyness or nervousness? Why could she cut into a living person to perform intricate surgery with never a moment's qualm? Being introduced to her fiancé's family was another matter, monumental and intimidating.

Louis chuckled. "Well, you've already met Marc. He should be there, but we never know for sure about him. Journalists...." He rolled his eyes, as if his brother might have joined a circus troop.

"Okay. And Françoise… will she be there too?"

Louis nodded.

Camille had found her story touching and unbelievable. She was anxious to meet her, this girl whom Louis's father had rescued during the war, shipping her from a Nazi-occupied France to Switzerland in a trunk. Louis had always referred to her as his sister.

———

Françoise had grown up with the two Duchêne boys. When her early schooling was finished, she had chosen to become a chef. With a heavy heart, Louis's father Henri Duchêne had given his blessing and support as she began the intense study and preparation that was required before she could even apply for the entrance examination to the Cordon Bleu.

She would leave their family forever, they were certain. Once cultivated, her talents would be in demand by exclusive restaurants. She worked exactly one year after completing the many various apprenticeships and graduating from the school's rigorous training program, then, without any forewarning, she'd returned, suitcases in hand, to Place du Chêne. "I want to come home," she'd said.

Henri had stared at her, relieved but also disbelieving. Later he admitted he'd felt a surge of protective anger.

"No, I haven't been treated badly," Françoise reassured her adoptive father.

Henri's doubt must have been evident to her.

"The fact that I'm a woman wasn't a source of discrimination either," she said. Then, as though closing the subject, she repeated firmly, "Or part Jewish. I just want to come home. Cook for my family. That's all."

Louis's parents Henri and Cécile were delighted to have her back, but the family remained bewildered.

"I'll pay you, of course," Henri said. "Surely, we can't provide what the *grandes établissements* can give someone with your talent and training. What about the recognition you deserve?"

"I know, but this is what I want to do... Papa."

With a tremulous smile that reminded Henri heartbreakingly of the one she'd shared years ago, the day they were allowed to return to their damaged home in 1945, she embraced him and kissed him. They all wondered whether her heart had been broken in some other way, but would never know.

"She's never explained why, but she wanted to come live with us again," Louis said. "I think my grandparents from Normandy will be there too." While he and Camille had lunched, as they frequently did at the same inn overlooking a mountain lake, he had shared the story of the Bertrand family's daring escape from St-Etienne-des-Près across the Channel to England.

"And so, they were safe?" Camille had asked. "They were so fortunate."

"They left with what they were wearing, their pockets and clothes full of gold, the *Louis d'or* and Napoleonic gold the family had traditionally been saving for a serious emergency." He adjusted his grip on the steering wheel, then hugged Camille closer with his other arm. "Even in the First World War they hadn't touched this cache. They paid the Danish captain with one gold coin. Just one of those large coins was worth more than a dozen weeks' fishing."

Camille shook her head; Louis was full of stories it seemed.

"They spent the rest of the war in England," Louis said. "Their beautiful home in Normandy was completely demolished. I've told you about the old estate in Normandy, right? Apple orchards and horses and a huge stone barn. Grandpère Maurice's grandfather was the equerry for Napoleon. What the German's didn't first destroy the Allies finished off—part of the nature of war."

Her family's life was so simple by comparison. With the exception of the one day the German general had come to their home, they had experienced nothing so dramatic in the small village of Douvré.

"Grandmère Hélène and Grandpère Maurice—they lived very simply. They endured the same hardships and dangers that all of England suffered. A couple of times a year he'd take the bus into London. He'd convert one of the gold coins into money for their living expenses. They were glad to be alive and relieved that my mother—she's their only daughter—was safe in Switzerland. Marc was born there."

Camille smiled, wondering whether Louis had been right. Was it really better not to know or to hear the many gory details and relive all the pain? Had her father kept secrets too? Had he really not been touched in this traumatic way? Hearing Louis's stories she knew she would ask her father more someday.

"And that brave man—the Danish captain—did they ever have a chance to thank him?"

Louis looked uncomfortable, a rarity for him. "They thanked him with gold." He shrugged, staring ahead at the road, and cleared his throat. "Rasmussen saved their lives, but his motive was probably greed." Early in the war, tiny Denmark, once overrun, had found it necessary to cooperate with their country's German conquerors. "I think that motive and deed are always connected somehow. He must have had some good in him, but I'm not sure."

They drove in silence for several minutes.

After clearing his throat, Louis spoke softly. "He was finally caught, helping a Jewish family escape. I don't know if they made it to safety, but I'm guessing not. It was highly publicized to discourage others. The German patrol executed Rasmussen and his crew on the spot, then set the *Kirsten* on fire and left it floating in the Channel. It drifted into one of the German mines and blew up."

Camille retreated to silence once more: war was kept alive in so many ways, in so many different memories, so many years later.

IV

After battling the crosstown traffic of Paris to reach the 16ième Arrondissement, Louis pulled up a slight rise and into the circle drive of a substantial, classically designed, two-story mansion. A row of mansards and four tall chimneys complemented the elegant proportions of the house.

Camille looked around, concerned. "Where are we? Aren't we going to your home first?" She was anxious to get the dreaded moment of meeting his family over with. Why had they made an extra stop?

"But, *ma chérie,* this is home."

It seemed as though he was out of the car and bounding inside before the engine had come to a full stop. Pulling a startled Camille behind him, he leapt up the front steps, threw open the tall double doors, dashed into the foyer, and galloped into the central hallway.

"Maman?" he called. *"Papa?* We're home!"

Two huge dogs loped up to greet him, enthusiastically placing their paws on his shoulders and licking his face.

"Where Odysseus returns from war and is recognized by his faithful hound." A pretty woman with light brown hair had stepped into the hallway, laughing at the scene and quoting the classic line from *The Odyssey*.

"Maman!" Louis pulled free of the canine welcome committee and embraced his mother, picking her up and twirling her around. Her shoes flew off, skidding across the room.

"Put me down, Louis!" Laughing and breathless, she collected her shoes and smiled apologetically toward Camille. "Sometimes it seems like we have one son who's never really grown up. Like having a grown dog that still acts like a puppy." She straightened her dress, which Louis had bunched up during his rambunctious greeting. "But our dogs are better behaved," she said, *soto voce*. She smiled and extended her hand.

Louis accomplished the semblance of an introduction. *"Maman,* my fiancée Camille Mauriat. Camille, this is my mother."

"Camille—at last! You're every bit as lovely as Louis told us." Cécile Duchêne dispensed with the formality of shaking hands and embraced her future daughter-in-law.

Camille studied this delicate woman: the soft, light brown hair, the smoothness of her skin, and the perfection of her complexion. This was clearly where Marc's features had come from, except he was much taller. Who did Louis resemble?

Then she noticed his father, who had quietly joined them in the hallway. He was more like Louis, tall but not like Marc with his extraordinary height of well over six feet. Henri Duchêne's eyes were the same dark blue as his son's, lively intelligent eyes surrounded by a dense fringe of black eyelashes. His neatly close-cropped, wavy hair had once been as dark as Louis's, but was softened to a gentle gray. The two men embraced, clapping each other on the back.

"Camille, welcome," Henri said, taking both her hands in his. "You're the new flower for the gardens of Place du Chêne."

Blushing, she realized too where Louis had learned at least some of his gallant flirtatiousness.

Cécile pulled her away from what felt like a crush of men and dogs, but Camille turned back to look, fascinated. Would Louis pick up his father and twirl him about too?

"We've given you and Louis the middle guest room," Cécile was saying. "It's the largest and you can see the gardens. Louis's old room is still full of university memorabilia." She glanced meaningfully in his direction, an indication it might be time for him to discard some of it.

Camille found their forthrightness intriguing. While her parents must have known she and Louis were sleeping together, they chose to pretend and ignore it. The Duchênes accepted the matter and addressed it as a given.

Camille had visited places like the house at No. 1, Place du Chêne before, usually as a school girl waiting in a queue with classmates, some school outing to tour historic chateaux and monuments in the vicinity. There was always a hushed expectancy in the presence of history. She had been awed, entering what appeared a dream world, always wondering about these people, those who had once lived in such elegance, richness, and beauty.

Always before there had been velvet cords and little signs everywhere: *Prière de ne pas toucher—Please don't touch* or *Don't walk on the rug* or *Don't sit on the furniture.* Here, at the Duchêne home, the family lounged about in the antique chairs and settees, casually placed wineglasses on a mahogany sideboard that should have been preserved in a museum, and dined at a table fit for kings, while two large white dogs lolled and gamboled about the place, oblivious to the historical treasures around them.

Here she was, entering the home of her fiancé, a home that would possibly be hers one day. She had known places like this existed but could never have envisioned living in one.

V

Camille was changing before dinner, bracing for the next group she would have to meet, and Louis had gone downstairs earlier to discuss some business matter with his father. Henri and Cécile seemed both charming and unpretentious. Still she was nervous, wondering what would happen this evening.

She glanced one final time in the tall pier mirror, took a deep breath, murmured a prayer for courage, and started down the staircase.

Downstairs in the spacious salon, a tall woman with soft billows of snowy white hair, piled atop her head in the style of a bygone era, smiled kindly in Camille's direction. She was standing by the grand piano where a slender, older gentleman was playing a Schubert improvisation, his fingers fluttering over the keys gently as a butterfly. The woman stepped away from the piano, beckoning for Camille to come closer, and then Camille noticed there were nearly a dozen others in the room.

The woman with the soft white hair took Camille by both hands, guiding her back to the piano as the last notes of Schubert trilled away. "Albert," she said, her eyes sparkling in a way that belied her years, "this is our Louis's Camille. Camille, my husband Albert. And I am Gertrude."

Camille was certain she'd heard their surname but quickly forgot it, distracted by the opulence of the room and overwhelmed by the growing crowd. More guests were arriving, pausing to hang their coats in the foyer. The knot was returning to her stomach. She hadn't anticipated that Louis would trot her out for display and approval like this, like a heifer at market.

"Mademoiselle?" The pianist Albert spoke to her softly. "Camille, is it? Ah, a lovely flower for the son of a beautiful family." The pianist half-stood from the piano bench and then sat down once more, flicking his suit coat out behind him in the unconscious gesture of a formal concert performer. "Surely you are accustomed to comparisons with Dumas's works—*La Dame aux Camélias*—but I offer you something different. This is 'The Flower Song' from *Lakmë,* one of the most exquisite duets in all opera."

She was preparing to back out of the grand salon, ready to flee and take refuge anywhere and to seek Louis and find out when this humiliating inspection would end. However, it would be rude to leave the elderly gentleman at the piano; she nodded and smiled.

He was pushing his starched white cuffs high above his wrists, another automatic and unconscious gesture of a concert pianist, his fingers poised, flexed, above the gleaming black and white keys. That was when she noticed the numbers. She gulped and swallowed with difficulty. They were not just any numbers. The unmistakable series of small black numerals—the impersonal identification on his lower forearm—was how the Germans had marked their human cargo in the nightmare existence of concentration camps.

She smiled back at him, watching the delicate, long-boned fingers create magic from the keyboard. Although willing herself not to, her eyes strayed to the tattoo again and again. The man, Albert—*what was his last name?*—clearly had a heart condition too. She could read it in the high-walled chest, his struggle to breathe, each shallow double-breath an effort, the bluish-purple, translucent tinge of the finger tips and pursed lips, and the knobbing of the joints of the fingers. *Congestive heart failure,* she thought. *Possibly rheumatic heart disease as well.*

Yet he was smiling, glowing and transfixed by dedication to his art and the tenderness of the melody. His wife Gertrude leaned on the piano, beaming at him, her eyes suffused with love. The last perfect notes finished, and Camille applauded, joined by several new arrivals waiting in the foyer.

"Oh, Monsieur, that was lovely!" she exclaimed. Albert again bowed—half-sitting, half-standing—before resuming his seat and letting his fingers soar lightly, effortlessly, over the keys, a simple Mozart melody trilling in their wake.

Gertrude grasped Camille by the arm and gently tugged her away from the piano. "We're so glad to finally meet you," she began, making Camille wonder exactly who "we" would prove to be. Hadn't she met most of the immediate family earlier?

"Henri tells us you're from Lyon." Gertrude hesitated for a moment, her smile fading. Her eyes brimmed with tears, glimpsing in memory another time and another place. "My poor child… how awful for you." She reached to brush Camille's cheek with hers, the touch of a kiss on her left cheek, then the right.

The awkward realization came to her. *Oh, my goodness,* Camille thought, *these good people somehow think that I've shared in their suffering.* She felt like an imposter. How to explain that she had been barely four years old when the worst had started? What should she do? There had been hardship, shortages, inconvenience, and fear, but no one in her family had been captured, herded to a concentration camp, or tattooed. No one was wounded or tortured—or so she had been told.

She was starting to protest, but Louis's boisterous appearance rescued her from trying to explain to this sweet elderly couple. With typical exuberance, which everyone else seemed to take for granted, he scooped Gertrude into his arms, hugging her tightly and kissing her firmly on both cheeks. He bent down to greet Albert but embraced him more carefully, as though conscious of his innate fragility.

"Angel?" He grasped her hand and pulled her toward him. "I want you to meet—"

Camille interrupted him. "No, Louis, I need to talk to you."

"Is something wrong, Angel?"

She guided him away, down the length of the grand salon, where she could face the fireplace, away from the group gathered by the piano. "I'm… I'm very uncomfortable here."

Louis shrugged, appearing genuinely bewildered. "Yes? What is it?"

"You never warned me that I was going to be put on display for approval like this. Like goods in a farmers' market. It's embarrassing—awkward. It's humiliating too. I want to leave. Now. I'm sorry." Finished, she stared down at the floor and waited.

Louis, for the first time since they'd met, did not respond with a quick and witty rejoinder.

She turned, murmuring "I'm sorry" once more, and was stepping away from him when he reached for her arm.

"Angel, don't leave. Kiss me. Please?"

She couldn't deny him her love, what she had never really known with Pierre. She was drawn to Louis as inevitably as iron filings were drawn to a magnet. He wrapped her in his arms and kissed her.

"Oh, *mon Dieu,* that's better." Louis sighed in relief. "Now, wait. I want to show you something." He pulled a book from the tall shelves flanking the fireplace—one book, then another and another—all first editions of the greatest writers of two centuries. She studied the names: Proust, Alfred de Musset, Jean de la Fontaine, Dumas, Hugo, Stendahl, Dickens, Goethe, Wordsworth, Emerson, and Sir Walter Scott. "And the portrait up there—" He pointed over the mantel. "A Fragonard, 1747, and that one—over there, a Chardin, 1728, I think. That next one's by Monet, about 1870-something. And the ceiling." He waved generally above his head. "A student of Watteau, I believe. These are all *things* of beauty and great value—*material things* our family has loved and valued, like precious jewels."

He glanced around the room for a brief moment, searching for other inanimate examples for comparison before continuing. "And I've told you about Françoise."

Camille nodded, with no clue whatsoever where he was going with his line of reasoning, but she'd grown accustomed to his ways. It was not a result of his head injury as she'd first diagnosed, but she had rarely seen him this serious.

"There are *people* who are of great value to my mother and father too. In the same way they wanted you to like our family and our home, they wanted you to like and approve of the people whom *he*—it was mainly my father—cared enough about to...." He shrugged, hands resting on her shoulders, and then stared down into the Aubusson carpet as if searching for someway to continue.

Camille waited, trying to meet his eyes.

"They're some of the people he could help. Back then. They're our family now too." Louis hesitated for just a moment. "He doesn't like to talk about any of it, but he risked nearly everything he had to help those he could. Some he didn't know as well but was certain they offered great promise, for the future. Others were loyal friends whom he treasured and trusted. In many ways the bonds are as strong as those of our blood family." He paused, surveying the group gathered in the salon, and then faced Camille again. "They are all good people of talent and beauty and intelligence and grace—something he values more than any jewel or painting. He treasures them all." Louis gulped, finished, and looked up into her eyes uncertainly.

Camille still hadn't spoken or acknowledged any of his explanations. She'd never before heard him discourse on anything, not even an automobile, with so much heartfelt passion.

"I know it must have appeared the other way, but they've come tonight for *your* approval. My father wanted you to know what matters to him and hopes that you will value these good people too."

The image of the ragged line of tattooed numbers on the elderly pianist who played with such delicateness and perfection swam across her vision. She tried to imagine the other stories that might be represented tonight in this home. The tattooed numbers, the salon, the people gathered there blurred before her, fading in and out of focus. She blinked at her tears and nodded.

VI

For Camille, a family dinner, at home in their modest cottage in Douvré, might have included three more people at the most, besides her mother and father. Her father's brother or his cousin might have been there and her mother's niece, everyone crowded into the kitchen. Theirs was a small family, left smaller by wars.

The table in the Duchêne dining room had been extended: Camille counted twenty-six place settings, with crystal and silver glittering in the soft candlelight. In a large household like this, furnished as elegantly as a palace, she would have expected servants, but there were none. Later, she would recall dinner that evening with a sense of dreamlike disbelief.

Françoise, a de facto sibling but also their Cordon Bleu trained chef, removed her apron and joined them at the immense table, taking a chair nearest the kitchen. Camille had finally acknowledged that everyone present was actually Louis's family. Henri Duchêne sat at the opposite end, Cécile on his right. He was engaged in deep conversation with the pianist Albert, seated to his left. Madeleine, Marc's girlfriend, sat between the attorney Hervé LeBlanc and his son, Eugène. Marc had come late, rushing in, out of breath.

Cécile leaned down the table and spoke to Madeleine in a stage whisper. "Be prepared for this, *ma chérie,* he's always late." Madeleine laughed with her. She, like Camille, must be relatively new to this unique family group.

Seated next to Gertrude was Hélène Bertrand, Louis's maternal grandmother, arrived in from Normandy the previous night, while her husband was seated beside Albert. Camille was struggling to keep straight the faces, names, and bits of stories she had gleaned, but with few exceptions they were a hopeless jumble.

Louis was seated across the table. Beside Camille, to her right, was a man whom she guessed was only slightly older than Louis and who'd earlier been introduced as Dr. Christophe Rossignon.

"Louis tells me that you've finished medical school and your residencies. Congratulations!" he was saying. "Where did you study?"

There were certain parts of her life that Camille was uncomfortable discussing. Would they ask anything that might lead to a need to a mention of Pierre? This was a hesitancy she must learn to overcome. "At Paris, for early studies. Then Grenoble for my residencies," she replied courteously. "And you, Monsieur?"

"Please, please—" he broke in. "It's Christophe, *s'il vous plaît*. I was going to start here, but I finished at the University of Chicago, in the United States." He passed the platter of *filet de sole Véronique* and held it while Camille served herself.

"Oh?" She tilted her head, curious. "Why there?"

"I'm two years older than Louis. It was easier for youngsters like him to run away to Switzerland... but I shouldn't joke about that." He laughed anyway and winked at Louis, seated across the table. He leaned down, nearer her ear, and spoke softly, answering her question. "Because of him." He nodded toward the far end of the table where Henri was savoring a first bite of the fish course.

"Françoise, ma chère. Délicieuse, as usual!" Henri was saying, raising his voice to be heard over the genial hum of chatter.

"I don't understand." Even as Camille spoke, she'd suspected what Christophe meant.

"Somehow he was able to manage my family's safe passage to Canada. He had a business associate in Toronto. From there, I was accepted in the medical college at the University of Chicago." He shrugged and grinned broadly. "When my parents were able to come home, I stayed on so I could finish and graduate." Turning back to his dinner, he became serious. "If I'd stayed here, my studies would have been interrupted... the classes always unpredictable. I probably would have ended up as a field medic treating German wounded. Maybe something worse. Serving Himmler instead of Hippocrates." He picked up his knife and fork and neatly sliced off a morsel of sole.

The Algerian girl Leila, who helped Françoise in the kitchen, was already placing bottles of red wine on the table, readying for the meat course. There was a low, gentle hum of conversation, voices softened out of respect for the excellent meal. Camille studied the others around her; obviously, everyone present knew everyone else. There was a genteel clatter as Leila and Françoise cleared the table in preparation for the next course.

Much to her relief, Camille was relaxing at last. Her dinner partner Christophe helped. It seemed they had much in common, and she enjoyed talking with him about his studies elsewhere and then his practice in Paris. He was a tall man, as tall and lanky as Marc, and his warm brown eyes sparkled with a passion for his work. She was not surprised to learn he was the Duchêne family's physician.

She tried to listen to other fragments of conversation. Everyone seemed to owe Henri a debt of gratitude and respect and loyalty and love, although she never heard it mentioned in those precise words. Everyone wanted to share news with him too, news in which he showed deep interest.

Henri modestly affected to concentrate on his plate, studying it with deliberation and dipping a crust of bread in the sauce of Françoise's savory *Boeuf bourguignon*.

Almost twenty years after the war had ended, like many he seemed reluctant to even mention his contributions. During Camille's relatively short time in medical practice, she had met others like him: those who had tried to help and survived would ache with the pain that they had never done nearly enough.

Christophe was speaking to her again. Smiling, Camille turned toward him, listening closely to his question. Christophe's wife Monique had just uncorked another bottle of a particularly outstanding red Rhone and was progressing around the dinner table, refilling wineglasses, just like any wife might do in her family's kitchen.

Françoise's assistant Leila entered the dining room, cleared the table, and delivered several more platters. The guests passed the tureens and serving dishes themselves, as if seated at their family's table. The cheerful background chatter was that of extended family with no spoken references to what had brought them together and united them under this one man's roof. With the exception of the luxurious surroundings and Leila's brief appearances, it could have been any dinner table at any home, dining *en famille*, the family of friends that Henri had chosen.

"Friendship has no intrinsic survival value; rather it is one of those things which give value to survival." Camille recalled the quotation from someplace, something she'd read, and couldn't recall the author's name. How fortunate those in this gathering were to have each other, and how fortunate Henri Duchêne was to call them his friends.

In the dim candlelight Camille squinted to read the label on the wine bottle. It was a Chateauneuf-du-Pape, 1945. Laid down and protected for over twenty years, but where and how? It was already known as one of the greatest vintages of all time. How had Henri Duchêne managed it? The family hadn't returned to France until 1945. Monique was standing beside them now, wine bottle raised in question. Christophe broke off what he'd been saying, nodded absently to his wife, and gestured toward his glass, his attention still focused on his dinner partner. Camille glanced up and into Monique's eyes. She gasped, recognizing something she had experienced and known so well, not that long ago. There was the hurt of lost love, something it seemed only a woman could identify in another woman. Monique had recognized immediately what Christophe himself might not have known had happened.

Camille allowed the doctor to finish, added a polite, general comment in response, and then turned to the dinner partner on her left, the civil engineer and architect, Stéfan Croisier.

After dinner, Françoise joined the group in the salon. She was seated on the rug beside Cécile's chair, her legs tucked to one side, while one of the family dogs nuzzled in beside her. She addressed Camille eagerly, smiling up at her future sister-in-law. "And so, do you think you'll like it here?"

"It's lovely, but I'm not sure of our plans." Camille tried to attract Louis's attention but he was typically engaged in a passionate discussion of cars, always his other love. Monique was close by, coffee cup in hand, and had rejoined their conversation. Relieved, Camille thought that perhaps she had only imagined the brief glimpse of sadness and betrayal.

Christophe was talking with Albert. Camille wondered whether he was the elderly pianist's physician too. Gertrude, Marc, and Madeleine formed another cozy group. The architect Croisier was chatting with Maurice and Hélène Bertrand, sketching something in a small notebook and displaying it to them. Those gathered around the dining room table had regrouped in the salon, a family once more.

VII

By 1969 Camille and Louis had been married three years. The family she had hoped and prayed for stubbornly evaded them. She suspected it was her fault, although she sternly objected when her patients referred to physiological functions as anyone's "fault." Research had shown that inadequate nutrition, such as the inevitable deprivations of wartime during formative years could adversely affect future reproductive ability. Soon she and Louis ceased to mention the children they had wanted to have.

Camille continued working for the nation's relatively new health care system. She loved her work no matter where it was, but she missed the beauty of mountains and open countryside always accessible in Grenoble.

It was 1969 also when Henri Duchêne declared that he and Cécile were moving. "The winter in Paris is too cold for my old bones now," he stated decisively. "Any business I conduct here— everything I do—I can accomplish from the villa in Cap Ferret. Place du Chêne is yours, *mon fils*, for you and Camille and your family to come." He clapped Louis on the shoulders, one of those rough hugs so typical of men, and then he had embraced Camille, kissing her tenderly. "You're the flower of our family, my dearest girl. You will blossom here, I know."

❖

8 *Forgiven by a Horse*

Louis Duchêne and Hélène Bertrand, Paris, 1982

I

URING THE YEARS FOLLOWING THE WAR, their family's
routines inevitably altered and shifted; like days of summer
slipping into autumn, the changes were imperceptible at first.
New traditions would slide in to occupy a void, replacing other
rituals when death, extreme age, or disability robbed the family
of a particular beloved connection.

After his Grandpère Maurice died, Louis and Camille hired
an architect to convert the loft over the old carriage house into
an airy and comfortable apartment for Grandmère Hélène.
Considering his grandmother's age and the safety risks of stairs,
Camille had insisted they also install a lift. The spacious area
below, where the Germans had once stored ammunition and
sheltered armored vehicles, still housed Louis's collection of
classic automobiles and racing cars. Louis's regular visits with his
Grandmère Hélène began two years ago, evolving into more than
a filial obligation: she was his last surviving relative of that gen-

eration. She was one of the few who could still talk about the past; furthermore, she was the only one who would talk about the war. Most, even over forty years later, would not.

When Louis was a young man the subject was avoided and not discussed at all. War's aftermath lay all about them. Rebuilding homes and lives consumed their energies, while silence avoided reliving their pain. A collective spirit of denial permitted everyone to move forward.

Later, in the flush and rush of youth, what young person would have wanted to listen to stories from parents about a dismal past anyway? The early 1950s were no different than any other postwar generation; in their defense, its youth were no more self-absorbed than any other. Impatient, they had pushed on. Only in the past decade had Louis sensed history vanishing around him, slipping from his grasp.

II

On his way home on Wednesday, Louis routinely stopped at a local *patisserie* for a selection of small pastries, and then he and Grandmère Hélène would spend the rest of the afternoon together. He would go up directly to the small kitchen of her apartment over the old carriage house and then fill the kettle, waiting for the water to boil for tea and considering the remarkable woman who was Hélène Bertrand.

His mother's mother.... Louis studied the delicate, still beautiful silver-haired woman, today warmly dressed in a gray, cashmere cardigan over a slender, black skirt, tiny pearl-drop earrings, and the inevitable classic shoes with their nearly doll-like, miniature heels. He had difficulty imagining her pregnant, carrying and giving birth to a child, or facing any of the challenges she'd been forced to endure. Women like her were different: they were fighters and survivors.

His grandmother and her contemporaries—there were fewer and fewer of those each day too—had been forged from sterner stuff than his generation. From the perspective of maturity, he could admit to that now, but he'd learned that the secrets of survivors were not easily surrendered. Speaking of them and sharing them seemed more painful than any physical wound.

III

Hélène de Louriston-Drouin was a country girl, born to an old Normandy family that had farmed and worked the lush countryside for centuries, breeding its elegant thoroughbred horses. They had also owned many of the region's prime apple orchards.

Until before the previous war, they'd also managed a dairy farm for the production of cheeses for which the locale was renowned. When young Hélène married Maurice Bertrand, the only son of a neighboring family whose historic roots extended into Normandy's soil nearly as deeply as her own, the two large estates had combined. The conjoined farms had become known simply as the Bertrand Estate, which would continue to produce the famous Bertrand Calvados—the region's distilled spirits known 'round the world, the always popular and refreshing Bertrand *Cidre Bouché*, and, of course, operate both internationally renowned horse breeding farms.

Throughout centuries, the two large properties, singly and then together, had provided a steady source of employment for the villages of the surrounding area, most particularly the small hamlet of St-Etienne-des-Près. The bucolic life had been their anchor and refuge, the home of their hearts. All that would change forever, one day in 1940; the region would continue to suffer during the next four years.

Others displaced by the intrusions of war were allowed to return to their homes by late 1945, but Louis's maternal grandparents had had no where to go. Everything they'd ever owned—from the manor houses to the stables to most of the orchards—had been destroyed by the concerted efforts of two armies surging across this critical terrain.

Immediately postwar, his Grandpère Maurice had hired local workers to replant and rebuild the orchards, much to the relief of nearby villages who would once again have work. Hoping to rebuild one day, they had salvaged blocks of stone, prying from the earth shattered, blackened chunks wedged among skeletal remains whose sturdy woolen uniforms had sometimes stayed intact.

Meanwhile, Louis's father Henri made certain that Hélène and Maurice had a suitable home in Paris, near their family and in the same *arrondissement*, always close. When the initial reconstruction in Normandy was completed by early 1951, his grandparents returned to their rebuilt home. However, after living at the estate only one year, Hélène pronounced, "It is simply too painful here," and after 1952 she had never returned.

Hélène Bertrand was one of those rare individuals who'd been seared by two wars, although she hadn't been toughened by their fires as had many who'd survived nearly identical horrors.

Despite pain and heartbreak, she'd maintained a soft inner core and an unfailing sense of humor.

When others would comment on the extent of the family's losses, Hélène would reassure them all: "It is of no consequence, *mes enfants.*" They were always "her children," no matter their age. "Besides, most of my treasure was saved," she would add cryptically, smiling through tears into her husband's eyes or lightly touching her daughter's hand.

Only once in all the years after the upheaval of war had Louis ever glimpsed a crack in this outer wrapping she wore as effortlessly as her classic Channel wardrobe. The single event had happened some years ago.

Everyone had gathered in the foyer of their home following a family dinner. His father had already called for the taxi to drive them to their townhouse. Grandpère Maurice and Louis's father hung back a few steps, still engrossed in an animated discussion of politics, speaking passionately about some issue that concerned them both.

His mother leaned forward to embrace her mother in farewell, tender *bisous* brushing cheeks. "You'll call when you arrive home safely, won't you, *Maman?*"

Louis had heard his mother make this request at least a hundred times before, so there seemed nothing unusual about it, nothing ominous cached within the simple request. However, it was as if the words, at that very moment and at none other, had traumatized his grandmother, piercing a chink in her armor, breaking through the careful adjustments of time and opening the edges of a wound they imagined long ago healed.

"Home was in another world." Her voice was dry, flat, and devoid of emotion; she shook her head. "It is someplace else… a word from another language. At *home,* I would wake up and I'd see a clear sky from my bedroom window, hung 'round with birds singing in the hedgerows. And there would be my horses...." The sentence trailed away, lost in a nearly inaudible small sob. "Oh, my horses...." she'd whispered, her voice breaking with emotion.

Just then, Grandpère Maurice had come up and taken her arm, helping her slip into her coat, quite unaware of what she'd been saying. Hélène's warm smile returned and her eyes sparkled with the animation that Louis had always considered an essential part of her. The transition out of and back into her former self had been completely without guile.

One unguarded remark had touched a depth in her that remained fragile and vulnerable, what could still be penetrated, after so many years. The single word "home" had erased all youth and cheer from her face and that was the only time he could remember because then, only then and never since, for a matter of seconds, she had appeared *old*.

Tires crunched against the gravel and cobbled drive; their taxi had arrived.

"Of course, *Maman*." Louis's mother had sighed, perhaps knowing more of the pain that her mother had hidden and buried so well it couldn't be touched, what she would not allow herself to feel.

IV

Louis had known her all his life, and she'd forever been a part of it, her presence and voice imprinted on his earliest memories. Only now was he discovering that he'd hardly known her at all. Like the strata of a delicate pastry, layers that he'd previously savored together as one, he'd just begun to recognize his grand-mother's many separate layers too.

She was a remarkable woman, still as strikingly beautiful as her daughter, his mother, had been. Both had been endowed with that rare complexion which certain women are destined to keep throughout their lives. Velvety soft, without wrinkles except for a fine webbing at the corners of her eyes, and the lightly-tinted warmth she'd been born to—qualities women envied and men admired.

"It's because I was raised on a farm," Hélène would always maintain. Calling the vast De Louriston-Drouin and Bertrand Estates and properties a "farm" seemed whimsical, an under-statement typical of her. By 1982, she had outlived not only her husband and most of her contemporaries, but her younger grandson, Louis's brother Marc, then her son-in-law Henri, and, just recently, her only daughter Cécile.

On these rare occasions she would allow Louis to look deep into her soul and glimpse the history she'd carried throughout a lifetime. Every time they were alone together, like today at tea, he would discover something new, something totally unexpected about the complex woman who was his grandmother.

Two years ago she had begun sharing her life story with him, one chapter per afternoon at tea. Louis once considered bringing a small tape recorder, because his memory wasn't nearly as sharp as hers, but he'd discarded the idea, instinctively sensing that its presence would intrude into the intimacy of their time together. Instead, he would try to listen more carefully.

How he wished his grandmother would return—even once more—to the newly renovated manor house in Normandy, but he was certain it would never happen. The property hadn't been seriously maintained since the earlier, hasty postwar rebuilding, but Louis expected the fully restored home would be completed within two years. Eventually, the management of his father's Herculean endeavor had passed to him: Henri Duchêne had hoped to present the restoration to Maurice and Hélène as a sentimental gift, a return of their family home.

In 1949, a scant dozen tiny photographs had been all they had to work with—except for memories—because the destruction of war had been so complete. If the photographs hadn't been in his mother's possession when the Duchêne family fled to Switzerland, those would have been lost too. Everything left behind was ruined—either bombed, burned, destroyed, or looted. What remained was a sad and blackened countryside, but the Bertrand work crews had begun replanting the historic orchards before 1946.

Louis had seen the pictures of his grandmother as a young girl. One of the snapshots had shown Hélène, a small-boned, petite teenager standing in a pasture. She was holding the halter leads of two horses who towered over her, one on either side, huge gray-white creatures either one of which could have stomped out her life with one massive hoof.

Puzzled, he'd examined another small, speckled, black and white square print. "What kind of saddle is that?"

"That's not a saddle, *mon petit,*" she'd patiently explained to Louis, who at six feet was certainly not "her little one" anymore. "That's me. I was reading."

Louis peered through the reading glasses he now needed and squinted at the pale and tiny image, two inches by two inches. He finally made out the miniature figure of a young girl, stretched the length of the animal's broad back, her head propped on the horse's withers, which she seemed to be using like a pillow. There was a book in her hands, and she was holding it above her face.

Yes, Louis decided, she did appear to be reading.

"I think that was Soucie. They were all so gentle, but she was the gentlest mare of them all."

"But, Grandmère, how did you possibly get up there?"

"She would lower her head, and I pulled myself up by her mane. She'd wait without moving until I was settled, and then she'd resume grazing."

The photos—all dozen of them—were small, crumpled, water-damaged, and faded. Later Louis had them enlarged and restored, their details enhanced, and the resulting fine-grained images framed for her.

———

One part of her past he knew quite well: his maternal grandparents had spent part of the war years in England. Unlike the Duchêne family who had left France quite early, Maurice and Hélène had been one of few in their region to escape, for they had waited almost too long. Hitler's armies had already occupied France.

Hélène had visited their property immediately after their return from England when they had all driven up together. Henri parked in the remnants of the long entry drive, its outline vaguely sketched by ragged plane trees.

She turned back to them as they stood around the car. "I think I'd like to go alone—at first, if you don't mind." She started forward, then came back. "Maybe Louis could walk with me?"

He was almost fourteen at the time, and he hadn't questioned why she wanted him—not her husband or not her daughter—to accompany her. Occasionally she had gripped his arm more tightly or sometimes there would be a sharp intake of breath. They'd walked on in silence for nearly an hour before she spoke.

"Louis, most of our orchards—over a thousand hectares—are *gone*. Vanished. We at the Bertrand Estate were known for our horses and our Calvados."

Louis had smiled at the mention of Calvados. When he and his mother, father, and young brother Marc returned from Switzerland their grandmother would quiz the two boys periodically, as if the time spent outside their native land might have changed them inside and made them less than they should be.

"What are the four most important things to remember about our Normandy? Never forget, *mes petits enfants—les chevaux, la crème pour le camembert, les crêpes, et le Calvados!*"

"Horses and cream for the Camembert, crêpes and Calvados!" they would chant for her benefit, parroting the words, sing-song, like a nursery rhyme.

"Who can forget the world famous distilled spirits made from Normandy's apple cider?"

"But no one!" he and Marc would chorus.

"There are only sticks," she'd said that day, staring at the stark land all around them. She walked carefully across the uneven terrain, holding Louis's arm and pausing occasionally to survey the surrounding hills. It had once been beautiful countryside, soft and lush and green. "There are charred black sticks sticking up here and there like burned skeletons…. Some of our tree stock was over a hundred years old." Over the years her family had grafted and created some of the most unique and outstanding apples not only for Normandy, but for the world. It was all gone.

Where they were standing there had been fighting from hedgerow to hedgerow, from orchard to pasture and back again to hedgerow. He had read accounts about those battles and pictured the hedgerows stained red: the flow of blood, the flare of gunfire.

They paused at what remained of their rambling old farm house with its many fireplaces and high-pitched slate roof. There were piles of rocks, as if a house had never stood there before. Part of one wall—just the one—was standing, about up to his waist.

She gestured with one hand. "And the stables—*pouf!*—vanished, their stones all scattered. I can't imagine how." She'd shrugged, and her tears had flowed on that day of their return years ago. "I can't bear to look at it… not ever again."

But Hélène had returned when she'd visited the site, the summer of 1949 when Louis was seventeen before he continued on to university. She and Grandpère Maurice had stayed with friends in the nearby village where rebuilding was proceeding more rapidly than at their family's country house. Louis had joined a cadre of local young men who were glad for the summer's work: the hard task of hauling rock and digging up thousands more stones. And they'd uncovered bones, so many bones… sometimes in scraps of woolen uniforms, the soldiers' metallic buttons or insignia scattered amidst the munitions.

V

The tea kettle was impatiently shrieking its readiness. Louis poured the boiling water into the tea pot, loaded the tray, and carried it to his grandmother's sitting room.

On these afternoons, they typically settled into her favorite, lovingly worn, overstuffed armchairs. His grandmother was so small and the chair so vast that Louis imagined hers might swallow her up someday. Tucked into a gracious window alcove, the chairs overlooked the Duchêne family gardens in one direction and the cobbled courtyard in the other. Below, young trees struggled to fill the space that had been crowded with oaks centuries ago; they never would dominate as had their ancient predecessors. Streaks of late afternoon sunshine filtered in, refracting and bouncing the warm hues of autumn up through the windows.

He reached for the heavy ceramic teapot, filled his grandmother's cup first, added one lump of sugar and tipped in a small drop of milk, just as he knew she preferred. He filled his cup and set the pot back, covering it with the faded, quilted English tea cozy Hélène had used for as long as Louis could remember.

They sipped their tea in silence. Fallen leaves skittered about the courtyard below, scratching softly at the cobblestones. The sun had reached both her chair and his, lazing across the table and enveloping them with the gift of light and warmth on a brisk late November day.

Hélène sighed and set the cup and saucer on the table between them. "Very good, as usual, *mon cher.*"

He shrugged and smiled. "Brewing a pot of tea doesn't require a tremendous amount of skill."

She laughed, and then turned to him, her lips parted in a playful half smile. "Have you ever been forgiven by a horse?"

At first, Louis thought he had misunderstood.

Unlike others who had achieved the dignified and delightful age of ninety-two, Hélène rarely repeated herself. On occasion she would mistakenly use one word in place of another. They would be near in sound, but far distant in meaning. Had she meant to say "Have you ever been given a horse?" Louis wondered or perhaps, "Have you ever forgotten to lock the house?" Both sentences contained approximately the right number of syllables; he silently practiced and compared them. Another possibility might be, "Have you ever ridden a horse?" Surely, she remembered that.

Despite her advanced years, his grandmother wasn't at all forgetful. This word switching—or was it confusion?—was one of those idiosyncrasies of speech that had occurred only recently. Their family first noticed these little episodes almost six months to the day following her stroke (a "mild one" they'd been told) of late last year. Why it hadn't happened earlier, none of her doctors could explain. Louis's wife Camille, a physician herself, informed him that this condition had a name, one which he promptly forgot because it was impossible to pronounce.

"How exactly do you mean that, Grandmère?" he asked with what he hoped was a wide-eyed, convincing air of innocence. For a moment his reply hung briefly between them, his conditioned response, inane words waiting for an answer.

The charming tease of Hélène's smile, the bright smile of a much younger woman, faded quickly. Her posture was always perfectly erect, but she seemed to have drawn herself up even straighter. The sudden flash of vivid blue from under the arch of her silky white brows that matched the neatly-coiffed silvery hair warned him. The forthright manner she met his eyes was answer enough. His grandmother had not slipped and chosen the wrong words, not this time.

"Bien." Louis shrugged and smiled in apology for his inappropriate choice of words. *"Pardonnes-moi, Grandmère."* He settled back into the armchair and waited for her to continue.

"I asked you, Louis," she repeated, emphasizing and enunciating each word carefully as if he might be a child or the one with questionable mental acuity, "Have you ever been forgiven by a horse?" She lifted her teacup, glanced down into the puddle of creamy tan, and replaced it on the table between them: it was Louis's cue to pour out.

Louis chuckled and set his cup on the table beside hers. "A lot of people have forgiven me for a lot of things, Grandmère." He grinned and raised an eyebrow, hinting at youthful indiscretions. "I've needed it, to be sure! When I was a boy and still had the nerve to go to Confession—"

He hesitated, supposing that now, safely approaching sixty, he should probably start again. Perhaps his sins had diminished sufficiently in severity, and the old ones, like staring back through the wrong end of a telescope, might have shrunk in size and significance.

He imagined stepping into a confessional, once more parting the curtain, kneeling, and beginning the standard confession of: "Bless me, Father, for I have sinned. It has been more than forty years since my last confession." He might spend most of a day there, cramped and on his knees.

Hélène was studying him closely. She waved one hand toward the teapot, then rested a finger along the edge of the empty china cup, thoughtfully tracing its delicate curves.

As he refilled their cups, Louis shook his head. "Back then a priest always told me I was forgiven." He winked at his grandmother and then regretted his flippant disregard for one of the Holy Sacraments. She took her religion much more seriously than he did his. He believed; he simply didn't participate.

"No. I've never been forgiven by a horse, of that I'm sure." He smiled, anticipating the story to come, what his grandmother would share today. She was an excellent *raconteur,* which was another fine skill of the past deserting the world day by day. It would be something he'd never heard before, because her memory remained precise, her voice sure, strong, and controlled. Hélène would never repeat, not unless she deliberately intended to. He placed his hand on hers. Only there could the true message of age be read in the transparent fair skin and fine, blue crisscrossing of veins that branched across the back of her hands.

Hélène smiled and drew her hand away from his and back onto her lap. Sunshine poured through the glass and shimmered across her silvery hair, as if granting its benediction on their time together. She sampled a circle of puff-pastry dotted with a swirl of *chèvre* cheese and then raised her cup from its saucer, sighing at the simple pleasure.

"A horse forgave me... once," she said, resuming where she teased him with her question. "You do remember my father and his father before him were royal equerries." Hélène's eyes narrowed for a moment while she studied Louis's puzzled expression at the term she'd used. "That's right, they weren't teaching that kind of history where you were." Her voice carried a note of disparagement, as if the professors in the first levels of school in Switzerland were incapable of this basic and quite simple task.

Louis, his mother, and father had crossed into Switzerland from France in early 1938, one year prior to the disasters which would overtake their country. They were safely settled there by the time he would have studied history of any sort, and in a modern era, the use of the antiquated term had faded from usage.

"An equerry maintains the royal stables for the king, the emperor—whatever excuse we might have for government at the time." She shrugged, a casual gesture of dismissal. "Our estate dated from the seventeenth century, when the large breed pedigreed horses were still needed for war. Then, after that, horses became a way of showing off. Men demonstrating their power and wealth—like you with your collection of cars, Louis." She shared an impish smile with him. "Of course, the formal Bertrand grant in perpetuity came from Napoleon. Our tall, muscular, thoroughbred horses from Normandy…. Ah, there's nothing more beautiful."

Hélène glanced to her left, staring out the window, and Louis recognized one of those times when she would step back into the past, reliving and recapturing some treasured moment she alone could experience and seeking comfort there.

Was she sprawled in some grassy meadow perhaps? Studying her books while surrounded by the wide-eyed curiosity of gentle, young foals? Were there scents from flowers, the new apple blossoms bursting forth on the trees above her? Somewhere, the little girl Hélène was enjoying the precious gift of peace and solitude, surrounded by the chirping of birds in the hedgerows on the morning air or the soft neighs of their brood mares.

"They were some of the most beautiful and gentle horses in the world."

Louis had been right. That's where she'd been for a few moments. He thought her eyes brimmed and glittered briefly, but she blinked and turned back to face him. Hélène raised the cup to her lips, sipped meditatively, and replaced it in its saucer, then turned to gaze out the window again, into the fluttering golden leaves of the courtyard, either searching for a word or peeking back once more into a distant past.

He glanced down, studying his hands. The calluses and blisters from that summer when he'd worked on his grandparents' estate were long-healed, but he was trying to recall something else about that time.

"Louis?" His grandmother's dark blue eyes softened with tenderness and looked up into his.

They'd all inherited her striking blue eyes, what always seemed more natural on his brother and his mother with their fair Norman coloring and light brown hair than on him, with his once black hair, thick black eyelashes, and the devil of a heavy beard.

"It's all right now, *mon fils,* whatever it is."

"Sorry, Grandmère. Daydreaming."

"Was that what it was? Hmm...." Hélène tilted her head knowingly but didn't pursue the matter. "I know all about daydreaming." She sipped at her tea, grasped the saucer firmly in one hand and the cup with the other, and eased back into the embrace of her armchair. "Even living that far out in the country, we knew they were coming."

When she referred to "them" or "they" there was no need to explain further: it was the German Army. She'd survived and endured two wars with them, wars fought nearly on her door-step.

Louis reached to refill her cup, but she ignored him.

"At first, we'd been promised we had nothing to fear, and we believed them. We were just a farm, out in the country, with no place to house troops, no wealth to plunder, no food stores except oats and hay for the horses. Apples, of course." She finished the half-piece of pastry and wiped her hands on the napkin she'd spread across her knees. "Those were excellent, Louis." She smiled, thoughtfully. "They always are. And you're always a good grandson."

Louis said nothing.

"Of course," she continued as if she had placed a bookmark in her story, "the vats of Calvados for the season were mostly kegged by then. We had stored those.... Around... here and there...." She shrugged. "It doesn't matter now—in other places."

Louis had heard these stories, about distributing stores and personal treasure throughout the countryside, in various locales and with various friends. According to family lore, his father and his ancestors had done the same thing, through war after war, even before the Revolution.

"Then one morning they came. They took all the...*eh*, the thoroughbred riding horses... *eh, les Selles... français....*" She hesitated and seemed uncertain of what to say next. He recognized one of those moments of searching for the right word she now encountered.

"The French Saddle Horses, right?" Louis supplied. Those had come from his grandfather Maurice's estate. Louis had ridden them with his mother and only once by himself—both times when he was a very young child. His mother had used no saddle and no bridle, yet the horse responded to her commands, her light touch, and the pressure of her knees as if they were one. The memory of the animal's magical power, grace, and gentleness had stayed with him.

She sighed and frowned. "Yes, at least they weren't in foal. Like so much, I would never know what happened after that. The soldiers forced two of the grooms to go with them. They threw all their tack into two trucks—just in a tangled pile." She shuddered at this disrespect of equipment oiled, polished, and maintained with such loving, meticulous care. Briefly resting her teacup on her lap, she gestured, trying to describe the wild disorder of the moment. "Another group of men put hay and oats in a third truck and used the trucks to herd our precious horses away. An officer saluted us, that way the soldiers in Hitler's army did." She shuddered again, recalling the moment. "He thanked our family for our service to the Third Reich and they left."

"They were all such beautiful animals, *Mamita,*" Louis said softly. Listening to this story as it unfolded, he wondered how she could tolerate talking about these events at all, and he understood now, whenever she shared something deeply emotional, why she had not mentioned it before. Some stories could be told but once, and sometimes that was too much.

How she had loved those horses. Any person who valued and admired natural beauty and grace couldn't help but fall in love with them. Years later Louis discovered that the meticulous records maintained by most of the country's official breeding farms had been stored and catalogued elsewhere, where looting soldiers couldn't destroy them. He had visited the National Archives and researched the Bertrand's stud and breeding farm records, finding the fascinating historic records remarkably intact.

Hélène raised the teacup to her lips and tilted it, sipping slowly. She held the cup close to her face, just a few minutes longer than was really necessary, hiding her tears.

"The next day Maurice traveled into town. He had business in Caen, too, and was trying to get more news. Then I discovered our telephone lines had been cut. That's when I knew *they* were coming back. I didn't have any idea when—but it would be soon."

"You were completely alone?" Louis asked in dismay and reached for her hand but the demands of recounting this chapter must have kept her focused, for she ignored him. The network of fine blue veins on her hands stood out as she grasped the delicate china, as if in a vice, one hand supporting the other with the cup and saucer trapped between. The tension required to maintain control was driving her forward, if she were to finish her story. Although Louis wasn't sure why, he felt that this part was only the beginning.

"I began trying to provide for the safety our workers and tenants, the best I could. There was no way to guarantee them anything. If they were on the estate when the Germans returned, the men would be pressed into service, captured, or shot. I was certain of that. Maurice and I had discussed what to do, if this should happen, but we couldn't do enough for them. It was never enough, Louis. We both knew that." She sighed, as if she'd been holding her breath, then inhaled deeply once more, bracing herself.

"Three days later, they came back for our Percherons. Maurice hadn't returned yet and I began to fear for him too. What had happened? I prayed to God, thanking Him that Cécile was safe—with you and Henri in Switzerland." Hélène was silent for several long moments. She gulped and swallowed, then reached for Louis's hand. "Every night, when I say my Rosary, I thank God that Cécile married Henri. He was part of our family's good fortune too."

"If only you had left then—" Louis began.

"Ah, yes…. Perhaps. If it hadn't been for the horses and the people who were counting on us, we would have left earlier too. Then I heard the trucks coming. Again." She was quiet for a few minutes. "You know, the air is so still out there in the early summer evenings."

For a moment, Louis's thoughts drifted away from his grandmother's apartment and the present. Yes, he could remember well the soft stillness of those evenings. *A gentle warmth that seemed to linger layered in the air, a chilled bottle of cider pulled from the creek, the aching muscles after a day of work in the fields, the filigreed shadows cast by the struggling new orchards, the cool grass under his bare skin....*

Hélène seemed not to notice his momentary preoccupation. "I started sending the last workers away, even if it was out to the orchards or to the far tool sheds so they could find a way back to their families. Old Giles stayed with me. He was too old and the Germans probably wouldn't take him or kill him. Clément was not quite so old, but he stayed on too, trying to calm the horses. They seemed to sense what was coming."

"Animals are unique that way, aren't they, Grandmère?" Not only horses, but their family's dogs had been that way too, often sensing impending calamity, illness, or disaster. Camille had tried to explain these extrasensory abilities scientifically, but he'd quickly become lost and floundered about among the many technical terms as she explained certain animals' nearly psychic abilities and heightened awareness.

Hélène didn't answer him, only nodded, because she'd pulled away again, turning to gaze out the window, her eyes unfocused, looking past the autumn trees that shimmered and reflected soft golden light up into the apartment.

She was watching and remembering something else. Could it have been the sight of those majestic, pedigreed animals with their rippling muscles and long, silky manes fluttering on the evening breeze? Did she hear the terrified whinnies as mares were separated from foals and herded away? Her gentle gray-white giants had been pressed into service for the omnivorous appetites of German invaders. Their prize-winning show horses, now mainly used in ceremonial parades, would once more haul supplies and heavy artillery for a warrior—for Hitler, not

Napoleon and others as they had in the past. What would happen to them afterwards?

"What broke my heart—right then, at least—were the foals. Some of them were less than a week old. If they didn't keep up...." She stared down at the teacup and saucer, still gripped firmly in both hands. "Sound carries too well on an evening like that. I screamed every time I heard a gunshot, I couldn't stop myself. I cried out each time." She looked up from her cup and faced Louis. "Clément would flinch too, but he kept trying to console me. We both knew the mares would turn back for their foals. They're massive, strong horses, *mon chéri*, but they're no match for a truck full of armed soldiers."

"They took them all? Everything? Every single one of the horses?" Louis pushed up in his chair, stunned at the large-scale brutality that seemed so unreasonable to his modern mind. Their country had been overrun by an armored German Panzer division and later by more Allied tanks and their armored vehicles. Why take the horses?

Hélène's smile, a slight ironic quirk, was Louis's clue that her story had been leading to this all along.

"But I wasn't going to let them take Tonette." She sighed. "When the workers were leaving I asked one of them to lead her back into the orchards and hobble her there, out of sight and hopefully where she couldn't be heard. I could hope. It was behind a small rise. I don't know why.... But I wanted to try, and if...." She stopped, her voice choked with emotion at the sadness of this day from so many years ago.

Louis turned to her. "Tonette?"

"You won't remember her, Louis, because you were so young. Tonette was a mare. She'd been a prize-winner too, but I'd kept her for sentimental reasons. She was old, but I loved her dearly and she loved me. I helped raise her and nurse her. She was her dam's last foal." Hélène hesitated, as if searching for a word. "Something happened to Caroline—that was her dam—after Tonette was born and she started having seizures. Toxemia— that's what it was. And she died from it. I helped raise and nurse her foal. She was my dearest friend ever. If you can remember your mother's age about that time, you can guess at Tonette's age. And I helped deliver her—when I was pregnant! It was a bad presentation too. Giles and I struggled and pulled the foal into the world."

Louis was unable to hide his amazement. "So, she was in her early twenties then, Grandmère?"

"*Oui.* Your mother Cécile was a born horsewoman, Louis. Well, she was nearly born with the horses at that!" Hélène's smile was one of genuine delight, remembering. "We named the filly Antoinette but your mother, as a child, couldn't quite say the full word. I think she learned 'Tonette' about when she learned 'Maman' and 'Papa'!"

Louis enjoyed the delighted, abandoned laughter of his grandmother, the free, easy laughter of a happier and younger woman, not of a ninety-two year old who had painfully managed to endure.

"Maurice arrived back shortly after the Germans departed— that second time," she explained. "He'd traveled the same road Hitler's forces had used as they left. He refused to answer my questions about our horses' fate or anything he'd seen… about along the road." Hélène swallowed hard.

They must leave the next day, Maurice informed her. Arrangements had been made with a Danish fishing boat to carry them to England. Denmark, which had acquiesced to Hitler early because it was too small to defend itself and had chosen relative shame and ignominy over total destruction, had more freedom in the Channel. Their fishing boats would know the placement of mines planted in coastal waters. However, there were always risks.

"I spent the next day up in the orchards, with Tonette. I was sewing."

Intrigued, Louis turned to face her and placed his cup and saucer on the table between them. He'd held on to it so long it had formed a ridge in his thumb and his fingers were growing numb. Somehow, he couldn't picture his grandmother sewing anything, yet he couldn't imagine her delivering a foal either.

"The gold," she supplied. "We could take nothing with us. 'Dress warmly,' we were told. So, I sewed gold coins into the clothes we'd wear. When I put on my coat I was afraid I couldn't stand up, it was that heavy…. I'm so grateful that I had that one day alone with her. We left the next day, early in the morning."

Louis had heard tales about the cache of gold coins, the famous *Louis d'or* from the early 1600s and 1700s, but had dismissed them as fairy tales. Each one would have been worth an unbelievable amount, even then. Modern collectors would pay over a million and a half francs for *one*.

"So it was true?" he asked. "Throughout all those years the family never touched that secret reserve?"

Hélène nodded and sighed. "I've always wondered," she said absently, "would they have taken our gold and perhaps left us alone? Then maybe our horses would have lived?" Her eyes appealed to Louis for reassurance. Surely she knew the answer. "Did I betray everything I loved for 'forty pieces of gold'? Our home and our horses." The pleading in his grandmother's voice was heartrending.

"Grandmère," Louis whispered. "You know it was a matter

of time. You could not have resisted for those next years. There was no way to know what the German armies would do or what the Allied armies gathering across the Channel would eventually plan."

"They might have rejected Tonette anyway as unfit for anything. But she managed to pull our cart, a bit unsteadily, through the countryside and back roads at night. We slept and hid during the day." Hélène turned to her grandson, again placing one slender hand on his. "Louis, never lose faith in the innate goodness of your fellow man. So many people were so good to us—and there was no chance we could ever repay their kindness. It took us five days—or nights," she amended. "At last, we arrived at the village where we would meet the Danish fishing boat."

"Where did you go? Was it up toward Picardie?"

She nodded. "I had those days to share my love with Tonette and tell her goodbye. It was painfully symbolic of the calamity unfolding around us. We'd abandoned our lovely old home. Clément would try to nurture the grafts from the trees, but there was only a slim chance that any of them would survive and that what we had done would work to save them. It was the end of all we knew and loved."

"But, Grandmère, you still had—"

She cut off his words. "Old Clément drove us north and up the coast to where he had relatives. He'd cared for Tonette since she was a foal, and then later he'd groomed her for competitions. But tonight, after we left, he would slaughter her to feed his family and their friends. The Germans must not get to her first."

Louis shook his head. He'd first thought that some stories should be shared but once; perhaps there were some that ought not be told at all. Hélène picked up a spoon and automatically, it seemed to him, stirred at her tea; the milk and sugar were long dissolved and mixed. It was the first since they'd been sitting together that she'd changed her solid grip on the cup and saucer, as though she'd been using the fragile china between her hands as an anchor.

"If they found Tonette at a poor worker's cottage, the Germans would know they had helped someone escape. Innocent people would be captured, tortured, or most likely, executed right then. She would put them all at risk."

Louis gasped. His grandmother didn't look right or left, but straight ahead as she continued, her grip on the cup and saucer tightened again, raising the veins on her hands.

"It was so cold that night. While we waited quietly—in total silence—for the signal from the boat in the harbor I heard them dismantling the old wagon. That was the only sound—nails screeching as they pulled the slats of wood apart."

"But why? Couldn't someone still have used the cart?" Louis's love for racing cars and cars in general seemed to have extended to embrace the protection of a humble wooden cart.

"The presence of a cart would suggest the presence of a horse." Hélène shook her head sadly. "They could use the firewood and it would be shared among many families. It was an old cart anyway…."

"But, what about other 'signs of a horse'?" Louis asked. *What a person might step in or slip on,* he wanted to add but didn't.

"Collected, dug into gardens behind their houses," Hélène responded, her voice flat. "It was so cold I could barely breathe. I had no idea it could possibly get even colder that night. I shivered while we waited for the flicker of light across the harbor. The signal a skiff was approaching to take us to the Danish fishing boat."

"How were you to signal back to the ship?"

"We had Tonette. Her gray had faded to pure white years ago. Like mine." Hélène brushed a hand through the soft waves and layers, a disarming gesture that enhanced her youthful appearance. "There was some moonlight—not a full moon though. She and I faced out toward the harbor. I would throw the blanket over her, then uncover her, twice. We couldn't take the chance with a lamp or any other signal."

At the National Archives, Louis had learned that some of the horses from the Bertrand Estate were seventeen, eighteen, and even nineteen hands tall. He couldn't imagine this small woman controlling an unbridled, unharnessed horse who might have weighed nearly a ton.

"While we stood there, waiting, I buried my face in my dear friend Tonette's mane. I wiped my tears in her hair—it was always like silk—and caressed her huge muzzle. She was velvety underneath the long white whiskers she'd grown as she aged. When she turned around to nuzzle me, her breath warmed my cheek and then, with each breath, it kept warming all of me… and I stopped shivering."

Louis reached for her teacup, but she raised one hand from her grasp on the symbolic stabilizer and waved his offer away.

"It was as though Tonette understood. She was consoling me, don't you see? Clément stood on her other side, holding the buckets—"

"Buckets?" Louis asked and then wished he hadn't.

Hélène looked up, meeting his eyes. "For her blood." Her voice had aged in an instant and turned brittle again, low and dry, like the fallen autumn leaves that scratched at the courtyard below. She whispered the next words. "The village had given sanctuary to a kosher butcher. They'd helped his family escape, but he was left behind. It's supposed to be painless, their way of slaughtering an animal." She blinked and looked away again. "I would be the only one to feel the pain."

Hélène inhaled deeply and held her breath for so long that Louis became concerned. Was she still breathing?

Finally, she exhaled, very slowly, and continued. "By the time we reached the Danish fishing boat, I knew there would be no evidence Tonette had ever lived. There couldn't be." Sighing, she leaned back into the chair cushions.

Louis hadn't been aware of how rigid her posture was until she'd suddenly relaxed. He reached one hand, offering consolation for this tragedy, but she had withdrawn back to that moment, living it again.

"I hugged Tonette and whispered to her, 'I love you, I love you. You'll always be with me.' And Tonette kept on sharing her warmth and her life with me, until the moment we stepped into the rowboat."

The Danish fishing captain Lars Rasmussen had rigged his boat for this purpose, she went on to explain. He continued to fish, and the cargo hold below held his regular catch as it would on any fishing vessel. Reels of nets clustered on the deck, and the *Kirsten* would work its normal fishing grounds, a zigzag pattern of laying down nets and pulling them in. Rasmussen had constructed a shallow space above the legitimate cargo hold, which often contained herring, with a false shelf of beams to support a token layer of fish that would be visible from the deck if the hatch were opened for inspection. That was where they would be hidden, lying down, for the duration of a Channel crossing, Hélène told Louis.

"Rasmussen warned us he would be challenged. At night he was always stopped at least once by the German patrols. He'd gradually gotten to know most of the men by name."

"He was caught, after that, right?" Louis had heard that part of the story from his grandfather.

Hélène paused in her story, again meeting his eyes, and for a moment Louis noticed a passing shadow of sadness. "Yes, but not with us." She looked down at her hands, rigidly grasping the empty cup on its saucer. "We were challenged only the once and a German crew came aboard the *Kirsten*. I thought we wouldn't make it then."

The clatter of boots on the deck above had echoed ominously below. Hélène and Maurice Bertrand, packed and layered in the shallow space between the legitimate cargo of herring, listened as the German patrol noisily boarded the ship. Muffled, surrounded by the omnipresent smell and icy insulation of fresh fish, they hadn't heard the patrol boat's challenge, only the high-powered engines and thump as their boat made contact with Rasmussen's. Then the big ship's engines began throttling down.

"I grasped Maurice's hand in the dark. 'Pray with me, dearest,' I begged. My heart was pounding so loudly in my ears I was certain the Germans could hear it on deck. Maurice couldn't answer, but he squeezed my hand in reassurance. Silence was our only defense… but after that?" Hélène shrugged, as if she were accepting the inevitability of their possible fate all over again.

"Those men sounded possessive and arrogant. They chatted with the captain, discussing weather and tides, the possibility of a storm. They shared cigarettes. I thought they would stay forever. And then one of them undid the latch and raised the hold cover."

The modest layer of fish, supported on a false shelf of beams, had come to light. The men studied Rasmussen's meager catch, and one stirred through the fish with the barrel of his rifle.

"'Don't do that,' another German patrol on deck ordered. 'The oil, fish scales, and salt water will ruin your mechanisms. There'll be hell to pay! It's enough bother keeping them clean without jamming herring inside.' The sounds of their laughter, concerned with nothing but their rifles, reached us in the hold. We held our breath, and another German spoke to Rasmussen. '*Ja,* indeed, the fishing, it is not very good, *Mein Herr.*'" Hélène paused for a moment.

"Whatever Rasmussen said in reply was unintelligible. We heard 'Permission to go....' but his voice trailed off and jumbled with the German voices on the changing wind. 'Why not?' their leader said. 'What good is beer without pickled herring?'"

Louis shook his head again. A thin shaft of golden light struggled past the house across the courtyard. It would soon be dusk, and Hélène's apartment had grown dim. He stood briefly, walking about the sitting room and turning on lamps, still listening. He returned to the armchair, but she didn't seem to notice he'd been gone.

"Then, to our relief—two humans layered with fish—the lid to the hold squeaked shut. The roar of outboard motors signaled the departure of the German patrol. The rumble of Rasmussen's diesels resumed and we were once more on our way to safety. It seemed to take so long, like it would be an eternity." She paused a moment. "What Rasmussen hadn't explained to us was how *terribly* cold it would be. The Channel is never warm...."

Louis grimaced. Even as a young man, playing water sports or boating with his grandfather, he'd found the waters thoroughly chilling. What was the average temperature there? The mid-40s and mid-50s, wasn't it? How people actually managed *to swim* it astounded him.

"The fishing grounds Rasmussen used extended up into the

North Sea. He couldn't use a direct route, the narrower crossing at Calais, because that would have aroused suspicion. That was filled with mines that were anchored floating just below the surface. It was under more surveillance than Rasmussen's per-mitted fishing grounds." Hélène pulled her sweater close around her, shoulders tightening against the remembered icy chill. "The cold sea water is allowed to splash inside and run through the fish and then drain out through the scuppers. It helps to keep them fresh. We were in the middle of it."

Louis remembered how his grandmother often complained of the cold; part of her story was already becoming clearer.

"I was so cold, my teeth were chattering. I'd bitten my tongue and cheek several times. I was bleeding and choking on my blood. I couldn't stop the shivering."

Louis reached for the teapot, surprised that it had kept hot under its cozy. "Here, this will warm you, Grandmère."

Hélène had begun shivering again as she relived those moments from so many years ago, but she handed him her cup. He prepared the tea as she preferred it and handed the cup back to her. She sighed, took a sip of the warming, soothing drink, and eased back into her chair once more.

"Merci, mon petit." She smiled and studied Louis, undoubtedly again considering there was nothing little about this grandson of hers anymore. "You're not going to believe this, I'm sure. Just when I was convinced I would certainly die of the cold, some-thing happened. A gentle touch of warm air brushed my face, then next it seemed to blow down my neck and back, and then all of me was warmed. There was a touch of velvet and then more warmth. Like happened waiting at the dock. It was Tonette.... That was when I knew she'd forgiven me... and she'd returned to share her warmth with me."

Louis said nothing. His wife Camille had once explained to him that belief can indeed be that powerful; he had no reason to doubt her or his grandmother. "Were you able to share it with Grandpère?"

"I don't know, but I tried. Every time the freezing and shivering started again, and my fingers and body started to grow numb or ache from the cold, Tonette's breath would come to warm me."

Hélène tilted her head and looked out into the courtyard, now grim and gray in the dusk. She sighed. "Once past his permitted fishing grounds, Rasmussen would extinguish all the ship's running lights, knowing only deep water was ahead, and set a direct course for a small spit of land where we would be set down, to walk the rest of the way to shore. The Germans didn't know how powerful his *Kirsten* was and what speeds her engines could achieve. He was experienced. He knew the water depths and the tides and when he could safely put his lights on again, off the coast of England."

"All we had were the layers of clothes we were wearing. Yes, our pockets and clothes were sewn full of gold—the gold our family has traditionally saved for an emergency such as this. Even in The Great War...." She hesitated again and looked to Louis for the correct word, eyebrows raised and brows furrowed in concern at this lapse.

"The First World War, you mean?" Louis clarified. "But it's still called The Great War too, because it was."

"Yes, but even then our savings hadn't been touched. We paid the captain with that, of course. Just one of those coins was worth more than many, many weeks of fishing. We spent the rest of the war in a small village on the coast of England."

Louis could not picture his patrician, gentleman farmer grandfather living in a fishing village and smiled at the thought.

"The only work Maurice could find was on a fishing boat. Can you imagine that?" she added. "We eventually learned our beautiful home in Normandy was demolished—apple orchards, horses, and all the stone barns. What the German's didn't destroy first the Allies finished. It's the nature of war." Hélène shrugged in resignation.

Total restoration of the historic country estate was nearly complete. It had taken years, partly because of the tremendous cost and partly because they'd wanted to use local labor and local material at all times. It was the only way they could think to repay the kindness shown Hélène and Maurice as they made their way to safety.

Louis often considered how deceptive pastoral beauty could be, disguising and forgiving the terrors of war. Hundreds had died and blood had been shed, right there.

"We lived very simply." Hélène picked up the cup and drained the last of what was now surely tepid tea. "We endured the same hardships, rationing, and dangers that all of England suffered. Once or twice a year Maurice would take the bus into London where he'd convert one of the *Louis d'or* gold coins into money for our living expenses. We were happy to be alive and we had each other. You and your mother and father were safe in Switzerland. We couldn't ask for more."

They had been among the fortunate, able to return and enjoy the beauty of home and to see their family reunited. Louis glanced up and realized his grandmother had fallen asleep. He reached to catch her empty cup and saucer, which had started to slide toward the floor. She had leaned back into the chair cushions and was smiling gently, the contented peaceful smile of a girl, not some ninety-two year old woman.

"I'm cold," she murmured in her sleep. "So cold."

"Grandmère?" Louis whispered and rested his hand lightly on her arm. "Grandmère?" She didn't waken. He couldn't leave her sitting here through the night. He bent to lift her in his arms, pulling her close and steadying her head against his chest. He noticed her reading glasses, coyly tucked down between the cushions of the chair, and bent to retrieve them. He grunted with the effort, even though she had become light, almost insignificant, and much lighter than he'd anticipated.

"Ah, that's much better, Tonette," she whispered against his chest when his breath touched her cheek.

Stepping carefully, he carried her into the bedroom and laid her gently on the bed. He leaned down, arranging her as best he could. In sleep, her face relaxed, but it hadn't taken on the flaccidity seen in normal sleep. Instead, it had assumed a sweet animation: she was still smiling. Hélène was visiting some better place again, somewhere warm and peaceful, some treasured place tucked away in memory.

Louis glanced around the room. He couldn't leave her like this either, not on a chilly November evening. He reached for the knitted throw and blanket, folded neatly over the end of the bed, and pulled them over her, tucking them close around her shoulders and up under her chin. His breath and hands must have touched her face, for she smiled again, accepting his gentle kiss on her forehead.

"That's good, Tonette." Hélène smiled and spoke to this treasured horse that lived on only in her dreams. "I always knew you'd forgive me."

He dimmed the lights in the sitting room, noticing that the lamps in the big house across the courtyard had come on and Camille was home. He watched the progress of lights and movement through the house, until at last the lamplight and warmth glowed from the windows of their bedroom. He checked on his grandmother once more before he left.

Hélène was speaking softly in her sleep again. "I should have saved them all...," she whispered to Tonette, the horse she'd treasured for so many years. "But I can't forgive myself."

❖

9 Christophe Rossignon

Paris, 1990

CHRISTOPHE ROSSIGNON STUDIED the pale yellow tie, knotted it, readjusted it twice, and still didn't like it.

His son, who had given it to him for his birthday last month, assured him this was the color that all men of power wore. "Just look at the politicians," he said. "They're all wearing ties like this."

Christophe had never considered himself a "man of power," and he was the first to admit that he'd never followed fashion closely. He jerked the silken strip from under his collar and replaced it with something more traditional: deep maroon accented by a subdued diagonal stripe.

The tie was not his only dilemma this evening. What should have been the prospect of a delightful soirée with Louis and Camille, surrounded by their close friends, had taken on different undertones. An evening with them was usually like relaxing at home with family, because they were his family.

He wasn't certain whose idea this new endeavor was. It might have been Louis's plan originally, but Camille had probably set it in motion. For their last several evenings together they had started including a single woman of the "appropriate age" for him. He would never hurt their feelings or the feelings of the ladies in question, but he had no intention of remarrying. He had been widowed twelve years and would surely die that way.

These lovely, eligible women would all generally have some loose connection to their intimate group: someone's cousin, a business colleague, a sister-in-law. All were intelligent and attractive, and one of them would undoubtedly make some man very happy, someday, but that man would not be Christophe Rossignon. He had loved two women in his life. One had been killed in an automobile accident on the busy Paris Périphérique highway and the other was happily married to his best friend: Monique and Camille.

There was an awkwardness to these evenings. How was he expected to treat them, these fine and appropriate ladies? On the first occasion, several months ago, he had made the unlucky choice of driving his car. From his home it was only a five minute walk to the Métro, and then he would emerge two blocks from the base of the steep, uphill climb to Place du Chêne. That was what he preferred. Now that he was expected to escort these ladies home, it placed him in the extremely uncomfortable position of not only the drive to their home or train connection but the more obviously awkward situation of not calling them back.

He was relieved he still had work to plead. "On call" could cover myriad imagined and mysterious medical obligations. The thought amused him: Louis and Camille were trying to see him settled before they moved to Normandy.

Paris without them—and without her especially, would seem empty—not a complete void, but they would vacate the vast terrain the entire Duchêne family occupied in his heart. What would happen to all of their extended, loyal family? At first, he had selfishly wondered about Françoise. Had she planned to move to St-Etienne-des-Près with them? Her *superbe cuisine* would be missed equally. Reflecting on this he considered how one conjoined with the other: fellowship with food and wine completed the perfect equilateral triangle.

Slipping on a tweed sport coat before grabbing his overcoat, he left to meet the next prospective candidate for the role of Madame Rossignon.

After nearly fifty years, the informality and casual atmosphere of Place Duchêne still came as a surprise. A liveried butler should have been greeting guests in the formal foyer, announcing their arrival in imperious tones, but it had never been thus. What resembled a small palace was simply the Duchênes' home. They employed a full time housekeeper who lived nearby (the place was huge after all) and a gardener who worked essentially when he felt like it, more on seasonal whim it always appeared to Christophe. But on the weekend it was typically Louis and Camille and Françoise, plus her two kitchen *assistantes,* who were doing more and more of the actual cooking these days.

Now, too, there was only the one dog, a great white creature that was the aging grandpup of one of the family's old favorites. The dog's only slightly younger sister had moved to Cap Ferret with Louis's mother and father and died with them there in the 1980s.

Cécile had had cancer and did not live long after her diagnosis. She had made Christophe promise, then actually made him swear on the Hippocratic oath, that he would not tell the rest of their family. "Henri and I have had a good life here. The doctors and the hospital are excellent." She'd smiled through her pain. "These things happen. There's no reason to distress everyone else in advance about what is inevitable."

At the time he had tried to argue with her. "Is this fair to the others?" But she had been adamant. Thus, he had agreed to her requests. After all, Henri and Cécile were his family too. Henri hadn't been well for years; he had died of heart failure shortly thereafter.

———

Tonight Camille answered his knock, having buzzed him through the sliding iron gates at the cobbled driveway. She helped him off with his coat, and then, standing on tip-toes, threw her arms around him, kissing him tenderly on both cheeks. *"Christo, bon soir!"*

It was good he was raised to be a gentleman, Christophe reflected, chastely kissing her in return. He would miss this too, for this was all it could ever be. It would be coming soon, the announcement: "There's someone we'd like you to meet." However, that wasn't what she said.

"Follow me while I hang this up," Camille said, urging him on. "Louis is in the library, on the phone with someone in Ottawa about an automobile part." She winked at him teasingly. "I have such terrific competition—carburetors, convertible hard tops, ignition switches, and even wheel rims!"

Christophe watched as she opened a massive armoire at the base of the grand staircase. Everything she did was graceful, even managing the full length coat of someone more than a head taller.

She turned toward him, soft brown eyes brimming with emotion. "Oh, Christophe!" She sighed. "I'm finally going to do it."

He wasn't sure what her announcement was, least of all how it concerned him. Hands deep in his pockets, he smiled and shrugged, drinking in the unique loveliness and charm that had always been hers and for the moment not really caring what she had to say.

"He's been asking me to retire. I finally rewrote the formal letter requesting an application for resignation. I've had it on my desk for over a year. I had to write a new one, the old one had gotten smudged and wrinkled and the dates were all wrong...." She shrugged. "I'll turn it in after the first of the year."

"But you don't really want to?" His question was cautious, hopeful, although he could read the answer on her face. The professions—doctors, lawyers, architects, engineers, professors, and others—were not obligated to retire at a specific age in France. A physician could keep on working as long as the National Health Service recognized his existence.

She said nothing for a moment. "I want to do what makes Louis happy," she replied simply.

Christophe regretted giving her the opportunity to say it.

"He's been upset with me, this past year," she began, "and now he thinks that—*pouf!*—it will all be over. But it won't. They'll need to hire my replacement. There are the interviews, then the training, then the reports I must complete."

Christophe wished that it was just a marriage prospect he was supposed to vet tonight, not deal with the personal issues of the two people whom he loved most outside what remained of his own family.

"Perhaps, if you talk with him, he might understand your explanation of hospital bureaucracy."

Camille knew him much too well. Yes, he would do anything for her. Fortunately, she did not understand why.

"Oh, one thing more. Louis doesn't like me to talk about him—but how is he?"

"Who…?" Christophe was genuinely bewildered by the vague, unreferenced pronouns and shook his head. "Louis?"

"No." Camille lowered her voice to a whisper, "Monsieur Armand? You know, Gérard, 'the miracle patient'?"

"Ah…. Oui." Comprehension flooded back. *"Ah, les Armands."*

The case had been a troubling one, nearly miraculous in its course—a complicated meningitis from a still as yet unidentified pathogen. The husband had been in a coma for eighty days, the wife strangely for only four. Their family was summoned and arrived in time for the hospital medical directors, of which Camille was chief of staff, to discontinue Monsieur Armand's life support. What had happened next would occupy scientific research papers and medical journals for years to come.

Christophe shook his head. As their personal physician it was only natural for him to think of them as a couple. "They're returned home. They have a daily physical therapist visit and round-the-clock nursing *assistantes* for the time. I'll see them in three months, I think." He studied her intently, pieces of the puzzle falling into place. "Louis was jealous of them, *non?* Not personally, but their claim on your time. Sad—and not at all necessary. It's our work." Again he resisted the impulse to reach out, caress her arm, provide understanding and reassurance and more.

More guests were arriving, among them Christophe's date for the evening he suspected, and the others the circle of friends that constituted the extended Duchêne family. Eugène LeBlanc was already there. He and Françoise would marry next month, which probably settled the question of whether she would move to Normandy.

———

In addition to handling all legal matters for the Duchêne family, Eugène's law firm had become involved in researching lost family connections from World War II, much of the work possible because of changes in international law that affected the statutes for reparations. Françoise had not been overly hopeful when she'd asked about her other parents; she'd considered Henri and Cécile her father and mother for most of her life. Eugène had dedicated much personal time and effort to her quest. He'd found one record, but of only Charles LeBourget, and that was on a train headed east after the infamous roundup by the Nazis known as "Fog and Night." His name, but not her mother's, was with a list of other prisoners only one of which he could trace to Natzweiler-Struthof in the mountains of eastern France.

One weekend nearly ten years earlier, Françoise and Eugène had traveled there to tour the preserved site. They walked slowly around the gas chamber, then stared silently at the furnace of the crematorium that had generated heat for the German officers' quarters, peered into the buildings where clay pots had once temporarily held cremains while they were allowed to compact, and finally climbed the hill to the soaring Monument to the Departed erected to the memory of all murdered there at the camp. The hill, American and British forces had discovered in 1945, consisted almost entirely of gritty ash and pulverized bone. Later, the mounds had been stabilized with retaining walls, allowed to remain undisturbed, then covered with thick layers of topsoil. Lush, neatly trimmed grass grew there now.

Eugène had held her hand as they stared out toward Les Vosges where clouds closed down on the distant mountains. "If they did come here, it was more beautiful than most death camps," he'd said for lack of anything else to say. He'd researched as far and wide as Yad Vashem in Israel and the Holocaust Survivors Memorial in the United States. Each time the answer was the same: "No such person(s) on record." Charles and Geneviève LeBourget had truly disappeared without a trace into the night and fog, Hitler's *Nacht und Nebel.*

Françoise had knelt down and pressed her hands deep into the grass, digging in with her fingers, but it was much too thick; there was no way to reach the gritty ash.

"I'm not even certain it was here, Françoise," Eugène said gently. "And the topsoil is at least four feet deep."

"I know. But I want to thank you for trying…. And I'd want to thank them for giving me life—twice."

He'd tilted his head, questioning.

"Giving birth, of course. Then having the courage to send me away when they did."

Over the years, their relationship had deepened. Eugène's young first marriage ended in divorce years ago. He had asked Françoise to marry him, for the third time, while they stood in the mountains of the old concentration camp. Her eyes filled with tears, and she had finally said yes.

***

"Félicitations, mon ami!" Christophe teased Eugène who'd emerged from the kitchen carrying two glasses of wine. He accepted a glass and raised it in toast. "I think a ten-year courtship is certainly within the bounds of propriety—a nearly Victorian propriety!"

"Nothing tempestuous about me, is there?" Eugène laughed. "One marriage in haste was quite enough."

Christophe could barely remember his first wife—a nice girl, but she had been a teenager, if he recalled correctly. After she'd left, Eugène, with the help of his parents and the Duchêne family, had raised their two children alone; Eric and Lisanne were accompanying him tonight. "Have you decided where you'll live yet?"

"We were considering—" Eugène began.

Just then Louis emerged from the library beaming in triumph. "Would you believe, a brand-new—*never* used—carburetor for a 1960 Corvette! *Quelle chance!*" he exclaimed and embraced his two friends.

Françoise and Camille joined them; Louis took the glass his wife handed him. "To retirement!"

They all raised their glasses, and Christophe noticed the shadow of sadness that fleetingly clouded Camille's smile.

How would their marriage fare, with both retired? Christophe didn't want to dwell on it, because the thought was inconceivable. Louis had little to retire from, actually. After university, he had done two years military service, some in the no longer existing alpine forces, and then worked several years with his father's investments and real estate ventures before starting his own business. Louis had never been obligated to anyone else, like he and Camille had been. Responsibility had forever ruled their lives—to family, to the hospital, to patients, to administration, to the system, to the country.

"Ah! Christophe?" Camille waved to him and he came around to her side. "I'd like you to meet Adèle Desrosiers. Adèle, Christophe Rossignon." She beamed as they shook hands. "She's Stéfan's second cousin, isn't that so, Adèle?"

The lady was quite attractive; they always were. *"Enchanté,"* he murmured.

"I believe Camille has us sitting together at dinner," Adèle said softly and laughed. "She means well, doesn't she?"

Christophe nodded and smiled. "That she most certainly does." He tried to meet Camille's eyes but she had turned away.

Christophe surveyed the group gathered at the dinner table: it had changed over the years, but a certain continuity remained. Louis and Camille occupied the chairs where his parents had once sat. Françoise was nearest the kitchen, but Eugène was now by her side. Although she had remarried, Marc's wife Madeleine was there with their twin sons, who so heartbreakingly resembled their father. Marc had died in 1975. As a journalist in Cambodia, covering the final days of war for *Agence France Presse,* he had been killed by a speeding taxi while crossing a busy street in Phnom Penh. Madeleine's husband Emile was a good sport, and he was there tonight too. The most recent vacancies were Camille's father Roger Mauriat and Louis's grandmother Hélène Bertrand.

The pianist Albert and his wife Gertrude had died shortly after Louis's parents, but their adopted children were always present at family dinners. In the concentration camps, Albert had played for the German officers' entertainment. "I need a *tourneuse,"* he had maintained. "Someone to turn the pages for me." He'd been sharing his meager rations with two children—a five-year-old Gypsy girl and a gaunt little French boy of six—and asked whether they could alternate for him. Sometimes the children would even be permitted the officers' table scraps. Now Rachel taught piano and violin, and Joseph was a concert pianist. Before they'd gone into dinner tonight, his music had filled the salon.

Other grown children of those Henri Duchêne had helped rescue were at their table, often even their own grown offspring. "So," Stéfan was asking during the first course, "when will the house be finished now?" He was one of very few non-locals Louis had hired, because his engineering and architectural expertise had been needed when a structural failure in the foundation threatened to destroy the entire restoration project.

The Bertrand property in St-Etienne-des-Près was frequently a topic of conversation, although not many would discuss Louis's planned departure. The thought of their leaving hovered like a gray cloud on the distant horizon, casting a shadow on the light and glow of camaraderie. Louis's dream of retiring to become a gentleman farmer in Normandy seemed far-fetched and impractical.

"They've finished the slate roof—again." He grinned sheepishly. "Let's hope the second time's the charm. I should have asked Stéfan the first time."

Stéfan modestly affected to concentrate on his soup plate, but the corners of his mouth twitched up in a smile. "Maybe it wasn't meant to be."

The others laughed. Christophe was familiar with the English term "the money pit" and that was surely what the Bertrand Estate's ongoing restoration was.

"When will you take the cars up there?" someone at the far end of the table asked.

Louis sighed. "When they finish the barn, I suppose."

"Would you like some advice on that?" A straight-faced Stéfan winked in Camille's direction. The barn, too, had crumbled down again recently, huge stones pouring into the cavernous interior.

"The plumbing's finally completed too, so we're hoping by spring of the next year—1993." Louis gestured expansively, nearly knocking over his wine glass and the glass of the guest to his right. "Everyone's invited to come up and spend the week of June 6 with us. Aren't they, Camie?"

"Of course." She smiled and turned to Louis. "But, *mon cher,* some of our friends and family have jobs and still work. Remember?"

Christophe chuckled. "He's turning into a true *normand.* Probably won't even celebrate Bastille Day any more."

"Oh, no. Life's a continual celebration for Louis." Camille placed her hand on his arm. "*Le six juin* is only one more excuse to celebrate."

"What about Place du Chêne, *mon ami?*" Christophe asked. "Do you plan to leave it vacant? Is that wise?"

Louis looked up. "No.... *Ah! Ecoutez!* This is what would be perfect. Eugène and Françoise—why don't you live here?"

Eugène and Françoise eyes met for a moment. "That's most generous, Louis," Eugène began. "However, we—"

"We're still working out some other arrangements." Françoise seemed uncomfortable. "*Vraiment, mon frère....* I don't know what to say."

Louis handed his plate to their kitchen helper. "Oh, there's plenty of time, I'm sure."

Camille was staring down into her plate of Coquilles-St-Jacques. She hadn't touched her food.

Christophe studied her for several more minutes. No, he was right to be concerned—about them, about her.

❖

10 Louis Duchêne

St-Etienne-des-Près, September 1993

SO, HER NAME WAS NICOLE. Had been, Louis corrected himself. He squinted into the slate-gray glare of the rain-splattered windshield and struggled to focus on the roadway ahead. Try as he might he couldn't remember her. It didn't make it any easier, and it certainly didn't make what had happened right. He could recall the camaraderie and the hard work of that summer, but he'd totally forgotten the girl. How many years later was it? Now he knew what happened, that was the difference.

A car flashed past him, faster than the marginally acceptable 100 kmh in good driving conditions. A dark blur of tires flung broad sheets of water against his windshield, temporarily blinding him.

Had he even kissed her goodbye before he left? That, too, must have faded from memory.

After that summer Louis entered university, facing an exciting world of new friends and new connections. Demands on his time changed, and he spent one year of college at Princeton in the United States, as a guest of Professor Croswell, the American army officer who had overseen the occupation of their home in a liberated Paris. His love affair with fast cars began then too.

Much to his own surprise, he discovered he was growing up and gradually assuming responsibility. Their family wouldn't return to his grandparents' country home in Normandy for three years, when the house was finally completed enough to be habitable once more. After that, for three weeks each summer they retreated to its peaceful isolation, far from the waves of heat and tourists that oppressed Paris equally in July and August.

His father would routinely tour the estate with him. "Those lower orchards were replanted and grafted in 1947 and the next section was finished in 1948." He pointed off in the distance, indicating what they'd accomplished so far and describing in detail what remained to be done. "Over there, those trees should be producing within the year." He soon included Louis in conference with the caretakers and the manager of the orchards. The Bertrand Cider Presses and Calvados distilleries were again established and thriving; their continued development after the war remained a priority: over half the village of St-Etienne depended on the local work.

Even then Louis had known he would eventually inherit not only the properties but the task of completing the ongoing restorations. As the older son, the responsibility would come to him much in the traditional way that had governed families for generations.

Occasionally he congratulated himself; he'd done rather well at the family businesses. The orchards, along with all the by-products of the cider industry, continued to expand and show a healthy profit. His grandmother would have approved. How he wished she would have come back to revisit her home. She'd adamantly refused, after those first few years when his labors as a youth had helped rebuild their home and make it habitable. She and his grandfather lived there two years, then returned to the townhouse in Paris.

"I'm sure you've done fine work, Louis. But the memory of what isn't there pains me too much," Grandmère Hélène had said. There was no way to bring back the many horses she'd so loved or to re-establish their world-renowned breeding farms.

Louis gripped the steering wheel and braced against the gusting wind and rain, alert to the threat of hydroplaning on this particular stretch of highway. The steeped banking on the curved portion ahead forced his thoughts back. *Back to...? Their plans?* "Their" plans to retire and move to the Normandy countryside were actually his plans. There remained the challenge of convincing Camille to retire, asking her to abandon her medical career and move from Paris to some isolated rural village.

What the hell! Another motorist skidded past him through the heavy downpour. *There's no way we can ever move up there—not now, not ever.*

The Bertrand home hadn't been maintained since the initial postwar rebuilding that started the summer of 1949 and continued throughout the early '50s. As the much needed renovations and modernizations of the old place neared completion Louis would drive up to check on the progress at regular intervals. A new slate roof, modern decent plumbing at last, a dependable water supply that would insure adequate water pressure, double-glazed windows, insulation, and central heating had been the principal necessities, while the plastering and painting were cosmetic, finishing touches. He had finally decided that here was where he wanted to retire, the idealized vision of life as gentleman farmer in the peaceful countryside luring him on, away from Paris. However, his decision had brought about their first major disagreement in almost thirty years of marriage. Camille was adamant; she did not want to retire, not yet.

Louis had found St-Etienne's lone inn adequate for the two nights he spent there each month. L'Auberge-des-près would never gain mention in any travel guide, which was probably for the best. Small but comfortable, it seemed frozen in some obscure, nameless, long ago era—not long ago enough to be charmingly historic, but simply old. The innkeeper was a plain woman of undetermined years who wore her severe black hair pulled back into a tight knot.

Madame Durocher would greet him cordially enough, and over the past year, she started to actually speak to him. She would often ask about the Bertrand Estates and his grandparents. Gradually, Louis began to comprehend that living in a small, insular community such as St-Etienne would involve much more than the physical move from Paris. Assimilation would come only with time.

Over breakfast this morning he'd felt Madame Durocher studying him as she read or possibly reread a two-week-old local newspaper. She'd offered it to him earlier as she served breakfast, and he'd politely declined. He glanced at the date and the bold headlines that screamed out from the paper. In small towns, news—in particular bad news—seemed to maintain its titillating allure long past any report of the event itself. He looked up from breakfast and met Madame Durocher's appraising gaze. She was pushing her spectacles back up the bridge of her nose but quickly returned to peruse the grim story before her. She nodded in his direction from time to time, acknowledging his presence.

"Simply dreadful, isn't?" the innkeeper asked. She held up the local weekly that covered the news and events of two dozen towns in the district and displayed the front page for his benefit. She continued to study him furtively as he sampled the apple crêpes she routinely provided each morning. "Such a tragedy. She was the granddaughter of Grandmère Annette."

Louis had noticed the headline earlier, DEATH ON THE CHANNEL, but glanced away. A casual glimpse at the leading story above the fold confirmed his initial impression of typically bad photography and sensational journalism.

"I beg your pardon?" Responding politely, he was uncertain to whom or to what Madame Durocher was referring.

Madame Durocher sniffed in indignation. "But surely, Monsieur Duchêne, she is now one of the oldest residents of our town." She peeked down at the paper and back up quickly, catching her spectacles as they skidded down her nose in freefall. "Ah, but of course. Your grandparents certainly would have known her. Her husband was Nicholas Chaumont—the very first name on the war memorial in the town square. Our bravest of those years and in the *Résistance* too!"

"Ah... I understand," Louis said, although he really didn't. "*Encore de café, s'il vous plaît?*" He raised his cup from the saucer a fraction of an inch in question. "Madame, this time, if you please, without the brandy?" This might be a charming local custom, but the routine splash of liquor in his morning coffee seemed too much, too early.

The innkeeper stood, moved slowly into her kitchen, and returned with the steaming pot to fill Louis's cup. Not actually believing him, she'd brought the familiar bottle with her anyway.

Louis smiled and held his hand over the cup long enough to prevent the addition of Calvados. "Thank you, but, no, Madame."

Settled once more in the window seat, Madame Durocher picked up the newspaper and quickly resumed her running commentary. "And Grandmère Annette… she must be such a strong woman too." She seemed determined to rattle on the litany of the town's woes and widows, while Louis was attempting to picture, without success, the peaceful, idyllic life in the country that awaited them, if he could only convince Camille.

His hostess continued undeterred. "Imagine that, Monsieur, her only daughter and now her granddaughter…."

Louis tuned out her sordid recitation, finished his coffee, and paid for his two-night stay.

Driving through town he reconsidered, deciding to circle around and return to the inn. What better time to start establishing connections with the village? Something more than supporting the townsfolk with the work of the orchards and the remodeling of his family's ancestral home?

He'd assumed that moving here and making themselves members of the community would demand such gestures on their part, his and Camille's. The Bertrand Estate was responsible for the livelihood of so many in the area. The thought warmed him although the weather outside had turned suddenly cold. Storm clouds had been building since breakfast, bringing with them the threat of heavy rain. By the time Louis finished his conference with the building contractor and concluded his routine meeting with the orchard foreman, icy rain, borne on a steady northerly wind, was spattering at his car.

Back at the inn, Louis asked, "Where did you say Madame Chaumont lives?" Madame Durocher hadn't said before, but that was always the easiest way to collect information. "I'll stop by and offer her my condolences. May I take this, please?" He indicated the old newspaper with its grim headline and grimmer story.

He found Madame Chaumont's small home after tracing his way through the cluster of houses and passing the war memorial in the town square. Next month he vowed to stop and search for her husband's name: there was important history right here that he'd ignored as a young man.

The wind was picking up steadily, the rain advancing on the town and stabbing at the countryside in icy spurts.

The Chaumont residence, with its pitched slate roof, crouched far down where the town's main street ended and dwindled away, vanishing into the countryside, an unimproved dirt road. The cottage was tidy, stuccoed and white-washed, although it hadn't been painted recently, with gray-weathered shutters and wood-cased windows that faced out to the street. A lone tree, its trunk and branches permanently bent by prevailing winds, leaned in beside the house as if attempting to stand guard against the elements.

Louis pulled his collar high against the blowing rain and wished he'd brought a hat, something he usually didn't wear. It would have been welcome today. A small woman answered his knock. She stared up at him, curious and uncertain, the clouded eyes of advancing age peering up through thick lenses.

"Bonjour, Madame Chaumont?" He proceeded to introduce himself before offering his condolences. "I'm Louis Duchêne. My wife and I are moving back to this area and I—"

That was when the thunderstorm broke in earnest.

Louis had never before met the elderly woman who opened

the door of the small house in St-Etienne, but this much was certain: she recognized him. She grasped unsteadily for the door handle and promptly fainted, collapsing in a heap on the slates of the foyer. Louis pushed through the narrow passage and managed to lift and carry her into the front parlor.

He arranged the unconscious woman on the sofa and went in search of water and a cloth of some kind. *That was what they always did in the movies, wasn't it?* He had the presence of mind to check for her pulse: it was weak, but there. *Damn it all, my wife's a physician,* he chided himself, annoyed at his incompetence. *I should at least know the basics about reviving someone.*

He turned. A stray flash of light flickered against glass, teasing at his peripheral vision, startling him. It was much like glimpsing one's reflection in a mirror where a mirror had not been expected. Instinctively he straightened, expecting to view himself, only to discover it wasn't his face at all. The photograph of a young woman, its frame cheaply glazed, stared back at him. She had the same black hair as his, the same thick black eyelashes and heavy brows and, under them, dark blue eyes like his, the same asymmetric dimple on her right cheek just like his, broad high cheekbones and a chin identical to what he negotiated with a razor every morning, the mouth shaped like his as a young man....

"*O Sainte vierge!*" he exclaimed. "*Mon dieu!*" He dropped onto the sofa beside Madame Chaumont who was coming around, starting to sit up, and clumsily searching for her spectacles.

"*Madame....*" His rehearsed, polite offer of condolence and sympathy was forgotten, forever driven from his mind. "That picture... up there, on the shelf? Who is that?"

Annette Chaumont cleared her throat with difficulty and tried to swallow. She accepted the glass of water he placed in her hands. Finally, her voice low and hoarse, she answered him. "That was my granddaughter, *Monsieur.* She was killed in a boating accident almost three weeks ago." Her eyes, distorted grotesquely by the magnification of corrective lenses, studied him intently, never turning away as she processed every detail of his features and the contour of his face. "I believe she was your daughter too, *Monsieur.* Her name was Louise."

He hunched forward and sat there dumbly, head in his hands, listening to the roar of thunder and the low voice of Annette Chaumont as she recounted Nicole's gruesome death and the birth of his daughter. Rain pounded and battered the small house in St-Etienne-des-Près.

———

The rain stayed with him as he neared the outskirts of Paris, but it was slowing considerably and at least the thunder had stopped. The windshield wipers slapped hypnotically against the windshield. Within the hour he'd be home. *Oh, dear God, what will I do now...?* he agonized. *There's absolutely no way we can move to the country... not ever.*

His dreams and planning of years had been for nothing. All his wheedling, trying to convince Camille to retire had been for naught too. The vague notions he'd suffered of late about the need to go to confession—more as a *pro forma* duty to the Church—had suddenly become an obligation of a different sort. Would telling his wife count instead?

He gripped the steering wheel and tasted bile rising in his throat at the prospect as he negotiated the northwestern suburbs and finally turned up the street leading to their house. Lights shone from the windows, so Camille was already home, quite early for her.

How can I ever tell her? he wondered as he pulled into the drive. *But I must.* There was no other way to consider what had happened: he had a daughter and a granddaughter and he was responsible for the death of the girl Nicole.

❖

11 Camille and Louis

Paris, September 1993

CAMILLE HAD INTENDED TO REMAIN working at the hospital for at least another five years, perhaps ten, since the country's rules governing mandatory retirement didn't apply to her profession, but Louis had finally won. It grated against her sense of personal autonomy, yet she'd finally acquiesced. At last she had asked what would be involved to officially apply for retirement from the National Health Service and the Ministry of Health.

Earlier this morning, the bulging packet of forms arrived on her desk. She stared aghast at the amount of paper involved and studied the four pages of nearly microscopic text. In a country where almost everything else about its citizens was documented on computer from womb-to-tomb, it seemed ludicrous that the final act of any civil servant's career would be handled thus, in writing, on these long, long pages of thick carbon-backed forms, filling in cramped spaces inserted amongst lengthy paragraphs of minuscule print.

After visiting three patients on her own medical-surgical service and assigning the rest to members of her staff, she'd succumbed to a throbbing headache, what reading ultra-fine print would sometimes cause. She'd left the hospital early and gone home, bringing with her the mountain of paper and bureaucratic tedium to battle.

The day was turning unseasonably cold for mid-September. A chill damp wind was whipping through the streets, too uncertain and undefined as yet to be called rain. Upstairs in their bedroom, with a pot of tea on the table beside her, Camille opened her briefcase and settled to work. She sighed, sipped from the freshly poured cup of tea, and felt about for her reading glasses. She didn't need the readers often, but the task before her would definitely require them. Couldn't these agencies realize that almost anyone filling out forms necessary to apply for a government retirement pension might not be able to read type this small?

She hadn't bothered to change but bundled into a warm sweater, pulled close against the chill of the afternoon, and tucked her feet underneath a blanket on the settee. Françoise and Eugène were downstairs in the library… or somewhere else perhaps. Eugène had come for lunch and hadn't returned to his office. She checked her watch: Louis would probably be home within the hour. She sighed again, picked up the first long form—she'd needed to fold it over three times to fit in her briefcase—and let it drop back with the others.

What she would have preferred today was a good book. A lazy rain began spattering at the tall bedroom windows, catching against one pane after another, small unsteady puddles held in place briefly by surface tension. Occasionally stray rivulets would break away from one pattern, forming new ones. Again she glanced down at the government forms that would change her life forever.

―――

"Wouldn't it be wonderful, just the two of us, living in the country?" Louis had worn her down with arguments like these. She wasn't sure even he would be happy in this new life he envisioned. She'd seen too many men as patients, freshly retired, and then listened to stories from their wives. Lifelong patterns could not be changed in an instant, dreams converted to a healthy, workable reality.

She was staring out at the gray sky, ignoring the work she brought home, vaguely aware that Louis had come in. His dripping coat carried the scent of rain and fresh country air. He stood silently before her, a clipping from some newspaper clutched in one hand.

"How was your trip, *mon cher?*"

He didn't answer. He gave no indication that he'd heard her, but turned and began pacing the length of their bedroom. Once he stopped to gaze out at the hypnotic path of the steady rain spilling from the gutters down to the leaf-spattered courtyard below.

Camille glanced up from the briefcase whose contents lay spread about her. She reached to shut it, hesitated, and removed her small reading glasses from the pile: she'd carelessly crushed them this way once before. She pushed the gaping reminder of work not done to one side of the settee. Something in Louis's manner concerned her. If only he would speak.

"Mon chéri?" She tried again, but his attention seemed focused elsewhere. What was wrong?

When Louis drove in from St-Etienne he usually arrived back

boisterous, re-energized, filled with new ideas, and talkative. She shared in his relief that the restoration was nearing completion. Over two centuries' work had been destroyed within a matter of days in the early 1940s. The restoring and rebuilding had taken craftsmen and arborists most of fifty years. Louis always rushed to her and kissed her, more than a habit after nearly thirty years, still a kiss of pulse-raising passion.

She gestured toward her briefcase. "I received the retirement papers from the Ministry of Health today."

Louis said nothing.

She continued. "It'll take me the rest of the day to finish them. But, if all proceeds in the Ministry's usual timely manner, I should be officially retired by this time next year. And by the middle of the following year, I should start receiving my government pension."

Louis finally spoke. "We're not going. I can't do it now."

"What?" Camille jumped up from the settee, the contents of her briefcase cascading onto the floor and, with luck, sparing the reading glasses. "This is all you've talked about for the past five years!"

The folded newspaper clipping, with the picture of a young woman named Louise who could have been his sister—their resemblance was that pronounced—he'd tucked in his pocket as he left town, but it didn't stay there. The drive back to Paris was torture: he'd reach into his pocket for the picture, then shove it back, the small scrap of paper taken out and replaced every few minutes. In his muddle of confused emotions it was difficult to separate his guilt from grim, confused thoughts that he was ultimately responsible for both their deaths.

And what would he tell Camille? Share with her he must. He needed to tell someone and, if anyone would understand, she would. Or would she? Tormenting questions spun in his mind.

Should he confess that even now he couldn't remember or picture the girl Nicole—the mother of this pretty dark-haired young woman—not anything remotely about her? He was seventeen; she'd been barely fifteen. Should he admit that when her name was mentioned he could recall absolutely nothing about this person whose death now haunted his conscience? That would scarcely be to his credit.

He was driving fast, but it never seemed fast enough. Was he driving toward home and someone to talk to—or away from the past he didn't want to consider but must.

Camille was automatically counting how many times he'd turned and paced the length of the bedroom and sitting room. "Louis, could I at least take your coat?" *Always start with everyday matters when a patient doesn't want to talk.* As close as they'd always been she sensed a chasm opening between them, but could not fathom why. He stopped, allowed her to remove his coat, and held out the piece of newspaper and tried to shake the folds and creases from the page. "It's this."

Photographs of a man and woman splayed across the top where a bold, black headline screamed: DEATH ON THE CHANNEL. Accompanying the article, another grim photograph showed a grainy image, an overturned sailboat bobbing against the tide where waves nudged the hull into a rocky shore. Behind it rose a sloping field crisscrossed by Normandy's hedgerows and to the right stretched a crescent beach where the shipwreck tossed, caught in the treacherous surf.

The page fluttered before Camille, the letters of the headline blurred. He waved the newspaper and held it out to her. "My grandparents knew this woman's grandmother, it turns out. I really didn't remember her, sorry to say." He hesitated, uncomfortable. "While I was checking on the house and the orchards I went to offer Grandmère Annette—that's what the entire village calls her, it seems—my condolences."

He turned away and faced the windows again, watching the rain drops coalesce against the panes, hit one obstacle, subdivide and join to form other patterns elsewhere on the glass. He swallowed, feeling Camille's eyes fixed on him.

"You see, Camie, I just discovered I've killed someone… long ago."

Camille didn't respond.

"Did you hear me?"

She was holding the newspaper clipping. "But Louis, you were no where near the Channel when this took place." She paused, clearly puzzled. "What are you talking about?"

That Annette Chaumont was shocked to see him at her door was an understatement. Furthermore, although they'd never met, she had recognized him immediately. He didn't feel he should digress to cover that detail at the moment. He braced himself for the hardest part.

"Many years ago, it turns out I fathered a child, the one summer I spent up there working on my grandparent's farm. This," he pointed to the newspaper photo of a woman, "is her."

He fumbled with the clipping, his hands trembling as he attempted to smooth the folds that remained from its journey crammed in a coat pocket.

"She's dead—this was my daughter!" Shock poured from his words. "She was killed, as you can see by the article. And so is her mother—my 'youthful indiscretion', as people would euphemistically like to say today. But now there's an orphaned teenaged girl, who is quite undeniably my granddaughter."

Camille said nothing. She remained quiet, as though waiting for more bad news to follow. "And what else?"

"What *else*? Like what? Oh, my God, Camie, I'm so sorry!" He was bungling even this attempt at explanation. Why were words so damn inadequate? Even carefully chosen, they could portend something awful. "I never knew. Never! I swear. Not until this morning."

Then Camille broke down, sobbing into his arms. "But it's *my* fault!" She repeated the words over and over, muffled into the thick wool of his coat.

Louis couldn't follow her reasoning. He and Camille hadn't even met until 1962. He shook his head. "No, no.... Don't you understand? I was seventeen for heaven's sake—and she never contacted me afterwards. I never saw her again! How was I to know?"

"No, but it is *my fault*, can't you see? Now I know it's my fault," Camille insisted.

Louis studied his wife, increasingly bewildered. "It can't be your fault, you weren't even there." His voice was kind and patient with left-brained logic.

"That we could never have children!" Her racking, gulping sobs began once more.

Louis held her tightly, shaking his head that even a physician, a doctor of medicine, could be such a puzzle to understand at times. "No, no, my Angel, who knows. It just wasn't meant to be. Maybe we weren't supposed to be parents." He grasped at any possible explanation floating through his mind, trying to console her.

"Did you love her?" She asked after several minutes; it had felt like an hour to Louis.

"How could I possibly have loved her? I don't even remember her!" He let go of the breath he'd been guarding, expelling the anger and frustration with himself. "I was a young, horny teenager!"

———

Later, perched together on the edge of the settee, Camille held the clipping in one hand at arms' length beside Louis's head, studying the two together. The late Louise Lessard was a perfect, female replica of her father. Camille had noticed the small story in the national papers too and grimaced at the sensational headline that screamed in bold type. She'd glanced at the first lines of the tragic story and passed on to something else.

A husband and wife sail-boating off the northern coast, a sudden storm, the boat capsized, and the choppy, turbulent, ever unpredictable waters of the Channel had claimed two more lives. Both were experienced sailors, but those icy seas were never intended for recreational boating, especially in relatively small sailing craft. According to the story, the bodies were recovered days later and their young daughter returned to a distant relative in rural Normandy. There was no picture of the girl, just the smiling couple. Why didn't she notice the resemblance then? However, Louis didn't notice it himself until faced with the reality, in person. Selective vision, it was called, Camille's analytic mind regained control of her consciousness and subdued her emotions.

She nodded but then shook her head in amazement. Genetics always puzzled her, especially how particular family traits could be so boldly proclaimed in flesh, again and again, generation after generation: Louis's father, Louis, his daughter, and now his granddaughter.

"And the girl? This woman's daughter, I mean," Camille spoke very softly, her voice no more than a whisper, and she touched the newspaper and the smiling face that was so much like Louis.

"You might as well be looking at her picture there." He indicated the news clipping and began another random search of coat pockets until he at last produced a small school picture of the younger girl, Louise's daughter. Even the severe school uniform couldn't disguise the bright blue, intelligent eyes heavily fringed with thick black lashes, high rosy cheeks, the dark almost black curly hair—all those characteristics that made foreigners ask Louis whether he might be Irish, maybe even part-Irish? Or perhaps from northern Italy?

The young girl appeared even smaller boned than her mother, but these things were difficult to judge from a photograph, Camille thought. She reached beside her and shoved the rest of the billowing papers and government forms onto the floor beside her briefcase. Retirement hadn't been her idea anyway; all of that could wait.

"Louis?" She patted the cleared space beside her. "Will you sit here and tell me? I want to know. I need to know. I couldn't give you children, but someone else did." She faced her husband, taking in the misery and guilt he couldn't conceal. "Will you tell me? Everything. Please?"

Reconstruction was well begun that summer of 1949 when Louis turned seventeen. University loomed in the fall, but a summer spent working for his Bertrand grandparents would be his vacation between school terms. True summer came late to Normandy, but under the afternoon sun, stripped to the waist, he sweated and strained and heaved stones from distant pastures, joining the cadre of other local young men who felt fortunate to have any job in those postwar years.

Come midday, Louis would stretch out on the welcome coolness of the lush grass. He had reveled in the freedom, away from the confines of a city classroom. Stone walls and the old *mas* were gradually taking shape, thanks to their labors. By summer's end the walls were solid enough that a master roofer could begin his task. Heavy slate tiles would once more shelter the central portion of the house.

Before summer's end, too, Louis had formed friendships with the young lads who worked beside him, distinctions between the owners' grandson and local farm boys eroded in their joint efforts. Muscles aching, hands calloused, the young group lingered on together in the evenings. Bottles of local beer and *cidre,* chilled in a nearby stream, were shared at the end of a long day of hard labor. And where there were young men, there were just as predictably young girls. There Louis met Nicole, romance blossoming as it would and nurtured by warm summer days: his first, Nicole's first, and her last.

Summer would just as inevitably end. Louis entered the Sorbonne and studies dominated his life. Accepting the invitation of Major Croswell, now Dean Croswell of the Department of History, he studied one year at Princeton. His time spent in America was the start of yet another romance and one which would never end: his love affair with the automobile.

At term breaks, his cadre of friends traveled to Cannes or to the Alps for winter skiing. Summer vacations he spent with his family at Cap Ferret. His maternal grandparents, Hélène and Maurice Bertrand, finished the farmhouse enough to summer in

St-Etienne once or twice, but joined the extended family in Paris for most of their year. After the summer of 1949, life took him miles away from Normandy and someone he easily forgot, the country girl named Nicole.

Camille leaned forward, intrigued. "This woman, her mother, Annette. She recognized you?"

"Angel, I thought she was going to have a heart attack, right in front of me. I hadn't a clue what was going on. She knew 'what' I was immediately, even though she didn't know my name. My mother married and moved away so long ago the name Duchêne didn't mean anything to her. But right behind me, on her mantelpiece, there were these two photographs, one of Louise and one of Louise's little girl. They could have been *me.*" He shuddered, then buried his face in his hands. "Oh, God, I killed someone, Camie. What do you say to a mother when you caused her daughter's death?"

What, indeed? For a moment Camille considered her own infertility, obviously *her* curse and not *theirs* for so many years: perhaps it was less a liability than its opposite. "Judging by what Grandmère Annette described, what happened to Nicole was either a placenta previa or placenta acretta. Both are difficult to prevent... both can have high mortality rates due to hemorrhage. And if there's no access to even basic medical care...."

She placed her hands on his and leaned closer to kiss his forehead. "Louis, you didn't mean to...." Her tone was that of a professional, reassuring a disturbed patient.

"No, but I did, all the same."

"My dear, you can't undo it. Nor can you make it right, in your conscience. I know you that well."

❖

12 *Christmas in Normandy*

St-Etienne-des-Près, December, 1993

I

EARLY IN THE AFTERNOON the day before Christmas Eve, Louis and Camille starting going from house to house in St-Etienne-des-Près, meeting and greeting the townsfolk who would soon be their new neighbors. A few had been part of the original restoration of the house in 1949, but many more had contributed to the most recent renovation of the Bertrand Estate. Some worked for the *cidre* presses and several others were employed by the Calvados distilleries.

For Louis, there was the pleasure of renewing acquaintances, the friends and neighbors of his grandparents from long ago. At each family's home they would leave several bottles of Champagne as a welcoming gift and for their New Year's celebrations. Surrounded by the easy camaraderie that was emerging at last, Louis would share the inevitable small glass of Calvados with the men while Camille sipped a cup of *cidre bouché* and chatted with the women.

Where had her terrible shyness gone, she wondered. Was it her background as a physician that made her at ease meeting new people? Theirs was a widely varied country, and this remote corner was vastly different from the village where she was born in Douvré near Lyon. Yet she was a small-town, country girl at heart. True friendships here would develop slowly, but the process of their acceptance was well begun.

It was Christmas, a time of peace and quiet and joy. Remembrances were spoken softly when spoken at all. One of the older residents, Erneste Branchet who was ninety-four-years old and now lived with his daughter and son-in-law, asked Louis whether he remembered old Father Guichard.

"Sorry, my friend." Louis shook his head. "To me, one black bird looks pretty much the same as another."

Branchet studied him uncertainly for a moment. "A shame. Guichard was a good man, I think. For a priest." He cleared his throat, adjusted his glasses, and peered at Louis more closely. "Now we don't know if we'll have a priest come Sunday. They're always changing, moving them around."

Guillaume Pomereau had been the Calvados distilleries' chief operator and the foreman for so many years that the title and duty had become almost hereditary. The German soldiers shot and killed him the day in June they captured Hélène's treasured horses. Hélène had insisted that all should try to escape and helped whomever she could. As a young man, his son Jules Pomereau was already well-schooled in the art of making fine brandy and when he returned in 1946, his father's job had come to him. When Jules retired last year, the position and responsibility was passed to *his* son.

Louis and Camille were relaxing in the comfortable home the Pomereau family had rebuilt when Jules raised his glass, not toasting *les Fêtes*, but in memory of Hélène and Maurice Bertrand. He held his glass high once more. "Louis, *mon ami*, there should be more like them in the world."

Camille blinked, smiled, and nodded, then lifted her glass. Hélène Bertrand had been an exceptional woman. Louis joined them in the toast, not responding. There were tears in his eyes.

II

Camille had been alternately dreading and looking forward to meeting Louis's granddaughter Annick-Louise. It would have to come some day, and Christmas seemed like a perfect opportunity. Apparently Annette Chaumont had kept her word, choosing to not share her discovery with the rest of the small town. What good would it be now, so many years later?

It was after five when they returned to her bungalow. Wrapped in a shawl, Annette had risen unsteadily from her chair to greet them.

"Louis?" Camille asked softly, placing a hand on his arm. "See how frail she is? She's not at all well."

He nodded. "I know," he whispered.

"*Ma petite* hasn't yet returned," Annette apologized. "It is starting to rain too."

Not a simple rain, it was freezing now, pinging and rattling off slate roofs in a steady tattoo. The wind was gathering momentum as it howled off the Channel and funneled through the low-lying hills of the countryside.

"Annick will stay with her school friend tonight and return in the morning," Annette was telling them. "It will soon be dark on the road. It is not safe, a young girl, in this weather. On just a bicycle." She raised her hands in further apology. "I am sorry to trouble you."

Camille smiled into the face that might retain vestiges of an earlier, younger beauty and perhaps the young girl Nicole's as well. It came to her naturally and unbidden: she wondered about her, Louis's first love—or at least his first. What had she been like?

Judging from the two photographs he'd brought back, the daughter and granddaughter—*his* daughter and granddaughter, she needed to remind herself—were cut from his identical genetic mold, striking feminine versions of her Louis. Dark wavy hair, deep blue eyes fringed with thick black lashes, broad cheeks that tended to flush. They were very pretty young women, sadly poignant reminders of the children she and Louis might have had but never could. She sighed, forcing herself to ignore the lingering regret.

She placed her hands around Annette's shoulders, steadying the older woman and attempting to reassure her that all was well. The faded eyes, magnified unnaturally by the thick glasses needed as a result of antiquated cataract surgery, stared back into hers, filled with concern and apology.

"Don't worry," Camille said. "Surely she's safe then. Louis and I can stay at our house tonight, can't we, *mon chéri?*" Meeting the girl was postponed for one more day, but it could not wait forever.

Louis answered with an uncertain shrug. "Of course."

The master craftsman Monsieur Collet was summoned, luckily before he started on his typical evening ration of Calvados. Their request took him by surprise, as if they were asking for something totally unreasonable. An obstinate man, he categorically refused at first, his position nonnegotiable. This was highly irregular and not possible.

"*Mais, non! Impossible!* But it is all fresh plaster. Too much heat at this time—and the plaster—she will crack—like so!" With expressive hands he demonstrated an explosion on the scale of a nuclear disaster. "*Pouf!*" he exclaimed, eyes widened to emphasize this impending catastrophe.

"Look here, *mon vieux*," Louis persisted, patient with the old man. "It is our house. Is it not? *Non?*"

Monsieur Collet nodded cautiously, eyes narrowed.

"We'll stay in the kitchen. There's no fresh plaster there. It's all wood and stone and that fireplace is big enough to roast an ox."

In the end Collet acquiesced and returned with them to the restored manor, grudging and grumbling. With large sheets of heavy plastic he sealed off the rest of the house from the kitchen, muttering and complaining as he worked.

After dinner that night, cocooned in their sleeping bag, Louis and Camille discussed plans and contingency arrangements for the following day. Timing would be critical if they were to arrive back in Paris in time for the festive Christmas Eve gathering at home.

Camille remained amazed at Louis's ingenuity, the resourcefulness he brought to most any unexpected situation. That dangerous mountain climbing was part of his background and training was something she tried not to think about. They never discussed the subject, but she worried. She strongly suspected that he included a mountain adventure whenever possible on some of his business trips.

She watched as he unzipped two subzero-rated sleeping bags, releasing the zippers so both were completely opened and flat. Their eyes met, the mutual understanding and instant communication of long-married couples, and then he looked away. She didn't ask, and he wouldn't admit to it, yet they both knew she had guessed correctly. Maybe he would stop climbing, once they were living in St-Etienne; he must know how much it worried her. She sighed and helped hold the pieces, the corners flapping like unfurled sails, while he brought the two zipper ends together, creating a single large, unified sleeping bag.

Next, Louis built a fire and discovered the huge iron damper was closed only when the room filled with a choking cloud of smoke. He struggled with its massive iron chain and finally opened the stubborn contraption, plaster debris and abandoned birds' nests collapsing onto his head.

The room cleared at last, while Camille curled up on their conjoined sleeping bags, coughing and laughing—at him, at the smoke, and at the absurdity of begging permission to spend the night in their own house. Sleeping on the frigid slate floor of the kitchen seemed so funny, and Louis was covered with bits of concrete, twigs, and dead leaves.

"Our first night, together in our new home," he murmured in her ear. "I don't intend to sleep alone." Camille snuggled next to him, pulling him closer, pressing his face against her breasts. She kissed the top of his head, still gritty with plaster. Outside, the fierce wind howled, flinging handfuls of sleet at the shuttered windows, sealing the house with ice.

"Your hair smells like wood smoke," she whispered, then wondered why she was whispering when there was no one around for several kilometers. She kissed his hair again, burrowing her face into the thick waves of salt-and-pepper. "It smells so good." Then she slid down beside him, into his embrace and the cozy world that was theirs alone. They had never made love in a sleeping bag before; surely at their age it wasn't just the novelty that made the night special. She fell asleep, cradled in his arms.

III

In the morning Monsieur Collet returned to the house, a flashlight grasped in one hand, an extension ladder under his other arm. Louis and Camille trailed after him as he progressed from one room to the next, fearful and guilty as two children who might be caught out in some mischief.

In each room he climbed the ladder and examined his meticulous plasterwork at the edges, where the walls met the ceiling, glaring along the flashlight's lighted path. "The heat, it rises," he muttered. "The damage will be up here, at first." Michelangelo, inspecting his work on the ceiling of the Sistine Chapel, would have been an amateur and a slacker by comparison. Collet seemed almost disappointed but, after an hour-long examination, he conceded that the house had suffered no harm from their one-night stay in the kitchen. His demeanor changed abruptly.

"Ah, bon!" he boomed, his manner amiable and expansive. "Now, *mes enfants, un petit déjeuner avec Maman*? You must be hungry? *Non?* Come back to our house and we eat a good breakfast like only Mother can cook!"

Louis shoved their sleeping bags into the trunk of the car,

sheets of ice cracking as it opened and closed. "That would be perfect, Collet! *Merci bien!*" Thoroughly chilled they huddled by Louis's car as the icy rain kept on, pinging off the slate roof of the house and the hood of Ferrari.

"I'm starved," Camille said. "Breakfast sounds delightful, Monsieur Collet."

Collet raised an admonitory finger and waggled it under Camille's chin. "But, Madame, every time you say 'Monsieur Collet' I look around, expecting to see my dead father! Just Collet, *s'il vous plaît?*" He kept his hand raised in gentle protest and admonishment, awaiting her response.

Camille smiled. "All right. I'll remember."

"A nasty sort of rain," Collet commented, studying the grim sky and massaging his lower back. "The back can always tell when it will rain and when it will stop too," he informed them with the authority born of years suffering with arthritis and sciatica. "It will stop by twelve-thirty—perhaps one—but then it will snow by early afternoon. The back and I, we always know."

Collet was but one of the richly colorful characters who lived in St-Etienne-des-Près. Amused and enchanted by their uniqueness, Camille was relieved they would not be her patients.

At the Collet house they crowded around the kitchen table, the warm, cozy room filled with the aroma of freshly brewed coffee, sizzling sausage, and apple crêpes, served topped generously with cream.

"What makes this coffee so good?" Camille asked. She usually preferred tea but hadn't protested when Madame Collet handed her the steaming mug. "You must do something special to it."

"It's the Normandy air," their host stated with absolute conviction. "To be sure. Sweet cream. And a *soupçon* of my secret."

Monsieur Collet waved a bottle of Calvados; Camille laughed but shook her head in disbelief.

"I have one more favor, Collet, if it's not too much bother." Louis had earlier thanked him for their hospitality and the hearty breakfast. "If we've not concluded our business here by about ten this morning, could you drive Camille into Rouen? She'll take the early train to Paris. It's Christmas Eve and we have family arriving at home. There are preparations for *le Réveillon*—so, perhaps?"

The big man's eyes softened. He smiled down at Camille. His reaction proved typical of the men they'd met here, and he seemed to welcome the opportunity to display his rustic country gallantry. "It would be my honor, Monsieur Duchêne. But you? How will you get back? It is a long drive. *Les routes?* They are so busy— So much traffic for *les Fêtes.*" His sing-song country accent suggested he would propose a long litany of further possible impediments.

Louis interrupted him before he could continue. "I have a plan. Don't worry, *mon vieux.*"

The other man shrugged, dismissing the problem. If Louis wasn't concerned, he wouldn't worry further, and he would enjoy the pleasure of Camille's company for half an hour.

IV

Just as Collet's arthritis predicted, the icy rain stopped before one. Louis would give the girl another hour, then, by two at the latest, he must be on the road if he was to catch the 3:22 from Rouen. The Bertrand garage where they stored one extra delivery truck and spare parts needed for other equipment at the orchard would be ideal. He could leave the Ferrari there, then be walking through the front door at Place du Chêne before six thirty.

In Paris their Christmas guests would probably have started arriving long before then, around two. Although Françoise surely had the cooking more than well managed, Camille would want to be home to greet their guests and family.

There would be Louis's aunt too, then Madeleine with her twin boys, with their heart-breaking resemblance to his brother Marc. She had remarried two years after Marc's death in Cambodia. He cursed the cruel unfairness that a war correspondent was killed not on a daring assignment but while crossing a city street. Madeleine's new husband—*my God, they've been married for years,* Louis reflected—must be one of the most understanding chaps in the world. He'd always respected her need to maintain a sentimental connection with the Duchêne family.

He checked his watch. He would visit the orchards once more and meet Millet, the new manager Eugène LeBlanc hired a year ago.

"Bonjour!" he'd called as he walked up to Millet's small field office. The rain was staying away but a freezing wind continued to howl through the trees; Louis was surprised to see the young man who waited for him wearing shorts, a sweatshirt, and work boots. They trudged over the windswept fields and between rows of Normandy's crouching apple trees, as Millet felt obligated to re-educate him about the property. Louis was learning more about agriculture than he ever imagined possible and, considering the foul weather, more than he really wanted to know.

Millet discoursed at length about the soil pH of the land. "Wouldn't the Domaine Dupont orchards down the road love to have our soil?" he asked smugly, chuckling at this bit of nature's one-upmanship, and then proceeded to expound further on his scientific philosophy of pruning. "Isn't this fantastic weather, Monsieur? We'll be guaranteed the best harvest of the region at this rate." He described the first harvest, the second growths, and his personal theory of grafting. Was it all right to use the *cépage* as they always had, selling half to pectin manufacturers and using the rest in composted mulch?

The energy of an educated zealot must know no bounds and must also be impervious to weather, Louis concluded. Numbed by cold and information overload he agreed, "Yes, that sounds great. You're doing a fine job, Millet."

The two men shook hands in farewell and wished each other *Joyeux Noël et Bonne Fêtes*. In any event, he and Camille would be back by March, when they moved to St-Etienne. Millet could reach him or the company's lawyer and business manager, Eugène LeBlanc, any time.

Louis checked his watch again. The rain had held off for more than an hour, and he began to question the predictions of Collet's arthritic back. He drove to Annette's cottage, the thick envelope from LeBlanc's law office crackling inside his coat, still safe and dry.

He wasn't certain whether he was afraid and, if so, of what. Was he anxious to meet the girl Annick-Louise? What had her grandmother—no, she was actually the girl's great-grandmother, the one who had raised both his illegitimate, abandoned child and now *her* child—told her about him? Who would be best prepared for this encounter? Did she want to meet him? Was this a terrible mistake on his part, only compounding a much greater one? He would introduce himself and leave the rest to Annette: that was the best he could do. The girl was probably somewhat prepared. She had seen his photograph and knew her mother all too well. Unless she was totally blind and had never owned a mirror, it would be obvious to her who he was, this stranger at their door.

Swallowing with great difficulty and wishing he was fortified by a glass of Calvados like old Monsieur Collet probably was, he was suddenly glad that Camille was not with him. He raised his hand to knock.

Annette must have been waiting for him, because the door was opened immediately. From behind the magnifying lenses, she peered up at him. "She's not here yet, Monsieur Duchêne. I am very worried now."

Louis stared down at this woman who had endured so much. In some ways she was much like his own grandmother, yet in others, extraordinarily different. He was unsure whether he should be relieved or share in her concern. Hoping the exasperation didn't show in his voice, he asked what seemed the next logical question. "Didn't she call?" Then, when Annette shook her head, he demanded, "Didn't you call to find out what happened? Why she didn't come home?"

With the pride that comes from years of relative isolation enhanced by stubborn, rural independence, Annette drew herself up the slightest bit straighter and taller. She answered him, her voice level, her tone bordering on the defiant. "Monsieur, this is the country. When there are ice storms, as we had last night, the telephones regularly fail us."

Louis walked over to the ancient black rotary phone and picked up the receiver. Even suspecting it would be useless, he punched the buttons in the cradle several times, a perfunctory gesture. There was silence, total silence, not even the smallest click.

"This is not Paris, Monsieur," she repeated softly, a quiet

reproach of his assumptions and a reminder of the isolation many rural communities faced routinely, as a matter of course.

"But… but surely she and her friend have cell phones!" He was grasping at what appeared to be his last hope. "Everyone in the whole damn country has a cell phone!" he exclaimed. "I think it's grafted to their arms at birth! Even those who have absolutely no need for one. *Un portable?*" he questioned her, repeating the word more slowly.

Annette shrugged and indicated with great deliberateness the unresponsive, quite dead, fixed land-line telephone of their home. "I believe her friend, Caroline, has one, but we do not." She raised both hands in dismissal of the matter. "If you have one…?" The sentence was left unfinished; her small shrug implied the request.

Louis nodded.

"So, I will try to find her number. Perhaps you could look at the phone line itself," Annette pleaded.

Why he had agreed to the unquestionable fool's errand, he couldn't say. Perhaps it was to get out of the house, to delay what he planned to say to this woman. Louis felt and must look absurd, his long overcoat cracking frost and shards of ice from the surrounding shrubs and short grass as he made his way around the old house. He knew absolutely nothing about phones, except how to make calls and answer them. If this were a question of an automobile, he might have been some help. Obligingly, he looked up and studied the eaves. There were three wires connected there, whatever they might be for.

By his casual and unprofessional observation, they appeared undisturbed by the ice storm, although multiple heavy icicles dangled from all of them. Whether or not three wires were sufficient, he had absolutely no clue. He did note that none of the wires dangled free, which even he could have identified as a hazard. He returned to the house.

In a back room the old woman was searching through the contents of what was clearly a young girl's dresser. He joined her, overwhelmed by a sense of violation and the certainty that this was where another teenager, Nicole, had died, bleeding to death because of him—the girl that he couldn't remember though he had tried so hard to do so for the past year.

Annette was sorting through bits of paper. "Ah! Here's her *agenda!*" She held up the young girl's address book. She placed the small booklet in his hands. "Your eyes are much better than mine."

Dutifully, he looked for the girl Caroline's name and, what he desperately hoped would be her cell phone number, not another silent black rotary phone.

"Ah, oui! That is her!" Annette exclaimed, sighing with relief, when he at last read off the correct name. The handwriting in the little book was neat, pretty, and, in a curious way, a pleasing match for the one photograph he had seen of the girl.

Louis hastily punched the numbers into his cell phone and handed over the unfamiliar machine to the girl's waiting grandmother. She regarded the gadget with suspicion, its smallness, its unfamiliarity, while Louis urged her to speak into it.

"Hâllo?" Annette asked uncertainly. "Caroline?"

A voice at the other end of the telephone must have answered in the affirmative.

"I was worried," she began, then paused to listen, holding the cell phone away from her ear as a volley of young voices poured explanations through the earpiece.

Louis witnessed a total change in her demeanor as concern and fear fell away from her face and she sank into a sturdy arm chair in the living room, overcome with relief. For seconds she appeared thirty years younger, and he glimpsed, for only a moment, what her daughter Nicole might have been like. She handed the cell phone back to Louis who could hear the girl Caroline still talking excitedly. *"Merci,"* he said into the receiver and flipped the tiny apparatus shut without listening further.

"She was returning, late this morning," Annette explained, "when she had a puncture. She returned to her friend's house and they tried to call here." She shrugged to explain this lack of communication. "And she has just left, again, now."

Louis looked at his watch, dismayed: it was 2:12. If he were to get back to Paris tonight at all he simply must leave immediately. He grasped a lower chair and pulled it directly in front of Annette. He had watched Camille do this, positioning herself directly before those she knew to have poor peripheral vision. There were only a few minutes to accomplish what he wanted to do, this delivery of a most important Christmas gift.

"Grandmère Annette," he said, "perhaps it is better this way. Perhaps, too, she doesn't want to meet me." He silenced the old woman's beginnings of protest with a gentle, but firm, gesture. "She has known I was coming, but it must be difficult to accept this new person in one's life, especially one who—" It was a sentence he didn't want to finish.

"No, Monsieur, you mustn't think that. This was to be very special for her. We have talked about it for the past two months, since we knew your plans." The words and the smile accompanying them were genuine.

"I'm relieved to hear that, Grandmère. There's no way I can make up for the past. But I do have a special Christmas gift for her." He reached into his coat and extracted the crisp white envelope, bulging thick with letters and bank documents.

Embossed in the upper left-hand corner was the address of Eugène LeBlanc's law firm in Paris.

He and Camille had decided it was best to do it this way. A fund had been established for the girl's education and living expenses, until the age of twenty-five. Also, the relative anonymity of the business arrangement, with funds deposited directly to their local account, provided an emotional distance for all concerned. When they were needed, funds for further education would come directly from LeBlanc. There was more that Grandmère Annette would discover when she opened the envelope. Camille insisted that a list of the best schools—and those most convenient for the girl—be included. There was also her personal letter of recommendation, hoping it might be worth something. There was a modest stipend as well, labeled "general funds," without the girl's name mentioned, assigned only to Annette Chaumont. Eugène LeBlanc's direct number was included if she had any questions about the arrangements.

"So, you can choose when it is best to tell her and how. We will return in March. Living here…. Who knows what will be the least awkward for her. It is up to you to decide." He patted her frail hand, feeling the knobbiness of each knuckle that spoke eloquently of a hard life. He stood to leave, then bent down to touch each softly wrinkled cheek lightly in farewell. *"Joyeux Noël et Bonne Année."*

"Joyeux Noël," she repeated automatically and squeezed his hand as he stood to leave.

Louis glanced back one last time as he closed the door behind him. Annette hadn't moved; she was sitting erect in the same low chair, staring at the unopened envelope in her lap. He started the car and checked his watch. The timing would be very close.

V

Although frost-singed to the pale gold and brown of winter, this remained beautiful countryside. Crisscrossed with hedgerows like a dull patchwork quilt, the gently rolling hills plunged in places to old stream beds. Even in drab winter garb this part of Normandy held the promise of a stunning spring to come: fruit orchards that would flower in a profusion of pink and white, followed by the lush green of summer, and next the glowing colors of autumn.

It was miraculous how the land could heal itself, not just from season to season, but following the desecration of battles, fire, and bombs. He thought back to the post-war summer he had spent here, over fifty years ago. The events of the past year had brought most of the memory vividly to life. The earth had been scorched, gouged, and burned; many of the trees, where they stood at all, were blackened, wounded, or traumatized by disease. For him it had been a glorious summer of hard work and camaraderie. With a fresh pang of guilt he tried but could not remember the girl he had seduced, late on a midsummer's evening. He'd started university after that summer; somehow new experiences must have blurred her forever from his memory: his first, her first, and the consequence, his only child.

At last St-Etienne-des-Près was behind him, but it seemed that an entire new life was stretching out before him. He had done what needed to be done; he would trust Annette to do what was best for the girl. That was his only choice if he intended to make the village his home. "My golden years," he said to the wintery country all around him. "Our golden years, Camie's and mine."

He had started leaving by this particular road well over a year before, when they were first discussing the prospects of renovating the old *mas* for their permanent, not just summer, residence. They needed another summer home about as much as they needed another car, Louis thought, almost guiltily. They shared the villa at Cap Ferret with what remained of the extended family. It was beautiful, but it was rented out for part of the year. Once a person has known Paris, the American author Ernest Hemingway once wrote, he will always have two homes—Paris and wherever else he might have been born. They would always have Paris, of course, but in this peculiar sequence of life events, they had adopted yet another home as well, and those who lived there were adopting him.

In this one corner of Normandy, the village of St-Etienne-des-Près, there was a special connection. The estate had belonged to his maternal grandparents. It carried their history, deep roots extending into the soil for hundreds of years, long past their connection as Napoleon's Chief Equerry, and their incomparable orchards (if he was to believe Millet's proudly exaggerated claims about the soil).

Haunting him again was a wave of remorse that he could not remember the girl Nicole, no matter how he tried and despite the old photograph Annette had shown him. He'd assured her then that he remembered Nicole fondly. Now his granddaughter represented one more bond, adding responsibility to guilt. Louis tried to analyze his feelings. Was it the death of the girl so many years ago? Or that he couldn't really remember her? Surely it was both.

The alternate route leaving the village was an uninteresting, newly paved, shortcut which dumped him unceremoniously onto the main autoroute, where four divided lanes roared past in a shocking counterpoint to the living history so near. Much shorter, it contained nothing of the countryside's charm, too abrupt in its convenience.

The surface he was driving on would have some difficulty even qualifying as a road; its continual deterioration over the past several months was appalling. It could usually accommodate one car traveling in one direction but in places it was barely wide enough for that. If two cars were to meet, one would have to back up quite some distance to allow the other to pass. To his right, clay and rocks crumbled toward a shallow ravine where a stream bed cradled the remains of stunted trees and chunks of monolithic boulders, more of Normandy's stone of cathedrals and castles.

Ahead was the raw charcoal-gray of a lowering winter sky, just as Collet and his back had forecast. The Ferrari's heater was more than adequate, but Louis shivered, surveying the frigid landscape, noticing that the gray sky was starting to deliver small flakes of the predicted snow.

At Place du Chêne, they would have built a fire in the grand salon, most everyone was already gathered by now and in a festive mood. Soon he'd be with them. Camille, radiant, would be wearing that cream-colored wool dress that he loved. It was simple, long-sleeved, high-necked, and with her creamy golden complexion, her soft blond hair pulled gently away from her face, she was as irresistible as a vanilla confection. *Ah, the warmth home. There's nothing like it on a night like this.*

His attention was drawn back inexorably to the road. In its increasingly primitive condition, hedgerows were creeping onto it, inch by inch, reclaiming that much more of the narrow surface and creating a visibility hazard.

It would take a while to establish complete trust with their neighbors in this country community that took such inordinate pride in its independence.

There might be an opportunity to offer help now and then, cautiously, of course. "Perhaps some of our crew might help with grading this road?" or "We have some extra dirt and rock." Once fields were cleared new rocks would appear, continually extruded from the earth. "This load could be used to stabilize one stretch of the road."

He vaguely remembered that the orchards did not own a road grader, but surely, couldn't they find some business excuse to get one? He would talk with the various property owners, lease a road grader if need be, somehow repair and stabilize the crumbling road edges. He hesitated to rob this precious corner of Normandy of its charm, but these were actions that would benefit all concerned. The road should at the very least be safe.

To his left, a short distance ahead, was old Madame Pencheret's place. A widow for many years now, she was trying to maintain her small property completely alone. There were a neat small stand of a dozen cherry and apple trees, a chicken coop, and a shed for one cow. But the Pencheret hedgerows were by far the most aggressive he had seen. He happily resumed role playing. "Madame, the crew at the orchard is finished for the day. Could they be of help to you?" he rehearsed. All a person could do was try, of course.

If nothing else, with a few of the proper words in the right ears he might be able to get the route on the *Département* budget, and the road would receive much needed maintenance. "Mine will be a voice for the community!" he pronounced firmly, with great vigor, as if he were running for political office.

This was something he hadn't expected. Not long ago he imagined he might have been happy forever, tinkering with his cars, finding those special, hard-to-find, exact replacement parts on the Internet while making contact with others who shared his passion. This was new and special and even better.

Opportunity spread before him like an unending landscape, full of promise, a future rich with new meaning. Because Camille had finally agreed to a full retirement, they'd overcome the one difficult period that had been filled with bitter differences and arguments, the only time they'd ever really argued about anything major. She would miss her work forever, but she was by far better adjusted to change than he was. Now, suddenly, retirement was becoming a marvelous new world, full of possibilities to make a difference.

It would take time, of course. They would become better known gradually, then accepted. Then there would be those gentle nudges from the Bertrand estate with offers of assistance.

"Monsieur, the workers have finished such-and-such project." Louis allowed his imagination to play. "They'll be passing by your farm on their way home. It's a shame to waste their time." Delighted, he practiced a variety of potential scenarios, liking them better with each rehearsal. The thriftiness of the Normandy farmer was legendary and perhaps the Duchênes' offers could be accepted in that spirit, that of preventing waste. Chuckling, he couldn't wait to share his scheme with Camille, unless she had already thought of it first, which wouldn't have surprised him in the least.

The road dominated his thoughts once more.

In the deep shade, where the route curved in and out following the craggy contours of the hills, there was ice—dangerous layers of partially thawed clay topped with thin ice that rested on a more solid layer of frozen run-off. Creeping along even at 20 kilometers he could feel the car's occasional skid, the uncontrolled spin of his tires seeking purchase in slurry. He should have turned around while he had a chance, but there was only a short distance between here and a decently maintained road. At the next drive he could turn around safely, although back-tracking now would put him home late. It was unfortunate, but that was what he would have to do. Snow had started to fall, larger flakes, soft and silent.

Ahead were the hedgerows that marked the beginning of Monsieur Daumier's large holding. To the left were the untended rock walls belonging to the farmer, the crumbling stonework of a retaining wall had finally collapsed, intruding into the road. A perfectly vertical slab of hillside soil remained, staying upright more from habit than from any structural support. Daumier was a nice man, stubborn as they come, with a brood of half-grown children. It amazed Louis that none of the older boys would help shift some of the rocks at the very least.

Ahead several boulders lay in the middle of the road. One rock was over half a meter high; the others were not much smaller. Swearing softly, Louis slowed, gently easing toward the inside curve of the road to avoid them. With its low suspensions, the powerful Ferrari was vulnerable underneath. In spite of his precautions he felt a sickening crack and thump: he had hit one of the rocks.

Directly ahead, Daumier, his wife, and family were backing out of their uphill drive. The tiny pickup truck of unknown and long-forgotten vintage was piled high with little Daumiers. With too much weight in the truck bed the rear tires had become stuck in the drainage channel created by runoff. The children instantly poured out of the truck and started milling about in the road, doing nothing in particular, while the two older boys and Monsieur Daumier surveyed the truck's predicament.

The loud clap Louis had felt and heard must have been the snapping of the front tie rod. Somehow he had managed to get safely around the boulders, but with no ability to steer and no safe place to steer to. He tried to pull away from the group of children directly in front of him. Nothing happened. The car continued to skid crablike, sliding forward unimpeded and accelerated by the layers of partially frozen clay and mud.

"Oh, God! No, no!" he begged, struggling with the car. "Turn, damn you! Turn!" He pressed down on the car's horn, hoping to at least warn the group ahead of him. Didn't anyone hear him? Were they swallowed up in the muffled snowy silence? The children hadn't budged, but smiled happily in greeting, and Monsieur Daumier even turned and waved. The skid continued for what seemed a lifetime until finally he felt the car start sliding the slightest bit to the right. It wasn't enough to clear the family: he was going to kill them all.

Focused on the impending disaster before him, Louis had barely noticed the lone bicycle rider cresting the rise beyond the Daumier's driveway. Dry flakes of snow were falling steadily now, blurring the landscape and softening the world to a uniform shade of gray; the cyclist in the distance was a darkened silhouette. Knowing it was not the safest of driving techniques, but the only one he had at his disposal to avoid mass carnage—killing the family that hadn't budged an inch and whoever was coming toward him on a bicycle, head tucked down against the blowing snow—with all the muscle he possessed he jerked the steering wheel to the right and pulled on the emergency brake.

With the clarity that accompanies times of absolute terror and finality the next thirty seconds seemed stamped with the vividness of a slow motion film, the timelessness of eternity. The Daumier family remained transfixed apparently, like bundled statues in the falling snow, standing in the road as if carved from the stones around them.

The lone bicyclist was upon him too, gliding silently up to meet him in the snowy stillness. As the car plunged over the crumbling edge of road he glimpsed the cyclist's face when she passed inches from the driver's window: bright blue eyes wide with horror, long, curly black hair windblown away from her face and flecked with snow, and above all, her intense effort to stop the bike.

———

The stunned group on the roadway watched as the Ferrari caught briefly in the skeletal branches of two trees, tumbled off a boulder whose bulk protruded down lower, ricocheted back and forth across the narrow ravine, then finally came to rest, upside down, in the stream bed below. Reverberations of its descent continued, echoing and rebounding through the hills like the deep, throaty bells of a cathedral ringing in the New Year.

Then all was silent and white with snow.

VI

"Where is Louis? I must see him! Where did you put him? Oh, my God!"

"You must wait, Madame. The doctor said he must first speak with you." Without success an anonymous voice was striving for authority and control.

"I'm a doctor," Camille snapped, ignoring whoever was speaking: Louis was here, somewhere. Determined, she plunged forward through the jumble of hospital corridors on a single-minded quest to find her injured husband. She recognized Christophe's voice at last, heard as if he were speaking from somewhere far away. Why would he be here? That he had driven her to the hospital was temporarily erased from her memory.

"No, please, Camille. You must wait."

Soon she was making noisy progress through the radiology holding area, pushing back privacy curtains that rattled along their tracks, startling other patients on stretchers and leaving chaos and disarray in her wake. Finally, there he was, at last.

"Oh, my God! Louis, are you all right? What happened?"

She noted with approval the cervical brace. *Les Pompiers*—the Emergency Team—had done the right thing. Applying a cervical collar was always appropriate after any kind of trauma. With dawning horror she registered that this was not the temporary inflatable collars emergency teams used, but the stabilization device used for a documented spinal injury.

"Angel? Angel is that you? You're here at last." His words were terribly faint, hard to understand. "I'm strapped down so tight I can't move. Where's your dress?"

Somehow, he must have imagined that she'd be wearing his favorite dress, the creamy white one. When the call had come and Christophe came running upstairs to get her she'd slipped back into the jeans that she'd worn in from St-Etienne-des-Près. She'd been preparing for the evening's festivities and the arrival of their family and house guests. Now she regretted that she'd tossed the dress aside, the dress he always liked so much.

Something was wrong, ever so wrong. Her ears were ringing, sounds weren't coming through correctly. Instead there was a terrible buzzing in her head. Nurses and orderlies were running about. There were voices here and there, explaining things, but they might have been speaking some unknown foreign language, rebounding and echoing from a great distance.

She was holding his hand, but Louis kept asking her to hold his hand. His words echoed back and forth in her head, the situation becoming all too clear. She placed her other hand on his thigh and stroked his leg through the hospital drape.

"There, there," she crooned. "How does that feel, *mon chéri?*" she asked. The confirmation that he could feel nothing at all dawned too quickly.

Louis was pleading. "Please, won't you just hold my hand?"

And Camille Mauriat Duchêne, who had dissected hundreds of cadavers early in medical school and who, during her residencies, had sought out and plunged into one bloody, challenging surgical opportunity after another with never a hint of squeamishness, felt her legs dissolve under her. She collapsed, fainting onto the floor of the MRI holding area, the certainty of her husband's cervical transection and inevitable paralysis already confirmed.

VII

"What happened?" Camille mumbled. She regained consciousness, cradled in Christophe's strong, slender arms. He was holding an ice pack to her head.

"Why—? What—?" She couldn't seem to manage a complete thought. An intravenous solution was dripping into her arm. "What are they doing to me?"

A nurse hurried close, alerted to her voice. Christophe waved her away. "Just fluid. Lactated Ringers and normal saline. You're not drugged. You've had a terrible shock and a nasty fall."

"But?" She was remembering. "But Louis?"

Christophe was one person she could always count on for the truth: he could not and would not lie to her. Besides, she already knew. He didn't say anything, but held her as she turned into his arms, sobbing. "Oh, no!" Anguished words spilled out and then she would cry more. "What if I'd stayed with him and not rushed back to Paris? What if we'd postponed the visit until after Christmas?" They were useless questions, never to be answered.

"Camie." He stroked her hair again and again, his expert, gentle hands exploring the rising lump on her head. "I'm so sorry."

Finally, her sobbing eased. "Will you tell me what happened? Then, I must see him."

"His car went off the edge of that road. You know, the one going east out of St-Etienne. There was a bicyclist who they sent for help. Apparently the nearest house didn't have a phone. No cell phone service either." Christophe helped steer her gurney closer to Louis.

"Do we know who? Was there another car—a collision?"

"Camille." Christophe spoke to her ever so gently and grasped her other hand, the one not clinging to Louis. "No, I almost wish there had been. This was much more tragic." He swallowed, pressing closer to the stretcher and lowering his voice to a whisper, then helped her to sit up and cautiously ease down from the gurney. Together they listened to Louis's breathing, irregular and labored. He didn't respond as doctors and nurses crowded around him, working.

"He'll need a tracheotomy, of course, and a vent—something to breathe for him," Christophe said.

"Of course." Camille nodded. "Louis, I'm here." She stroked his forehead, but he didn't open his eyes.

"There were people in the road apparently," Christophe was saying after they stepped aside, allowing the doctors and respiratory team to do their work. "They might have all been killed, but he succeeded in avoiding them. I think they said it was the Daumier family and a bicyclist too. The EMTs arrived within twenty minutes. They had to pry him out of the car. It's a miracle the car didn't catch on fire."

"No. It wouldn't." Her words were bitter. "That was once a racing car. It has some special feature. It's designed not to burst into flame."

"Angel?" Louis's voice had become fainter as he tried to repeat his simple request, muffled more around the whoosh of oxygen and the rhythmic noises of a ventilator. "Hold my hand?"

Camille bent over him, clinging to what remained of her husband, cradling his hand in hers and stroking it, again and again, leaving kisses on his face around the oxygen and the tubes. Could he feel her touching his face?

"Home... Normandy...," he mouthed the words with difficulty. "Thinking... so... wonderful...."

❖

13 *Camille and Christophe*

Paris, 1994

I

LOUIS SURVIVED FOR TWO MONTHS and three days, succumbing to the complications of quadriplegia that life support, no matter how sophisticated, could not prevent.

"There is always swelling to be expected around the spinal cord," she was told rather unnecessarily considering her medical background, but the formula, the rites of communication with family members must be repeated, the rituals of non-specific reassurance observed.

She had even perpetuated the charade, telling Louis about progress in current research for spinal cord injuries. Louis, pragmatic even in the face of disaster, had recognized the truth.

Camille mourned him by forgetting to live, drifting alone around their big house and forgetting to eat the meals that Françoise prepared for her when she came by every day.

Françoise and Eugène had taken the Duchênes' old dog Bijou to live with them. In mourning herself, Françoise insisted

228

Camille see a doctor. She called to set an appointment with Christophe and promised to accompany her, but Camille refused to go.

Feeling helpless, Françoise hadn't known what to do next. "Did anyone send in her letter of resignation?" she asked him. "She needs to go back to work—wouldn't that help?"

Christophe accompanied her to the hospital and finally was allowed into Camille's office. The letter was still there. Relieved, he learned that administration was considering her absence an extended sick leave.

II

On a morning in late March, Camille rushed into Christophe's office. She had finished the last of Louis's tranquilizers and muscle relaxers that he'd needed against the rage of agonizing muscle spasms. The spasms were one of the acutely unfair consequences of quadriplegia, considering the rest of his body did not respond as it should. Not only would his neck and upper shoulders suffer in agonizing grips of muscle tension, but, most unfairly, his legs that could walk no more would often twitch so violently that even the specially designed heavy hospital bed would shake.

She hadn't called their family doctor but just appeared in the office—telling the secretary what she needed—displaying two of Louis's empty prescription bottles as if their presence and emptiness were the only message needed.

The polite but efficient young woman in Rossignon's reception had taken the two containers and then returned in a few minutes. She leaned toward Camille, whispering so the waiting patients would hopefully not overhear her. *"Le docteur* said to go on back. He'll see you in about fifteen minutes."

Camille, in her single-minded quest, hadn't lowered her voice. "But I don't need to *see* him!" She waved the bottles again. "I just need these."

The secretary had already opened the door to Rossignon's inner sanctum, and was ushering her inside. To continue her frenzied protests Camille would need to follow.

Down the single long corridor of the office, Christophe, as ever immaculate in his *de rigeur* white lab coat, was writing on a chart outside the closed door to a patient room. He glanced up, smiled politely acknowledging her presence, and then hastily looked away.

He would need time to master his emotions. He picked up the chart he had just completed and feigned deep interest in what was printed there. He had had many years of practice at this, disguising his feelings, not letting them be read on his face, because there were some thoughts patients should not be allowed to discover. And Camille must not be able to read his now. Neutral—that was what it must be. He looked up once more and motioned for her to come in. Camille closed the door behind her, leaving the waiting patients to murmur and grumble at this interruption by some deranged interloper without an appointment.

The warm greeting that was traditionally theirs was stifled in his struggle for neutrality. "Here." He waved toward a vacant treatment room.

"I don't need to see you," she maintained stubbornly. "I just need these—" She waved the empty bottles in his face.

"No, *ma chérie,* you do. My office?" He motioned to the other side of the narrow corridor. "Or this room?" She glanced in at the stiff, leather-covered table, metal stirrups protruding from its corners like stylized antlers, obviously used for gynecology patients.

Turning, he waggled the prescription pad over his right shoulder, the only bait and lure he had at his disposal. She simply must stay: she now needed help infinitely more than before Louis's death: she'd been using his powerful tranquilizers and muscle relaxers, in strengths recommended for someone twice her weight.

"Your choice." Again he waved the prescription pad as he turned to see his next patient, waiting in privacy behind another door. He would need these next minutes to gain control over his emotions. He would listen to the heart of the frail old Madame Canette, he would chide her about taking her medications, he would do what he regularly did… and then he would need to face Camille Duchêne.

Where had the time gone? It was trite and an oversimplification, but bad times, those filled with misfortune and stress, seemed to last forever while the good slipped by incredibly fast, as if in a blur. He had last seen her when Louis had been moved to a private room. Only a month or so ago, but by Camille's appearance it might have been years. The soft blond hair, once so lovely, straggled in unkempt strings and clumps around her face, escaped untidily from a clip at the back of her head. She looked as if she hadn't washed or shampooed in ages—surely that was just his impression.

Her complexion had lost its glow and was now sallow, almost gray, instead of her usual exquisite, pale golden-peach color of health. The tender brown eyes that had captured his soul and his heart were dull, bloodshot, and rimmed by dark circles. She had been slender for as long as he'd known her, but now she was gaunt. How much weight had she lost? She was clutching an ill-fitting sweater around her shoulders, which he realized only later must have been one of Louis's.

This was the woman for whom—if the Duchênes hadn't been his lifelong family and close friends and if he hadn't been married at the time—for whom he would have broken every oath he had ever taken to try to win her love, even if it had meant wreaking her own marriage. Always immaculately coiffed, elegantly dressed, even at her most casual and in jeans like she was on Christmas Eve—the person today was barely recognizable. This is what he feared would happen to her... and now it had. And she was taking medications not intended for her.

Christophe escorted the elderly Madame Canette from the office, with avuncular affection reminding her again about the necessity to take her medications and the next time to please wear her hearing aid so he wouldn't have to shout her medical conditions out for all to hear. He handed her an envelope, his usual missive to the granddaughter who visited her twice weekly, with details of treatment, should the old lady forget what pill she was taking for which condition and when she should take it.

He sighed and pushed open the door to his office. Camille had collapsed into the chair facing his desk and fallen asleep. He walked around to sit down opposite her, settling into the leather chair with a whoosh and creak. Camille awoke, startled, the two empty bottles still clutched in her hand.

"Here," she said.

Where had her radiant smile gone? Things were not only as he feared, they were worse.

"I need these... they were for Louis," she said.

Rossignon ignored the bottles at first, then took them from her outstretched hand, and nudged them with a long forefinger slowly and deliberately toward the middle of his desk. Studying the two objects he aligned them precisely and regarded his handiwork critically. He removed the half-glasses he used when writing and, with care, added them to the arrangement. Finally he took a deep breath, let it out slowly, and with studied deliberation replaced the prescription pad in his coat pocket.

Christophe shook his head. "*Non*. Louis is no longer my patient, but you are. Camille, I must speak bluntly—we'll ignore the matter of taking medications not intended for you, for now. Your condition is more serious than his. Louis is no longer suffering."

"But... But—"

He silenced her protests, dismissing them with a wave of his hand and a deliberate shrug. "You must listen. Now. To me."

She slumped back into the chair.

"You are not sleeping. You are not eating. You've not returned to work. Is your mourning all in the name of love? The end result will not be a good one. By not taking care of yourself, you will destroy your immune system. *Non?*"

She was starting to protest again, but in the end said nothing.

"Now, this is not like talking to someone without a medical background." He paused and looked directly into her eyes. "But there are harsh realities that you and I both knew. The body of any quadriplegic patient is immediately at risk: the lack of mobility, then the presence of urinary catheters, ventilators, and other technologies that allow bacteria to enter the body. The entire body is compromised—you can massage and turn and do God only knows what—and the outcome will usually be the same. The fact that Louis had already had pneumonia twice and four major urinary tract infections, prior to this last one involving the kidneys, each requiring a different, stronger antibiotic, each requiring longer treatment…. That was not a good sign." He paused a moment to allow Camille to process what he was saying, what he must be leading up to.

"Let me repeat this. No more of his tranquilizers. I have only one patient now: you. We've lost Louis." Tears were brimming in those tender brown eyes that he had always loved and still loved so much. Automatically, he pushed a box of tissues in her direction. He swallowed hard; his pathetic efforts at neutrality were wearing thin. "I don't want to lose you too."

At last, Camille nodded. Christophe replaced his half-glasses and withdrew the prescription pad from his pocket and deliberately, slowly, and clearly wrote something and then signed it with a sprawling, underlined *C. Rossignon.* He handed her the slip of paper.

For a moment, she didn't move or glance at the prescription, only continued to slump down in the chair.

"Read it," he encouraged her.

She plucked the note from her lap, then looked up at him, puzzled. "It says 'May I come to dinner tonight?'"

"Well…. May I?"

"Of course, dear Christo." She smiled. It wasn't very much of a smile, but it was a start. "Should I call Eugène and Françoise?"

"If you wish. That'd be nice." He studied her for a moment. "Just the two of us would be fine too."

He stood at last and came around the desk to tell her goodbye. He reached down to assist her out of the deep chair that had practically enveloped her. He was a tall man, never big and muscular like Louis, but he had the impression he could have lifted her up with one hand. And, had his hand slipped, she might have sailed through the air; she seemed to weigh no more than a bird. They embraced, tender *bisous* on the other's cheek.

He tried not to dwell on the feeling of tiny bones, the fragility of vertebrae, ribs, wrists, and forearms that reached him through Louis's sweater, nor think too much about the immediate future.

❖

14 *Family*

Paris, December 1994

CAMILLE GAZED INTO THE FLICKERING CANDLES, past the sparkling crystal and antique silver serving dishes, and down the long table, the faces of their friends and dinner guests blurring at the edge of her vision.

For a moment she imagined all was just as it had been the day Louis brought her home to meet his parents. It was the same, she thought, although some of the faces were not. The odd part about family was that despite change and time, it would stay constant in other ways. Especially their kind of family. Although some of the faces around the table were new or had changed, more than thirty years later the essence of what held them together remained intact.

How she wished she had been more observant, that evening she met the extended group whose allegiance and hearts and lives belonged to one family, the steady warmth of the Duchênes. The elegant pianist Albert, with the tattoo from one concentration death camp or another, had died years ago; his struggling heart had failed him. Afterward, his widow Gertrude, by then elderly and in poor health, rarely came to the dinners they hosted at Place du Chêne. It was Gertrude's brother, Camille would learn later, who had been arrested for the excellent forgeries of many a Frenchman's papers, their passports to freedom and safety. The Gestapo had captured him and executed him in Lyon's city square in a hail of bullets and blood.

Theirs was a reconstructed family of friends, relatives, and associations that had developed, emerging when blood relatives were killed or lost to war. Tonight, listening to the hum of chatter around the table, Camille noticed one special difference from her first evening with the Duchênes: everyone was sharing stories and memories.

Unlike the reconstructed family gathered at the Duchêne house to meet Camille in 1964, which had not wanted to talk about the humiliation and pain of their personal wars, those gathered tonight were distanced by time, representing a freshly awakened curiosity and need to know. In more modern times it was considered therapeutic to talk about the past; it had not been an accepted behavior for those who were recent survivors of pain and stress and fear.

Annick-Louise was there that evening, smiling, seated where Christophe's wife Monique had sat that evening in 1964; she was flanked by Marc's twin boys. One of them—they were young men now—was asking her whether she liked to ski. Camille smiled. What a convoluted family relationship that would prove to be, if it were to develop past friendship. What were they— second cousins? Was Annick-Louise actually the boys' auntie? Or were they her uncles? Camille was encouraging the girl to stay in Paris for school, but she had chosen and been accepted at another excellent college, nearer her Grandmère Annette and the village of St-Etienne-des-Près.

During Annick's visits, which were more and more frequent, her questions were about Louis and his family, deeply curious about what had happened during the years before and after the war. "So they were trying to rebuild his grandmother's home that summer?" she asked disbelievingly. "It's such a beautiful house. Was it really completely destroyed?"

Camille would try to explain, as much as she had learned from Hélène Bertrand, but she was not the one to describe the circumstances of Nicole's death. That was Annette's responsibility, if she hadn't told her already.

"And what about where you lived? Near Lyon?" Annick had pressed on eagerly with her questions. "Did anything happen to you and your family?"

"No, not really." Camille gasped, holding her hand to her mouth for a brief second. She'd just told her first lie concerning the war years, what she vowed she would never do, not after hearing what her father finally admitted, about the day of the German general who had come to their home and raped her mother. There was the pain of knowing her father had never forgiven her mother—and for what, to what end? He had claimed to be a man of God. "Actually, could we talk about it? Perhaps some other time?" She didn't want to repeat all the details, but knew she must sometime and she should be honest. It was a difficult choice: the anguish of war would live on as long as there was anyone to remember it, but its lessons were important too.

Thinking about the Bertrand Estate always brought back the heartbreak and agony, haunting her with "what-if?" The distilleries and cider presses remained part of the Duchêne business conglomerate, so they would always have that to manage and a share of the income. Thanks to the fiscal wisdom of Hervé

LeBlanc and then the continued management of his son Eugène LeBlanc and others she need never concern herself with more than appearing at an occasional board meeting now and then.

———

The manor house, where she and Louis would retire to the country.... *Oh, dear God!* Sometimes when she smelled wood smoke, the memory of sleeping on the kitchen floor would return, so real.

One night in particular a whiff of fragrant smoke had drifted up the hill, seeping down through the chimney of her bedroom. Camille turned toward the scent, imagining the warmth of Louis's breath against her ear, the familiar mouth touching her cheek, even a hint of stubborn beard that by evening was part of him, and the strength of his arms around her.

She had grown up in starkly realistic times, the child of stern Calvinistic parents, but she whispered into the night, "Please— just once?" fearing that if she asked for more, it might be denied, like a child wishing for too much at Christmas. She inhaled deeply. The scent of him was there too: a blend of coffee, hints of his morning's aftershave, cigarettes, and the lingering, apple-tinged aroma of Calvados.

Camille hadn't dared move at first. "I love you," she said to the darkness punctuated only by numerals changing on the bedside clock: 2:17, 2:18, 2:19.... "Thank you for coming back." She adjusted her breathing to the familiar rhythm of his, so that nothing would disturb the feel of him, the solace of his touch. She breathed in the wood smoke in his hair: perhaps if she breathed deeply enough she could hold on to the remaining essence of him. When she awoke again an hour later, Louis, his scent and the sensation, had vanished.

Come morning, she would call Christophe and give him the answer he had been wanting and waiting for.

———

Eugène had negotiated the sale of the manor house and barn to a young, wealthy, French and English couple from London. They planned to use it as their summer home. Camille hoped they would be good stewards of the land and that they would respect its history. She never wanted to see the place again, although, once recovered and out of mourning, she would visit Annette Chaumont in the nearby village. Louis's collection of racing cars and classic automobiles was scheduled to be sold at auction in March of the coming year. One life and many eras were coming to an end.

Tonight Françoise and Eugène, now a married couple, had parked in the back drive near the old carriage house early in the evening, part of the curious regrouping of what constituted their family. They would probably be among the last to leave.

Two months ago she and the courtly, gentle Christophe, who had been by her side since the day she arrived at Place du Chêne, were married. She was content, although the changes they faced in the coming year would require many painful adjustments.

———

"I know you have many regrets. *Non?*" Christophe said as their final dinner guests departed.

They were standing on the front steps of No. 1, Place du Chêne. She stared out into the quiet darkness, the security lights

winking off, one by one, as the last cars drove through the automatic iron gates. The gates slid shut, but the lights by the
portico's double oak doors remained on, glowing down on them.

After January 6, the magnificent old house and its treasures
of art, architecture, and antiques would belong to the com-
bination of entities which was the closest France had to a
National Trust, joining the list of *musées* and historic estates
preserved as property of the state. Art experts had already
visited, evaluating what would need to be done regarding preser-
vation, conservation, and security.

"And the ceilings?" Camille had asked the curator. Together
they viewed the delicate paintings, their eyes drawn inevitably to
the one black hole that had been deliberately left after WW II. It
was subtle, but there—the bullet-shattered navel of a cherub
holding two candles which, when viewed from three corners of
the room, had blended with the lights of the crystal chandelier.

"Certain art forms are more easily maintained," the curator
was saying. "It has always been thus. Fresco will fade. Add extra
humidity, acids and oils from human skin, chemicals—even those
dissolved in the air—and it will break down quickly. Over two
hundred fifty years old! It's had a good life. It has seen much."
The young man tilted his head back to study the cherubs, the
birds, and the *trompe-l'loeil* forest which blended into the blue sky
of some unknown, incredibly talented artist, who had dated his
work in one corner, but not signed it. "If ceilings could talk...," he
said at last, straightening up and rubbing the cramp in his neck.

The art conservators had debated at length, about whether or
not to cover the remaining bullet hole in the Watteau-era ceiling.
In the end, they had decided to proceed with repair of the
damage. It had been the Duchêne family's "reminder."

Curators and archivists from la Bibliothèque Nationale had

begun to catalogue and preserve the Duchêne collection of rare books. Certain pieces of the silver and china, some dating back centuries, would be left on display within the setting of the house; other pieces would be stored and brought out for rotating exhibits.

The carriage house would eventually be converted, after much reinforcing and the installation of systems for security and climate control, to another display area attached to the museum. Should she and Christophe choose to live there, the apartment in the loft could be theirs, but would revert to the state upon their deaths.

Camille said nothing for a moment, but turned to examine the bronze plaque one historic commission had already mounted to the right of the entry way. It listed, as briefly as even quite a large plaque could allow, the history of the property. In 1585, there was a much smaller house, indicated in old records variously as a cottage in *"un parc des chesnes"* and later as *"la place du chêne."* The spellings and terms were a history lesson in themselves. Hanging in the foyer was a worn tapestry, which dated from the mid-1600s and illustrated the lands, trees, and various structures, that visitors could compare with a more modern map, dated 1918, of the Paris environs.

She placed her hand on one date, *1940–1944—German occupation, headquarters for the Sicherheitsdienst, Communication and Intelligence Service of the SS.* The next date read: *1944–1945—Allied Forces occupation, The United States Army.* The final lines included the birth and death of Louis's father, his mother, and his brother. The last was Louis Duchêne, 1932–1994, the end of their family line.

Camille had asked Annette Chaumont and Annick-Louise Lessard, Louis's granddaughter whom he'd never actually met. "I feel Annick's name ought to be there too," she'd suggested.

"I appreciate the offer, of course," Annick-Louise had replied kindly, politely. "The Duchêne family has been most generous, but it wouldn't seem right." She'd made a long weekend, two days away from school, and had come to Paris for these final days in the old house. Camille liked her: she was bright, witty, and her pretty blue eyes reminded her of Louis.

"I would have liked to meet the major, Professor Croswell. Louis spoke of him sometimes." Camille shrugged. "I write to his children from time to time."

"Is that all?"

"Oh, no.... Most of all I wanted a family." Her voice caught. "I'm sorry, Christo.... I miss him."

Christophe nodded and took her in his arms. "I know... I do too. We always will."

It was very cold now but they continued to wait on the front steps, absorbing the spirit of the old house. An unexpected light snow had begun to fall, silent, delicate flakes twinkling against the remaining lights, swirling gently before settling, vanishing, on the cobbled drive.

"Camie, dearest, you may not realize it, but you have a family. Most of them were here tonight. Not all families are the same. The people who will stand by you—without flinching—those are your true family."

She said nothing for several minutes. "But what will happen to all of them when we.... When all of this is gone?" She gestured toward the big house above them and leaned back into the comfort and warmth of Christophe's arms.

"There's no way to know. Times change, but I have faith in all of them." He was silent for several long moments.

They remained there, staring out as the last of the timed motion-activated lights winked off slowly, announcing the very last car—Eugène and Françoise—had left the courtyard and begun the descent down the hill that raised Place du Chêne slightly above the neighboring houses.

"It existed before us," he said. "Not just Henri and the self-lessness he shared throughout the war and always, even after. He learned it from others, good people and examples of sharing. Generations before have done the same. Then and now, we try to carry it on."

"But our home?" Sometimes she was unable to hide her anguish at the prospect of leaving. When she'd first arrived she could never have imagined living in the vast house that seemed as big as a palace. Now it contained memories, what had changed it to a home.

"My dear—" Occasionally Christophe slipped and used this American expression. It would always make Camille smile; it also helped to separate him from memories of Louis.

"The house is symbolic, *oui.*" Christophe wrapped her snuggly in his arms. "It has a marvelous history. But it is, too, just a house. What pulls people together—gratitude and loyalty and caring and goodwill—will continue to pull them together."

"Sometimes I think you have more faith than I do."

"Perhaps," he said. "I'll concede that."

"I know you're right."

"I also believe that every ending begins something new."

"You're very wise, dearest Christo." Camille turned and raised up on her toes to kiss him. "I'm cold. Let's go inside now. I want to enjoy what time we have left in our home, together."

❖

Ends

About the stories

T HERE'S ALWAYS ANOTHER VIEW OF WAR, personal, intimate, and close to those not on the battlefield. The famous Polish writer Stanislow Jerzy Lec, who fled Poland in 1939 when Germany's armies invaded his homeland, once wrote: "You can close your eyes to reality, but not to memories."

War is what happens to people, one by one—in any war, in any place, at any time. Not all war stories involve bullets or bombs or bloodshed: there are other wounds of war that run as deep, leaving scars that never fade. Where there is war, there will always be stories, because there will always be memory.

Furthermore, no single memory stands alone, by itself. According to the American western writer Louis L'Amour: "(Memory) is at the end of a trail of memories, a dozen trails that each have their own associations." It's also been said that war is a story of ordinary people doing extraordinary things. Just as much it can be ordinary people doing ordinary things while they survive to remember.

Another View offers the reader insight into one extended French family, partly what happened during the war, partly what happened as a consequence of war, "at the end of a trail." No matter the story, war will be kept alive as long as there is one person who remembers.

I'm grateful to my parents who taught me a love of history and an awareness of the past. I'm especially grateful to the French side of my family, some quite distant, some very close, who shared with me and entrusted me with the great honor of writing their stories. In particular, *un grand merci* to Georges and Arlette Lessard, and to Janine, Amélie, Robert, and Natalie.

❖

About the Author

MICHAELE LOCKHART brings a diverse background to her writing: a passion for history, a fascination with human drama, and a love of literature. Her education combines early and secondary schools in Europe, in addition to college at the University of Arizona and the University of Maryland.

Embracing a variety of genres, her versatility extends from her favorite periods of history to contemporary social issues. A retired teacher and a talented nature and landscape photographer, she often inserts elements of visual lyricism into her writing. Her short stories and novels encompass historical fiction adventure to romantic magic realism to suspense.

As an editor, she works with writers, helping them produce their best by publishing the most professional books possible. As an author advocate, she encourages clients to spend resources wisely, where their dollars will most benefit their books and careers.

Michaele lives in Tucson, Arizona. Current projects include a mystery-suspense series set in the scenic beauty of the Southwest. Book One in the series is *Focused on Murder,* to be followed by Book Two: *Murder Out of Focus. A Maximum Focus* is Book Three.

Connect with her online at MichaeleLockhart.com.

❖

Made in the USA
San Bernardino, CA
27 June 2015